A CENTURY
OF STORIES
NEW HANOVER COUNTY PUBLIC LIBRARY
1906-2006

HOLLYWOOD
STUFF

SHARON FIFFER

HOLLYWOOD STUFF

ST. MARTIN'S MINOTAUR ❧ NEW YORK

www.minotaurbooks.com

Library of Congress Cataloging-in-Publication Data

Fiffer, Sharon Sloan, 1951–
    Hollywood stuff / Sharon Fiffer.
        p. cm.
    ISBN-13: 978-0-312-34306-4
    ISBN-10: 0-312-34306-X
    1. Wheel, Jane (Fictitious character)—Fiction. 2. Women detectives—Illinois—Chicago—Fiction. 3. Antique dealers—Fiction. 4. Hollywood (Los Angeles, Calif.)—Fiction. 5. Screenwriters—Fiction. I. Title.

PS3606.I37H65 2006
813'.54—dc22

2005057852

First Edition: June 2006

10 9 8 7 6 5 4 3 2 1

For Steve …

WHO PICKED ME OUT OF THE CHORUS

AND MADE ME A STAR

ACKNOWLEDGMENTS

Thanks to the usual suspects who read, listen, and laugh at my jokes: Cas Rooney, Steve Fiffer, Kate Fiffer, Nora Fiffer, Rob Fiffer. Thanks to my friends who share their expertise: Judy Groothuis, Dr. Dennis Groothuis, and Dr. Arnold Robin for medical stuff; Emory Schmidt, who knows a lot about cigars and being a big brother; Chuck and Lynn Shotwell, photographers extraordinaire. Thanks to my West Coast friends who drove me around, fed me, sheltered me, and spilled their stories: Fred Rubin, Alan Rosen, Thom Bishop, Alice Sebold, Glen Gold, Jane Franklin, Marley Sims, Ingrid Willis, Sheldon and all the folks at The Mystery Bookstore in Westwood, and tonight's special guest star, Bob Lowry. Thank you, Gail Hochman and Kelley Ragland—you both make business a pleasure.

HOLLYWOOD
STUFF

1

Nothing good ever comes from a conversation that starts with "babe."

—from *Hollywood Diary* by Belinda St. Germaine

Jane Wheel knew better than to speak on the record. One month ago, when asked if she would be interviewed for a newsmagazine program by the journalist who had written last summer's story of Johnny Sullivan's murder as a syndicated feature, coloring it as cautionary tale of small-town grift and aging Americans in rural isolation, which, truth be told, Jane had thought a bit over the top at the time, she could have and should have said no.

And if her mother, Nellie, hadn't agreed with Jane's first impulse, telling her that she would look like a fool, going on television bragging and yammering about other people's business, Jane might have remained firm in her refusal. But something about Nellie's advice to say no turned Jane's no into a yes.

That's how she ended up in a small television studio, miked for sound and pancaked for glamour, all of her instincts for self-preservation, her obsessive desire for privacy, her almost paranoid fears of self-revelation conspiring to stop Jane from talking. She choked on a glass of water, causing her to cough unattractively for the first five minutes of the pre-interview. She then felt her muted cell phone vibrate in her pocket. She excused herself, explained that her husband was out of town, she had to answer it in case it was her son calling . . . and left the room. There, she explained in an angry whisper to the actual caller, Tim Lowry, her media-curious best friend, that the interview had barely started, she could hardly tell him how it was going. She returned to the set with her lipstick freshened—Tim did know his stuff when it came to cosmetic reminders—and, when the camera rolled on her return, answered each question posed about the murder, about the experience in Kankakee at Fuzzy Neilson's farm, as directly and as cautiously as she could. Jane paused for a drink of water, remembering to allow her lips to stay moistened—Tim's voice in her ear again—and relaxed, just a bit. It was going well. She hadn't cursed, stammered, stuttered, or blurted out anything negative about anyone personally. Then Marisa Brown, the journalist who had written the original story that had been picked up by newspapers in almost every city in the country, leaned forward, girlfriend to girlfriend, and asked Jane Wheel, on camera, the million-dollar question.

"One day you were haunting garage sales, the next you were solving murders. Do you ever feel that your life has become a movie?"

Jane forgot that there was tape rolling. Her throat suddenly cleared. She opened her brown eyes a bit wider, barely licked her lips, and leaned forward in her chair.

"That's exactly how I feel. Every time I find a body, I think somebody's going to jump out and yell, *Candid Camera,* or what was that new one? Oh yeah . . . *Jane Wheel. You've been punk'd.*"

After that, Jane couldn't stop talking. She described her parents, Don and Nellie, their tavern, the EZ Way Inn, the gambling scandal that had involved practically their whole town. She babbled on about her neighbor's murder and mentioned that she had been a suspect in that one because of an innocent kiss.

"Hey, it didn't mean anything," Jane said. "I mean, we'd been drinking, for heaven's sake."

Jane found that she liked playing to an audience. Marisa was smiling and nodding. Marisa's sister, Laura, who had taken the photographs for the print piece, was standing in the wings, doubled over in silent laughter at Jane's stories. Even the cameraman, all serious business when Jane was choking earlier, was now laughing and miming one-handed applause.

Only after the lights were off and Laura and Marisa were high-fiving each other on the piece did Jane wake up.

"I got a little chatty," Jane said.

"You were marvelous," said Marisa.

"Perfect," said Laura.

"Could you maybe edit out . . . ?" Jane paused. Where to begin? The loose remark about her mother, Nellie, being, at best, a difficult woman? The knock on Kankakee as the tavern capital of the world? Blurting out that Charley was an academic and everybody knew that academics were underpaid?

The Brown sisters did edit some of the interview. The carefully measured and thoughtful performance that Jane gave at the beginning of the piece disappeared. Instead, when the interview was televised nationally that week on a newsmagazine that Jane had never even heard of before, Jane Wheel appeared to be a cross between the crocodile hunter and the entire Ozzy Osbourne family.

Watching with Nick, she gave silent thanks that Charley was out of the country and hoped that Don and Nellie were still having problems remembering the numbers of television channels since they got digital cable. Besides, who had ever heard of this program?

Everyone. Jane heard from her former schoolteachers, Kankakee shopkeepers, her Evanston neighbors. Her personal worst was when she yanked the phone cord out of the jack and she looked over to Nick for some sympathy. He was staring straight ahead, almost comatose.

"I'm not going to school tomorrow," he said softly.

"What? I didn't say anything bad about you, honey," said Jane. "You're the one—"

"Ace," said Nick.

"What?"

"I'm the *ace* midfielder on my soccer team?" said Nick, not quite as softly. "Why would you say something like that? Why would you say anything about me?"

"*Ace* means that you're good," said Jane, feeling herself grow weaker and weaker.

"Do you know what this means? For the rest of my life, I will be called *Ace*," said Nick. "And I'm not even that good, Mom. I'm finished. I'm quitting."

"You can't quit soccer, Nick. Nobody watches this, nobody—"

"I'm not quitting soccer. I'm quitting school," said Nick, leaving the room. "I'm quitting this family."

Jane heard a kind of angelic choir, some kind of chanting, and thought maybe, if she was lucky, she had dropped dead. Of course, the way she had sworn and been bleeped on national television, she should have known immediately that the first thing she heard after death was not going to be an angelic choir. No, it was just her cell phone that Nick had switched to the *Seraphim* ring tone.

"It wasn't that bad," growled the voice at the other end.

Uh-oh. If Nellie was calling to comfort her, it was even worse than she thought.

Jane would have to quit the family, too.

Tim, of course, had taped the interview and edited it in such a way that when he walked into Jane's house that night and dropped it into the VCR, it played over and over in a continuous loop. Tim then reminded Jane that if she tried to turn off the television manually, without the remote, she would never be able to get the television, with cable, back on. When she asked him what that had to do with anything, Tim smiled, dropped the remote into his vintage leather briefcase, and walked swiftly and decisively out the door.

One week later, Charley called, asking Jane how she felt about Nick joining him for an extension to his trip. He had been asked to join a faculty panel heading to Peru for a three-week symposium. Students would be attending for credit, it would be a safe and sane trip, and, after all, he reasoned to Jane, wouldn't Nick learn more from that experience than from a middle school unit on magnetism or yet another introduction to the significant battles of the Civil War? Jane, no defender of the curriculum at Nick's school, where she had seen him read the same short stories in English class two years in a row, still didn't like to go through the permission request for Nick to miss that much school.

The last time Charley had whisked his son away from his battered desk, the principal had intoned, "Even if it is educational, Mrs. Wheel, surely you understand that Nicholas is missing valuable curriculum material here?"

Jane, feeling like she was the one being called into the principal's office for some infraction, had bent her head and shuffled her feet, mumbling something about Nick's straight A's no matter how much class time he missed, and somehow managed to exit without her voice breaking or any tears escaping.

This time, however, Jane leapt at the opportunity to get Nick out of the country. He would surely forgive her televised babbling if she got him out of school, out of the country, for a three-week period when something, anything, might happen to break the middle school news cycle of her idiocy. Surely, in twenty-one days, some other kid's parent would do something, anything, that rivaled her loose lips sinking ships, and Nick could return to school, happily under the radar, where any self-respecting fourteen-year-old longed to live.

Jane told herself that it was a good thing Charley had gotten Nick out of town. And it wasn't just to spare him the razzing of classmates for having a mother who didn't know when to shut up. Jane knew her son would learn more from his father and the travel experience than he would here, and when father and son returned, they would both be full of the excitement and knowledge of the dig, forgiving and forgetting all about Jane's televised shout-out.

But now, on this October evening, cool with just enough orange and red leaves crackling underfoot to remind anyone and everyone that this was autumn in the Midwest, with all of its promise of harvest moons and the smell of woodsmoke—which, let's face it, never made up for the snow and freezing rain and skin-numbing cold that would follow—Jane, walking the neighborhood with Lovely Rita, her big loyal shepherd mix mutt, was filled with . . . something. Longing? Maybe a little. In that sentimental, falling-leaves sort of way. But this feeling felt bigger, more momentous. Desire? Well, she missed Charley, but they had grown comfortable with the rhythms of his fieldwork and her treasure hunts, which often separated them. Restlessness? Definitely. Jane needed something to happen. No, she needed *to make* something happen. She no longer wanted to fall into a criminal case by tripping over a body. She didn't want to live from Thursday to Thursday, checking the local paper's classifieds for garage sales.

Back home in her kitchen, she unsnapped Rita's leash and buried her face in her dog's neck. Rita turned around and looked at Jane, mildly curious, then trotted off in search of food and water.

Jane phoned Tim but got his machine. She dialed her partner in noncrime, Detective Bruce Oh, and heard his wife Claire's efficient voice message, dictating exactly what the caller was to do and how long he or she had to do it. Jane hung up.

She paced the length of her living room, a large space filled with wooden trunks used as tables, a cast-off crystal chandelier which had never been wired for light, only hung for reflection.

She plumped the pillows covered in flowered barkcloth and stared at the bookcase filled with old hardcover books. Jane Wheel was not a book collector per se, but she was a collector who heard the small voices of objects that called to her. *Take me home.* That's what she heard from ceramic flowerpots and old autograph books, tins of buttons and battered boxes of office supplies from the thirties. She picked up a tiny matchbox with strong art deco graphics that held "gummed reinforcements" and wondered how many of Nick's classmates would know what a gummed reinforcement was. The tiny container had been propped up in front of a collection of books Jane had discovered at a house sale. She remembered the thrill of opening the carton in the basement and finding the cache of hardcover mysteries. No Nancy Drews, but hardcovers with glossy dust jackets intact. A Mary Roberts Rinehart. An Agatha Christie. A more recent, but also more raggedy Raymond Chandler. *The Long Goodbye.* Jane took it off the shelf and rubbed away a light film of dust with her hand, and found herself saying the title out loud. Such an exquisitely sad phrase, *the long goodbye.*

If Jane hadn't been holding the book, staring at the off-center column of stacked shabby suitcases filled with vacation photos, travel brochures, and maps, all gathered from rummage sales and thrift stores, all chronicling the lives and travels of strangers, she might have been more wary when she answered the ringing phone.

"Jane, oh, Jane, I feel I know you, may I call you Jane?"

Jane nodded, before she actually spoke.

"And what may I call you?" she finally asked.

"I'm Wren Bixby and you can call me Wren, but everybody out here calls me Bix." She paused for a breath or for effect or for both and added, "Including my buddy Jeb Gleason, who claims to be your best friend. Is he lying to me again?"

Jane felt all of her loneliness melt and be replaced with something else. She threw *The Long Goodbye* on the couch and curled up in a giant padded rocker and tucked her feet underneath her.

"You're a friend of Jeb's?"

"We worked together years ago and he was the love of my life. Luckily I've had almost as many of those as he has, so we've remained friends," said Bix. "Look, I'm just terrible at small talk and dancing around stuff, so do you mind if I get straight to the business of this call, then we can trade Jeb stories?"

"Fine," said Jane. She immediately responded to this stranger who disliked small talk, since Jane was so bad at it herself. In fact, she hated small talk as much as she hated talking on the phone, so the combination of telephone small talk was something she really wanted to bury. "Shoot," she said.

"I want to buy your story and turn it into a movie."

"Which one?" said Jane, looking up at the bookcase.

"The scarecrow murder, to start with. You've got a lot more?" asked Bix.

Jane claimed later to have gotten a little hazy after she realized that Wren Bixby was not talking about buying any of her old first editions. Bix explained that she wanted to buy the rights to Jane's life story . . . at least to the part that had become public when Jane got into the crime-solving chapter of her life and when she babbled like an idiot on that Chicago televsion newsmagazine. Apparently Wren had caught the segment on some early morning program in L.A. on a sister station to the Chicago channel that had carried it. That same morning, Bix happened to have breakfast with Jeb Gleason, mentioned the story, Jeb told her that he and Jane had been close friends in college, and since there are no coincidences, according to Bix, she knew she was meant to make a movie of Jane Wheel—PPI, picker, private investigator.

"So how about it?" asked Wren. "The sum we offer for rights is small, and I mean small, but if we move through the pipeline with the project, sign with a major studio, get a good writer, persuade a star to get involved, and the movie gets made, you'll get more. I mean, we'll put you on as a consultant or something. I usually give a fancy dog-and-pony show when I'm schmoozing someone for their story, but Jeb says you are strictly a no-bullshit kind of woman.

Jane took a deep breath. "I might need a little bullshit for this one."

"Fair enough. How about you come out to L.A. for a meeting with us—my partner, Lou, and I have a very small production company, Bix Pix Flix. Don't judge us on cutesy, we picked it in a moment of weakness. Kind of like people who pick their online screen names in homage to their favorite metal band, then have to give the contact name out during a job interview . . . you know . . . yes, I do have that MBA and you contact me at *stuckpig@fu.com.* Anyhow, BPF will fly you out here . . . oh, and we want Tim Lowry's rights, too, but they're not essential," said Wren. "You're the story here, Jane."

Jane called Charley's cell and left a message. She knew he'd say to do whatever she wanted on this. This was not the kind of thorny issue that Charley and she would need to sit down and thrash out. Charley would tell her to leave him out of it, Nick would make her sign an oath in blood to portray herself as childless, but basically, this would be her decision. Jane could take it or leave it. And she knew what she would do. She would leave it. She had done enough damage to her own privacy and to those whom she loved in a ten-minute interview. She was a monastic person, one who would be happy to live as a recluse, a hermit . . . if only the other caves would hold occasional yard sales.

Ay, there was the rub. Jane had to put up with all those other people because people begat stuff, and stuff, for Jane, was what brought people palatably to life. It made others interesting, warm, human. It was what people kept and what they discarded that guided Jane through the confusion of human emotions. But how could Jane go along on her anonymously merry way, scouting junk in alleys and yards, on rummage sale tables and auction house floors, if she was involved in some ego-wrenching nonsense in, for the love of Pete, Hollywood? What would ever make Jane leave her happy home, in the sensible midwestern time zone where you can catch the local news and Letterman and still be asleep by midnight, and head for loopy La-La Land?

Not Jeb Gleason. Not anyone who found her through Jeb Gleason, that was for sure.

Jane picked up *The Long Goodbye* and carried it with her to bed. She fell asleep with the book open next to her, content with her decision to call Bix in the morning and explain that she was not interested in any movie project.

Morning came slightly earlier than Jane had planned— announced by a ringing telephone.

"Wake up, babe, wake up. I've already booked our flight. We're going out tonight. I'll be there in a few hours to help you pack appropriately. Book a haircut and a pedicure. You'll be wearing sandals. This is going to be a first-class trip."

Right. Jane picked up her alarm clock and held it an inch in front of her face. 5:00 A.M. What was that she had asked herself when she decided that she would reject the movie proposal? What would make her leave her happy home? Wrong pronoun. Who would make her leave? Not Jeb Gleason, no.

Tim Lowry. Of course.

2

"Out of the question," said Jane. "I'm going back to sleep so that I can forget that you called me at this hour."

"You are so cute when you're sleep-deprived. Expect me in two hours."

One hour and twenty minutes later, Tim Lowry showed up at her door in Evanston wearing Ray·Bans and carrying a vintage Hartmann suitcase. He walked past Jane at the front door, through the house, up the stairs to the master bedroom, and opened her closet.

Shaking his head and clucking, he threw a few blouses and skirts on the bed. He held up a ridiculously expensive flowered chiffon dress that Jane had bought the summer before and looked at his friend, the top of the wire hanger forming a question mark in front of his face.

"I thought Miriam's daughter's wedding would be a good time to experiment with a new look," she said, shrugging.

"How'd that work for you?"

"It didn't. I wore my old black Lauren," Jane said.

"As I suspected, Miss I-am-so-comfortable-in-my-rut-I-will-never-leave," said Tim, tossing the dress onto a chair. Jane served up the excuses—the phoniness of Hollywood, the loss of privacy, her fear of flying—and as Tim swatted away everything, she waved in his face the flyer for the River Grove Rummage Sale that was coming up the next weekend.

"How about this, then? We can't go off and miss the biggest rummage sale in the Midwest, can we?"

"Darling girl," Tim said, "one word: *Pasadena*."

When Jane didn't respond, Tim practically began dancing around her bedroom.

"If we leave today, we'll be staying over the weekend, and this is the first weekend of the month. Pasadena City College Flea Market," said Tim, overenunciating each of the five words. "Not the Rose Bowl, but that's too big anyway. Time for us to see some West Coast flea, don't you think? Old film star photos, movie props, posters, good modern furniture, California pottery in its natural habitat . . ." Tim trailed off and took Jane's hand in his. "Do you good to get out of the Midwest, honey." Tim waved his hand around her bedroom, pointing to the pottery vases that lined the top of barrister bookcases under the window. "You're suffering from too much McCoy. Not enough Bauer."

Tim stopped for air and looked deep into Jane's brown eyes.

"Charley and Nick are off working and you will be lonely here anyway, so why not give this a whirl? We don't have to say yes. We don't have to sign anything," Tim said. "It's not like you to turn down new territory for scavenging, honey."

Jane took a deep breath and prepared to list all of her fears of traveling and public embarrassment, but none of that came out when she opened her mouth.

"Jeb Gleason," she said.

Tim shook his head.

"You met him when you came to see me at school. When I lived in that big pink stucco house on the hill? With those two blondes you called the Bobbsey Twins? Jeb was tall, thin, wore the big Panama hat?"

"Jeb Gleason," said Tim. "Yeah. Right. A lanky Dennis Quaid type, right? So what's the big deal? An old boyfriend. You're a grown-up girl now, all married and motherly. What's the problem?"

Jane shrugged. "I don't know. I didn't even know I was going to say that. It just hit me that if we go to L.A. and he's a friend of this Bix woman, I'll have to see him and it's been so many years. He didn't show up for my wedding. Remember? He called Marty's during the reception and a waiter called me to the phone?"

"Sorry, hon, I was drinking tequila and acting out my own little drama with Bill," said Tim. "I think that might have been our third-to-last breakup. The one before the one that finally took."

"He didn't say anything when I got on the phone. Just held it to the stereo so I could hear what he was listening to. . . ."

"Which was?"

"I don't remember. Really, I don't. But it made me cry a little."

Jane moved over to her dressing table and leaned into the mirror until her nose nearly touched the glass. "I thought it might be nice to stay twenty-one in someone's eyes."

Tim came over to stand behind Jane. Reaching over her shoulder, he placed his finger on the mirror, right beside her left eye. "See those fine lines there, baby? That's from the smile Nick put on your face when he was born. When you look at him, even now, your whole face just gives in and gives it up for him." Tim touched her lips reflected in the mirror. "And see, there's just a hint of softness around the mouth here? That's from whispering to Charley every night. And kissing. And being kissed. That'll do it, too. I mean, if you kiss someone like you mean it. And I've seen you and Charley, honey. You both mean it."

Tim moved his right hand from her reflection and pointed in the mirror to her throat. "Look at that neck. Still long and graceful, yes, but hmm . . ." He ran a finger down the side of the mirror along her neck. "Yes, maybe the skin here is a touch less taut. And why would that be? Because you've lived some of your life and you've laughed and cried and been busy singing your story to the world.

"Janie," Tim said, straightening up and placing his hands on her shoulders. "You aren't a pretty little twenty-one-year-old coed. You are a beautiful grown-up woman who has lived life deeply. If Jeb thought you were something back then, he will be blown away by the way you look now."

Jane smiled and put her hand over Tim's.

"You do have all your own teeth, right?" asked Tim.

"Okay, okay, I know. It's silly."

"And you wear the same size jeans?"

"Okay, I'm done talking about this. I'll go because you want to go and we'll find a flea market and take pictures of each other at the Chinese Theatre, but I am not signing away my rights for some ridiculous movie."

"Agreed," said Tim. "That would be a terrible idea."

Jane went into the spare room to get out a suitcase and Tim quickly looked over the makeup table. He gathered up Jane's pathetically small supply of paints and powders and slipped them into a worn makeup bag. "She's going to need every one of these," he said softly, shaking his head. "Should have been moisturizing," he added, giving his own firm chin an appreciative pat.

By noon, Jane had finally managed to pack a suitcase whose contents met with Tim's approval. He then drove her to a day spa in Chicago where he knew a friend of a friend. Jane was manicured and pedicured and, in his best while-we're-here-what-the-heck style, Tim convinced her to get her hair cut.

Jane had been letting it grow out from a very short experimental phase where she told people she was re-creating a kind of brunette Mia Farrow pixie. Her short hair directly coincided with her temporary separation from Charley, and Jane knew that her style choice had less to do with Mia's character on the sixties television show *Peyton Place* than her own feelings of guilt. She had to become shorn and penitent. Charley had finally convinced her that although she could pull it off—he admitted she had fine cheekbones—he would love to run his fingers through her hair, her long hair, once more.

"I promised Charley," she said, holding up her hand in a stop-sign position when the stylist approached with the scissors.

"He will approve, sweetie," said Tim, and nodded at Buzz, the stylist. "Just a cleanup, right?"

"Absolutely."

Jane had to admit, when she was all done, staring at herself in the mirror, Tim might have been right. Her fine brown hair, stretching to almost shoulder-skimming, had looked tired, accentuated her drawn face. Now, with soft layers, slightly spiky on the ends, her whole face lightened. Her brown eyes were bigger, her smile brighter. Jane's hands were smooth and her nails, red ovals, elongated her fingers. She kept staring at herself, waving her hands next to her head, smiling. Inside Charley's argyle socks, which she preferred to her own, Jane wiggled her deliciously painted apple-red toes. Although she had begun the ordeal feeling like the Cowardly Lion being groomed for Oz, she wasn't at all displeased with the result. And her new look did confer courage.

"Hello, Bix, good to meet you," Jane said, practicing. "And Jeb, how wonderful to see you again."

"Smile with your eyes, babe, and take the voice register down a notch. You can't miss with throaty," said Tim, taking her wallet and removing her credit card and handing it to the severe-looking blonde dressed entirely in black at the front desk.

The girl in black, whose red-shellacked lips barely moved, asked something which Jane heard as, "Could I ask what she thinks she's doing?"

"Naturally," said Tim, taking the bill and writing something with a flourish.

"Oh," said Jane, the translation of Lacquer Lips's remark hitting her. "Would you like to add a gratuity?"

"Yes," said Tim, taking Jane's arm and guiding her through the door that the receptionist had run out from behind the counter to open for them, "and you liked adding a big fat one."

By six o'clock, Jane and Tim were buckling themselves into first-class recliners and sipping Grey Goose with bleu-cheese-stuffed olives.

"How did you manage first class?" asked Jane. "Bix Pix Flix didn't spring for this."

"How do you know that?" asked Tim, holding up two fingers to the flight attendant to signal that they were ready for more. "They might be dying to sign us and want to wine and dine us royally."

"I know to you I'm a poor antique-picking partner who needs you to make all important decisions in my life, but you forget that I'm also a detective. I have my ways of finding out about people and their companies," said Jane, removing an olive from a toothpick and popping it into her mouth.

"You got some kind of spy network thing going now?" said Tim, digging into his briefcase.

"I Googled Wren Bixby. And the company. And her partner, Lou. They had one minor success about six years ago when they got the rights to that hot novel that stayed on the bestseller list for a million weeks. They didn't get to make the picture, but they made money when they sold the option. A few other interesting-sounding projects in the works and no outstanding red flags—I mean, they didn't get their start in porno or anything—but there was nothing that suggested that they had money to fly people out to L.A. first class."

"So you think I upgraded with my Visa miles? Nope. You might be a good little Googler, but I went a step further. I have a whole L.A. network of out-of-work soap actors who are friends of friends of friends and I called around. Bix Pix Flix has a development deal with a major studio. My source told me that if a producer wants life rights, a producer should cough up some royal treatment. Sooo . . ." Tim said, in his best bedtime storytelling voice, "when Bix called me to coax you into a yes, I told her that I thought you and I deserved a nice trip together. First class was understood. Look, I know you're a homebody at heart, but with Charley doing all this globe-trotting and now Nick going along with him, I thought you might need a little reminder of what the world looks like outside of Chicago and the suburbs and Kankakee, and besides . . ."

The rest of the flight was boarding and Jane heard a dog barking. Could one of those passengers have a small dog in one of their carriers? She smiled, thinking of Rita in a giant duffel bag beside her. No way her dog would stand for becoming a travel accessory. Rita was happy at home, with her buddy and second-best friend, Officer Miles, acting as dog-sitter.

"Janie," said Tim, snapping his fingers in front of her face, "that's you barking."

Reaching into her bag, Jane found her cell phone, apparently set on *Singing dog* instead of ring. Since Nick was gone, Jane glared at Tim, who shrugged.

"Who do you think taught Nick how to do it?"

Jane, trying to quiet the barking as quickly as possible since it was clearly not a first-class cellular ring, flipped up the phone.

"Yeah?"

Jane sighed. The electronic barking was stilled for the time being, but her mother growled louder into the phone.

"Yeah? What's this about you going to California with that damn Tim?"

"I'm on the plane, Mom, I have to turn off my cell phone," said Jane.

The flight attendant, bringing them their second round, shook her head. "No worries, we're fifteen minutes from take-off, so—"

Jane shook her head furiously at the woman.

"They're telling me now to turn it off, so I'll just call you when I—"

"You listen to me, young lady. Charley and Nick need you at home and you don't need to be flying off on some wild goose chase to Hollywood. Your dad told me what you said, that somebody's doing a movie or something, and I'm telling you, it's a scam. I saw this on a TV show. They'll ask you to invest some money, and pretty soon you'll have a condominium you can't pay for in the middle of a swamp."

Jane looked at Tim. He took the phone and immediately began his static imitation. ". . . *chchchchchch* . . . all electronic devices . . . *chchchchchc* . . . turned off now . . . *chchchchc*." Tim turned Jane's phone off.

"As I was saying, you deserve a peaceful paid-for vacation in a warm and sunny place where the flea markets are ripe for picking," said Tim. "I'm going to iPod, but I brought you a little present to keep you busy."

Jane read the title of the slim hardcover book. *Hollywood Diary: A Life Coach's Guide to Making It in L.A.*, by Belinda St. Germaine.

"Hey, this is the author of *Overstuffed*, that decluttering book I was reading, remember? What ever happened to that, I wonder, I didn't get to finish . . . ?"

Tim gave Jane the universal symbol that he wasn't interested in what she was saying by pointing to his headphones.

Jane sipped her Grey Goose, wiggled her well-polished toes encased in first-class slippers, and opened the book. Tim had said she deserved a vacation, and maybe she did. She had tried to call Detective Oh, her partner, Bruce—she really had to learn to call him Bruce—but had to leave another message on his machine. She told him she was taking a vacation, so she should just begin vacating right now. But if Tim really wanted her to relax, why was he giving her a guide to making deals in L.A.? Ah well, who said you couldn't have a vacation and be successful? Charley came home from his digs relaxed and tan and thrilled over whatever discovery the crew had made. Maybe she could have it all this trip. Sun, fun, and Pasadena flea. No Nellie, no dead bodies, no foot-in-mouth interviews. Jane smelled her first-class steak au poivre heating up and smiled. Maybe a movie deal wasn't such a bad idea. Maybe this was the beginning of a whole new adventure for Jane Wheel, PPI—picker *and* private investigator. She wriggled down into her roomy seat, overwhelmed with a sense of well-being, and finished her Grey Goose, known for its property of conferring a false sense of well-being on lightweight drinkers such as Jane. Maybe after L.A., her card, when she got around to having it printed, would have to be changed from "Jane Wheel, PPI—picker, private investigator," to "Jane Wheel VIPPI, *very important* picker, private investigator."

3

First Hollywood Commandment? Don't take that teenager dressed in torn jeans loitering in the hall for granted. He or she is the future head of the studio. And those distressed blue jeans? They cost more than your car.

—FROM *Hollywood Diary* BY BELINDA ST. GERMAINE

Tim had made all the arrangements with Bix Pix Flix. That was why, Jane told herself, she allowed herself to drink on the plane. Tim was in charge. When they landed, he guided Jane through LAX smoothly, and at the baggage area pointed at a short round man in a dark suit.

"Danny DeVito?" Jane asked. She had been trying to spot celebrities since she got off the plane.

"Read his little sign, honey."

"WHEEL," Jane said, looking over her shoulder. "Coincidence?"

Tim sighed and guided her to their driver, who had already retrieved their luggage.

Seated in back of the limousine, Jane shook her head at Tim's offer of a drink.

"Probably like a hotel minibar. Let's not spend all our money in the limo," Jane said, stroking the leather seat and pressing her face against the window.

"Palm trees, Timmy," Jane whispered.

"Last time I'm going to say this. We are not paying for this limo. Bix sent it. Sit back and enjoy."

Wren Bixby had made all the arrangements with Tim. Since they were arriving in the evening and traffic would be insane, she had suggested they have a nice evening at the hotel. She had booked them into the W in Westwood, an area she thought they might enjoy. "UCLA, bookstores, all that rot," was how she described the neighborhood. Tim and Jane's meeting would take place the next morning at Bix Pix Flix on the studio lot.

"Only if you're not all jet-lagged and loopy," Wren had said. "I know some people need at least a morning to recover from travel."

"Are you loopy?" Tim asked Jane, who had plopped onto her king-sized bed and was making a snow angel on the white duvet. He unlocked her suitcase and began hanging up Jane's clothes.

"Nope," said Jane. "Not loopy. Wary. I would describe my-self as wary." Jane stood and waved her arms around the spacious two-bedroom suite that Tim had assured Bix would be perfect for them. "What could I possibly have that would make it worth their while to spend this money? I've found a few dead bodies, and asked people the right questions. I have not, as far as I can recall, participated in any car chases, time-traveled, or averted any natural disasters with my cunning superpowers. Why am I in Hollywood?"

The phone rang and Tim promised to answer Jane's question as soon as he took care of the caller. To his surprise, it was not the part-time clerk at his Kankakee flower shop, nor was it a forwarded message from T & T Sales, his estate sale business. He shrugged and handed the phone to Jane. Her raised eyebrows were answered by Tim's shoulder shrug, so she gave her wariest hello into the receiver.

"Long time, no happiness."

"Jeb?"

"I told Bix to put you up in a nice room. Is it a nice room? Do you and the husband like it?"

"No, not the husband," Jane said, shaking her head at Tim. "It's a lovely room."

"And you've already got some guy in there who's not the husband?" asked Jeb, his voice still maddeningly low and measured. "My little girl is all grown up."

"Tim is my business partner who is also out here for the meeting. I am not your little girl and I grew up a long time ago."

Jane remembered now all the reasons she was crazy about Jeb and all the reasons she was driven crazy by Jeb. He was a womanizer, a shamelessly condescending chauvinist. He played the bad boy . . . and he was so good at it.

"Sorry, Janie. You can't blame me. You walked away from me twenty years ago and I've never recovered. It always brings out the pompous ass in me. When can I see you?"

"Twenty-five," said Jane.

"If it was twenty-five years ago, that would make the birth date on my résumé grossly incorrect. In Hollywood, we round down, darling."

Jane looked up at Tim, who also rounded his age down five years. He was now doing an elaborate pantomime of twenty questions about her mysterious caller. Jane turned to face the wall so she wouldn't have to try to read Tim's lips and respond rationally to Jeb Gleason at the same time.

"I have something tonight I can't cancel, but I thought after your meeting with Bix tomorrow, we might meet. We will meet. It's inevitable. In fact, maybe you and your little friend or partner or whoever would want to stay at my place for the weekend. Bix told me you guys were staying on a few days."

"Well, that might be . . ." Jane really didn't know if she was going to say *possible* or *impossible*. Now she would never know.

"Look, I've got to run. Emergency out by the pool. I'll phone you later or you call my cell. 'Bye, babe."

And it was over. The conversation she had imagined off and on for twenty-five or twenty years, depending on whose résumé one was reading, was over. Jeb Gleason had been the love of her life in college until one night when she knocked on the door of his apartment and was greeted by Linda Fabien wrapped in a very skimpy bath towel.

"Jeb's still in the shower. Want to come in and wait?" Linda had asked.

Jane remembered that Linda had been vigorously chewing gum. It was, in fact, the gum-chewing that kept her sane as she walked back across campus to her own place. Who ran around naked and dripping wet and popped gum into her mouth? What kind of insane idiot had Jeb hooked up with while she was out of town giving an undergraduate paper at a college history conference? She had taken a filthy all-night bus ride back by herself in order to surprise him by getting home six hours early. Surprise!

Jane called him the next morning and told him she never wanted to see him again and hung up while he was still asking why. Only later did she realize that even though she knew Linda Fabien, Linda Fabien did not know Jane. Linda was an art history major/local folksinger whose face was on a music festival poster that had been plastered on every possible vertical surface on or near the campus. Jane had not given the towel-clad Linda her name. She had politely said that she would not wait, that she would call another time. She'd still been wearing the navy blue suit she had worn when giving her paper, an outfit that Jeb would never recognize as belonging to her. Linda Fabien probably told Jeb that a census taker or a Jehovah's Witness had stopped by.

Despite the fact that every campus, even an enormous land-grant state university, was a really small world, Jane never saw Jeb again. A theater major, he ducked out of the program and skipped the degree when he was cast in a West Coast repertory company. Jane's heart had healed, albeit a little crookedly, giving her a slightly more cynical view of happily ever after. During Jane's senior year, a handsome TA named Charley had walked into her discussion section, and Jane found herself in the right class at the right time. Charley proposed on the night of Jane's college graduation. Jeb phoned Jane on her wedding night and it had been the last time they had spoken. Until today.

Cynda, Wren's assistant, not Danny DeVito, picked them up after breakfast and drove them to the studio. She gave them a mile-by-mile description of their trip, explaining that to live in L.A. was to learn to drive by your watch—avoiding rush hours, which were becoming all hours.

"And," she said, "never be without your *Thomas Guide.*" Cynda held up a thick book she had wedged into the door pocket on the driver's side. "This is the bible. Better, actually. Gets you where you need to go without any threat of damnation." Cynda smiled a perfect straight white smile and turned into the legendary gates of the studio.

"Here we are."

She parked the car and pointed to a row of bungalows.

"These used to belong to all the big stars on the lot, you know, when they were under contract to the studio. Can you just imagine what went on in them?" asked Cynda, who had been doing a running commentary as studio tour guide.

Jane didn't recognize most of the young stars' names or the TV shows Cynda mentioned. She tried to absorb as much information as she could—difficult, since she was still overwhelmed by real live palm trees outside the car window. Jane recognized these feelings of excitement. Hadn't she forgotten her own inhibitions sitting in a local television studio? Now here she was, weak-kneed at the thought of passing by Clint Eastwood's parking space.

Earlier, over coffee in the lobby, Jane had once again reminded Tim that she was not going to get involved in any movie deal.

"Right," Tim had agreed, smiling at a handsome waiter who seemed genuinely thrilled to be serving them coffee.

"Everyone's too happy here," said Jane. "I don't like it."

"Who would?" agreed Tim, nodding at the waiter, who offered a silver bowl filled with raw natural sugar cubes.

The receptionist, Jenna, introduced herself, offered green tea, free-trade coffee, and English chocolate biscuits, then excused herself to find Bix, who had taken a call on the back porch of what was really a tiny charming house.

"Tim? Look at these," Jane said.

Two glass shelves had been hung across the window. Each held mismatched Depression glass salt and pepper shakers. Three of them, missing their tops, were being used to root delicate cuttings of ivy. One of the green salts Jane recognized as green U.S. Swirl and there was a pink Miss America, but the others were less familiar.

"These are all firsts, I think," Tim said, his face an inch away from the glass door of the bookcase.

"Yes, they are," Wren Bixby said, coming in with her hands extended in welcome.

"My partner Lou's weakness. I don't think he reads them. Just buys them and locks them up."

Jane thought, *Typical book guy,* but gathered her wary self together, concealed her delight at finding out that Bix collected mismatched shakers, put on her I-am-not-making-a-deal face, and shook hands.

Wren Bixby did not conform to Jane's mental picture of a producer, but then again, Jane's mental picture was snapped sometime in the sixties, watching the late-late show on television with her mother. Typical producer? Maybe William Powell in *The Great Ziegfeld?* Nellie didn't have many soft spots, but give her a bowl of potato chips, a Pepsi on ice, and Victor Mature in a toga or Van Johnson in an army uniform and she went off-duty until "The End" floated on to the screen. Nellie interpreted old movies primarily as cautionary tales—if you fall in love with someone, he'll leave; if someone goes up in an airplane, he won't come back; and if you sign your name to a piece of paper, you'll lose your shirt. Shaking Wren Bixby's hand, Jane heard her mother's voice tell her this was all a scam. *Look at that girl, for Christ's sake, she hasn't even brushed her hair. Hold on to your wallet.*

Jane did not think the young executive was going to pick her pocket. She had, however, imagined that Wren, or Bix, as she insisted Jane and Tim call her, would be wearing a business suit and, perhaps, trendy glasses, lipstick, and have an expensive-looking haircut. Jane, in her past life, had been an advertising executive responsible for a talented creative team at a major agency and had done her share of supervising commercial productions. She wasn't exactly a mogul, either, but when she had to meet clients, she pulled together the businesswoman's fitted suit, high heels, and made-up look. Jane might have felt like a phony dressed like a grown-up, but she pulled it off when necessary.

Bix didn't bother with the homage to grown-up. At first Jane figured Bix for thirtysomething. Then a shadow fell across her face and Jane started thinking older—maybe she and Bix were about the same age. Nope. A quick toss of her head and Bix was back to Gen X or whatever letter of the alphabet stood for *not as old as Jane Wheel.* Bix wore a lavender embroidered silk tunic over torn blue jeans, red and purple strappy sandals, and what looked to Jane like small light fixtures hanging from her ears. Her long hair, braided into twenty or so skinny plaits, was swept up into a ponytail with bangs hanging down to her freckled nose. Tim had immediately impressed her by naming the designer of her chandelier earrings and complimenting her on her fabulous shoes. Jane thought she saw him heave a slight sigh when he looked back at Jane's feet, sensibly covered up in her most comfortable leather clogs.

"All settled at the W? Rooms okay? Flight okay?"

Jane nodded, since there wasn't really any space left for answers to the questions.

Bix led them into her office in the back of the house. She took the tray from Jenna, who had appeared with drinks and cookies, and closed the door, offered them their cups and plates, and then threw herself into a chair and smiled.

Jane and Tim smiled back.

Jane was afraid they would remain that way for too long. Smiling. Then Bix would produce the contract and Jane, not knowing what else to do, would just sign it. Somebody had better say something.

Somebody did, but it wasn't Bix, Jane, or Tim.

"You'll give him a message? Okay. Give him this. I'm going to kill him. I'll kill him and I'll get away with it. You know why? Because no jury in the world would convict me for killing that bastard. You want to give him *that* message?"

A very angry visitor seemed to be checking in with Jenna in the front office.

Wren didn't stop smiling, but she cocked her head to listen.

"I want everything back and I want acknowledgment. Got that? Can you fit that on your memo pad? You tell him Patrick wants acknowledgment."

"Ah, a writer," said Wren, as if that explained it. "Always unhappy."

They heard a door slam, and Bix started over on the smiling and the let's-start-the-meeting adjusting herself at her desk.

"Who do you see playing you, Jane?" asked Wren.

Jane was caught off guard. Not by the subject . . . she and Tim had played the who-would-play-me game since Bix's first call . . . but she had no idea that Bix would start the meeting with the same trip to fantasyland that they had taken.

"I hadn't really thought about it," Jane began, then stopped herself. Hadn't she decided she was too restless, and that she had to make something happen? Maybe this was it.

"Teri Hatcher?"

Tim nodded approvingly.

Bix nodded too. "Too bad she's tied up with a hit. Perfect choice. And she loves garage sales, too. When she was on Leno—"

"I saw that, that's why I thought of her," said Jane. "It was an accident. I never watch Leno, I'm more of a Letterman type, but I was flipping and heard her talk about driving around on Saturday mornings, so I—"

"Yeah, yeah, and she's so hot right now, we'd have to see how tied-up—"

Jane shook her head.

Bix looked from Jane to Tim, who leaned forward, acting as interpreter.

"Jane isn't a regular television watcher. She has no idea," he said.

Jane did watch television, but in a wise and wary moment she decided not to protest. She knew Teri Hatcher was on a hit show, she knew who her costars were, and she vaguely understood the show's premise. One could get all that from catching Letterman or any other late-night program and that's what Jane watched. She turned on television after ten and schooled herself on popular culture. No reason to explain all this to Bix, or to Tim, for that matter. Why not allow herself to be portrayed as the know-nothing and let them talk out the fantasy, tentatively titled *The Scarecrow Murder*? Since she was going to say no in the end, the less involved she got, the better.

Jane tuned back in to the conversation, buzzing along happily without her. Now Bix and Tim were discussing writers. Jane was impressed with Tim's ability to pretend that he recognized all of the credits Bix recited for each of the names floated.

"Oh, Tal Beaman? You know he was really hot after the *Ghoulie Boy* sequel made such a splash, but we hear he wants to get away from all the melting latex special effects and delve into character work," said Bix.

"Call me crazy, but I thought *Ghoulie Boy II* was so much better than one," said Tim. "Much more heart."

"Exactly what I'm talking about," said Bix.

"How about Patrick?" asked Jane.

Bix turned to her, smile intact, but with one braid twitching slightly, as if it were trying to escape the ponytail.

"Patrick?"

Jane gestured toward the outer office. "You know," she said, "the one who wants to kill somebody. Maybe he'd calm down if he got some work."

"It is true that most writers out here forget all about their outrage and their artistry being tampered with as soon as you offer them another paycheck, but I'm afraid Patrick's a different case. Not a writer, really."

"But I thought you said—" Jane began.

"Novelist." Bix shook her head and looked sad. "Couldn't write a second act if his life depended on it. I hear his books aren't bad, though. First novel won some sort of prize a zillion years ago. He and Lou are in some pissing match over some first editions that Lou bought from his uncle's estate."

A noticeable edge had come into Bix's voice when she told Patrick's story, and she began fussing with one of her many braids, so Jane refrained from asking any more questions. Still, she wondered why Patrick, if his anger really *was* over being out-bid on books, would demand acknowledgment. That was a new one. Dealers and pickers she knew, after losing an object of desire, would never be satisfied with a little tag that said the armoire had almost gone to Big Elvis, who, on another day, might have been the picker who got up the earliest and shrewdly went into the master bedroom ahead of Jane and slapped a red sold sticker on it.

The meeting went on to cover who would play Tim, who would play Nellie, and who they might get for the roles of Fuzzy and Lula. Jane tuned out deliberately when they got to parsing the qualities of aging character actors who might be perfect for the old couple. Jane realized that hearing the individuals who she knew and loved reduced to facial characteristics, height, weight, and voice quality depressed her.

Good thing this movie wasn't going to happen.

Jenna—or was it Cynda?—apologized for interrupting and stepped in to hand Bix two notes. Jane sipped her green tea and considered what would happen if she moved to Hollywood. First she would change her name to Jana.

Tim leaned over and patted Jane's arm. "Going well, isn't it?" he whispered.

"Yes, Tima."

"Looks like your lunch date with Jeb is on. He's meeting you at Has Been's," said Bix.

"It serves leftovers?" asked Tim.

"Owned and managed by actors who never made it past their first hit, or who didn't move on to another second-banana spot—you know, the Potsies and Ralph Malphs of the world."

Jane shook her head. She didn't get Bix's references, but she had a suspicion that she herself might be one of the Potsies of the world.

"You'll love it. You can play spot the child star for whom braces and rehab just wasn't enough. I'll have Cynda run you over there now, and then Jeb can get you back to . . ."

Bix was reading the second note. She allowed her face to go blank and she took a few breaths before she looked up.

"How about a studio tour, Tim?"

If Jane had known she had a firm lunch date with Jeb, she might have opted for open-toed shoes to show off her fresh pedicure, a fitted blouse to show that she had a waist, and a flirtier skirt that would showcase her still-slim legs. That morning, however, when she was dressing for the meeting she did not want to take, she had decided to dress down, show she could be casual and unimpressed by an interested producer. She had assumed she'd have a chance to change and prepare herself more for a meeting with Jeb. Her jeans were not expensively torn, but they did fit well. She had paired it with a loose-fitting pale yellow shirt and wound a rope of amber Bakelite beads around her wrist, passing Tim's wardrobe scrutiny with only a sniff at her insistence on sticking with the old hippie riffraff look. Tim had selected the earrings she wore, a tangle of loopy gold chains that hung from a small rough-cut citrine. And Jane herself had chosen to wear her old faithful rusty orange clogs, for comfort and luck.

Now, waiting for Jeb at a sidewalk table, she checked her lipstick and hair and thought just for a moment that perhaps she, Jane Wheel, a happy enough wife and mother, shouldn't be thinking about whether or not her pedicure was showing. Why was her heart racing at the thought of seeing Jeb Gleason again?

Jane quickly calculated the time difference between Los Angeles and the site where Charley and Nick were digging and sifting and cataloging. Charley's cell phone did not work there, but once a week they drove into a small town nearby and called Jane with an update. As accustomed as she was to Charley's absences when he was in the field, she needed to hear his voice now.

"I still haven't forgiven you for breaking my heart."

Jeb's voice was as deep and self-amused as she remembered. She had rehearsed what she would say to Jeb, but none of her well-thought-out witty words came to mind.

"Bullshit."

"Touché," said Jeb. He kissed her cheek and pulled up a chair. Within two minutes he had charmed the waitress, who looked vaguely familiar to Jane, into switching the flowers on the table, a tall vase of carnations for a low basket of violets— *all the better to see you with,* he had explained to Jane—and also secured an off-the-menu list of specials that the chef would make up for regular customers who knew enough to ask.

"May I?" he asked, gesturing toward the menu, and Jane nodded.

He ordered shrimp bisque for both of them, a basket of artisan breads, and a cheese plate, then asked for one lamb curry and a wild mushroom ragout with extra plates for sharing. "And a bottle of the Sancerre," he added.

"Isn't that too sweet?" Jane asked.

Jeb shook his head. "Not this one. Doesn't really go with the lamb, but it's too delicious to pass up. Might be trite to ask about the last twenty years, so I'll start with today. How was your meeting?"

Jane shrugged. "You first. You're not acting anymore, are you?"

Jane knew Jeb had begun writing as soon as he hit Los Angeles, but she didn't want to admit she had followed his career and his credits, if not the actual programs he wrote, for years. *Parker's Playground, Mr. Meek and Polly*—those were his early shows. Then the megahit—*Southpaw and Lefty*. Everyone watched on Thursday nights and quoted it to each other the next day. Viewers claimed withdrawal headaches when it left the air. After *Southpaw*, Jeb was executive producer of a badly reviewed comedy drama that limped along for one and a half seasons—*Merle's Place*. It had been off the air for two years.

"I better not be, since you don't recognize me from anything."

Jeb told Jane that he was writing a screenplay and working off a development deal. "I was a writer on a hit show, so I've still got some . . . and have an idea that will blow . . ." Jeb reached for the cell phone that was quietly vibrating in his pocket. "Sorry, I have to take this."

While Jeb answered questions and laughed at his apparently witty caller, Jane sized up her first love. He had aged well. Damn men. They all did. Tim, with his crinkly eyes, all Redford- and Newman-like, and Charley with his boyish grin and hair forever tumbling over his forehead. Now she had to add Jeb to the handsome-boys-to-handsome-men list—still tall, still lean, no loss of confidence in his smile, no fading of those intense dark eyes. Just enough gray to signal experience and wisdom, but not enough to make any girl half his age lose interest. Damn those men.

Jane watched Jeb drum his fingers while he listened to his caller. That was new. Jane had always considered Jeb's hands to be his most startling feature. He was tall and thin, with huge hands that he would lace in front of him on his lap. He always held them still. To Jane, loopily in love with him, his quiet hands had emphasized how capable and strong he was. The last thing you'd say about the Jeb Gleason she knew was that he was a fidgeter.

Jane heard angels sing and looked up. Down. Her purse was vibrating in celestial celebration. She'd ask Tim to change this ring—a lively mambo, perhaps? She sure didn't feel like she deserved a heavenly choir. She wouldn't have answered her cell phone while out to lunch with a friend, but what the hell? Jeb was so engaged in his conversation that he didn't even look up when she answered her phone.

"Yeah?"

Angels must have a sense of humor if they deigned to announce her mother.

"Hi, Mom," Jane spoke softly. People in L.A. got important calls on their cell phones. She looked around at the other tables. Half the people were talking not to their lunch companions, but into their hands or to the tiny wires hanging out of their ears. She doubted that any of the carefully downdressed, artfully made-up to look non-made-up, surgically enhanced women and men sitting around her were talking to their mothers.

"Your dad said you went to California even though I told you not to. You back?"

"Still here in L.A.," said Jane.

"I need those pictures."

"What pictures, Mom?"

"The ones in the sewing box you took. Your Aunt Veronica says we didn't wear hats for Bernice's wedding and I say we did. What? Get the ketchup from the other table. Yeah, you can get up off your behind and get it yourself. Jeez, what am I? Your maid?"

Technically, Jane thought, Nellie was the server of food and drink at the EZ Way Inn, the tavern she and her husband had run for thirty years in Kankakee, Illinois, and strictly speaking, since the person she was yelling at was a patron trying to eat his lunch, he was a paying customer, and if one subscribed to the customer-always-being-right theory of business, Nellie was, sort of, for the time being, his maid. Jane did not point this out to her mother.

"And the photographs?"

"There's some picture in there with all of us in big hats. Had to be Bernice's wedding . . . here's mustard, ketchup, what else you want? Egg in your beer? You still got those pictures?"

Jane smiled. Yes, she had those pictures. Upstairs hall, oak flat file, third drawer. She had recently placed all the wedding pictures of people she didn't know, the rescued photos from estate sales, flea markets, and rummage sales, into the top two drawers, and labeled them with a big N for *Not ours, Nick, not to worry*. The third drawer, the narrowest, the one that could hold the least amount, was reserved for O, *Our family, for better and/or worse*.

"Yup, I'll check it out for you when I get home."

"When's that? Tell Don you had a tomato slice on that. I'm charging you extra."

Jane could hear her dad laughing in the background. They didn't have a regular lunch crowd now that Roper Stove and all the factories were gone, but old regulars still stopped in around lunchtime and Nellie, if she was in the mood, would make sandwiches and yell at everybody for old times' sake.

"Better get home. Earthquake'll get you there in California," said Nellie before hanging up.

To some daughters, that would be an abrupt and unkind good-bye, but Jane felt warm and loved. Nellie had connected an actual place with an actual disaster and predicted it would happen to Jane. That was as concerned and protective as Nellie got. She must have been in a good mood.

Jeb finished his call at the same time and caught Jane smiling at her phone.

"The husband?"

"The mother. Charley's in South America. I only hear from him and Nick every four or five days, when they get into a town."

"He's digging for something, right?" asked Jeb. "Fossils? Dinosaurs? Something old and academic?"

Jane nodded. Jeb answered the question she started to ask. "I've kept track of you, you know. Married to Charley, a geology professor. A son. You are an antiques picker who has solved several murders—a regular Nancy Drew—and before that you were a hotshot ad executive with—"

"How?"

"I'm still in touch with a few people from college. You'd be surprised how many people want to keep in touch with someone who might be able to get them tickets to *The Tonight Show* when they bring the family out to Disneyland."

"But *I'm* not in touch with anyone," said Jane.

"True. You've retained your loner status, but Chicago's a small enough town for someone who knew someone to know a Jane Wheel who went to college with whatshisname and she used to work with whozit who married Phil who worked with . . . you know . . . on and on. Somebody always has some connection. Besides, I work with actors and you used to work with actors. A few of those beer-drinking types you cast in your producing days made their way here for pilot season. . . ."

"Then I saw you on the morning news," said Jeb. "Cute as can be, talking away about your family and your antique-picking and your crime-solving—"

"Oh God," said Jane. "You saw that? Wren said she saw it and mentioned it to you, but I hadn't thought about you actually watching it."

"Saw it. TiVo'd it," Jeb said, rearranging salad plates to accommodate the entrées being served. "I've watched it more than once," he whispered.

The first half of the meal, they played more catch-up.

Jeb suggested that all people over forty should have cards printed up—not to inform others of their business address and fax numbers, but to answer the basics.

"Married? Twice. First time, my fault; second time, hers. No children, but not opposed to having them. Income? More than I deserve. Health? Good. Faith? In a pinch. Major disappointments? Three . . ." Jeb pushed the bread plate toward Jane and picked up her hand. "Maybe four."

The sun was shining. It was, after all, L.A. Jeb was right about the wine . . . crisp and summery, not at all too sweet. Jane felt a flush of well-being. She was terrible at flirting, but it didn't count as flirting if it was an ex-boyfriend. It was more like remembering. Jane loved remembering.

Jane was about to ask some follow-up questions to Jeb's canned answers when his phone rang again. A tasteful soft bleat. Clear to Jane that he didn't have a smart-aleck son like Nick or a wise-ass friend like Tim who used her cell phone to make a fool of her every chance they got. He looked down at the number and some of the good humor left his face.

"Business partner," he said. "Sorry." He shifted in his chair and faced away from Jane toward the street. After only a few words, he turned back to her, his eyes wide, looking for an answer. "If this is a joke . . . Okay. Yes. I'm bringing a friend."

Jeb signaled for the check, while dialing another number on his cell.

"Marilyn, it's Jeb. Yeah, just now. I'm on my way over to their office. Sure, we should call everybody."

Jane tried not to look obvious as she tried to get in as many bites of the mushroom ragout as she could. Looked like they wouldn't be having dessert and the food here was incredible.

"Sorry, babe. I owe you another meal. Bad news." Jeb signed the check and stood, taking her elbow and standing her up with him. "Terrible bad news."

"What's happened?"

"Wren Bixby," said Jeb, as if he were questioning someone just out of sight, "is dead?"

4

Thou shalt not expect anything to happen in a meeting. People in L.A. take meetings like those in other parts of the world take breaths. If something is going to happen to your Hollywood project, it will happen after the meeting, and the results will be relayed to you by a third party. Or in a memo.

—FROM *Hollywood Diary* BY BELINDA ST. GERMAINE

"How?" Jane fastened her seat belt and stowed her bag under her feet on the inches allotted her in Jeb's Mini Cooper. Why did everyone out here drive these toys? Didn't they ever see abandoned furniture on the street? How would an oak schoolroom chair fit in this vehicle's backseat? "What happened?" Jane asked, picturing Bix as she appeared just a few hours ago, underdressed in current Hollywood style, her long hair a confluence of braids. This movie producer was just a kid.

"Something blew up in the prop shop. I couldn't really hear. I think that's what happened anyway." Jeb aimed the car toward the studio and fired. "Shit."

"Prop shop? Prop warehouse?" Jane felt her cool questioning mode melt. "An explosion?" Jane felt panic rising. Tim. Tim was touring the prop warehouse with Bix. "Was anyone else hurt?"

Jeb shook his head and shrugged. "I don't know. Gary only told me about Bix. It happened right after you left, though. A few hours ago. I don't know what the hell took them so long to call me."

"A few hours?" said Jane. Tim could be hurt. For a few hours, he might have been calling her name from a hospital bed.

The faster and more precisely Jeb drove, the more he mumbled and swore at other drivers. Twenty-five years ago Jeb had been too cool for the room, the guy who stood above it all. Jane had the feeling during lunch that he still maintained that persona, although it was getting harder. Being a hipster might work fairly easily in one's twenties, but at fortysomething, it just took more to pull off. A few extra pounds, the softening of the chin, the thinning hair . . . something made it harder to stay forever young. Wasn't it just an hour ago Jane was thinking that men escaped aging? Maybe they just didn't show concern, anxiety as often as their female counterparts. Now, upset and driving like a maniac, Jeb could have been any middle-aged dad hurrying to get to his child's soccer game.

She dialed Tim's cell, praying for him to answer. Message. She stared at the phone, willing it to deliver her friend instead of his canned voice explaining the many ways in which he might get back in touch with you if you left all your numbers for him.

Jeb drove past the main entrance to the studio.

"We'll take a shortcut. Better to avoid the police and all the chaos at the front gate . . . if there is any. Right?"

Jeb parked the Mini in a small private key-card lot around the corner and motioned for Jane to follow him to an almost grown-over passageway, covered in flowering bushes.

"Legend has it that the studio head kept this hidden entrance to get certain starlets on and off the lot in a hurry. In fact," said Jed, pulling out a small key and unlocking an ornate mechanism on the old gate, "it might still be used for—"

"How do you have a key to a hidden entrance in this day and age of security and surveillance?" asked Jane. "Impossible. . . ."

"When Bix and Lou got this office, they thought they were lucky, but they didn't know how lucky," said Jeb.

When Jane saw where they were, she understood. Once through the iron gate, they ducked through heavy hanging vines and foliage. She and Jeb were in what appeared to be a small backyard garden. It was the backyard of the Bix Pix Flix bungalow. Turning back, she noticed that the gate was invisible. If Jane hadn't known it was there . . . actually she did know it was there, and she still could not see it.

"Bix found it when they were assigned this office. There's a built-in desk in the entryway with a few bookshelves over it—"

"Yes, I saw this morning."

"She found four keys under the divider in the pencil drawer. There was an unsigned note that must have been thirty years old that referred to a backyard gate, so she looked until she found it. It was all grown over and we put this stone bench back here to mask it even more. We'd see other cars parked in the side lot, maintenance staff mostly. Sometimes I'd wait and watch until a driver got out. Always walked out the driveway and down the block to Entrance Four around the corner. Nobody except us. . . ."

Jeb stopped. Jane had never seen him break down, but she thought he might be close to it right now.

"Wren said you were old friends, but I didn't know . . ."

"We weren't lovers," Jeb said, leading Jane up the back steps to the door to the Bix Pix Flix bungalow. "We were closer than that. We were writing partners."

The back door wasn't locked. Jane saw the office she had sat in earlier. The door was open and the light was on. She could hear a woman's voice in the front office. Sounded like a phone conversation. The door to what Jane assumed was Lou Piccolo's office was closed, as it had been earlier. Jane moved ahead of Jeb, who had stopped to take out his cell phone and was punching in a number, and stepped into Bix's office.

No police, no crowds, no chaos.

Behind Bix's desk, perfectly at home, sat Tim. He was listening intently to someone on the phone, Bix's phone, and waved Jane in to a chair, signaling at the same time for her to be quiet.

"How dare you sit there?" said Jane, her relief at seeing him alive fueling the anger she now felt for Tim's callous appropriation of Wren Bixby's office.

"Thanks so much," said Tim. "I'll pass it along."

"What . . . ?"

"You missed all the excitement," said Tim. "And the prop warehouse is to die for. Aisle after aisle of candlesticks and silver tea services and furniture and statues . . . all tagged for future projects or sitting there, all spruced up and waiting to be chosen . . . just your kind of place, Janie—"

"Have you lost your mind? Wren Bixby's dead and you're sitting there talking about goddamn movie props?"

Tim shook his head. "Where do you get your news? The *Enquirer?*"

Jeb stepped in. He was grinning as he stuck his hand out and introduced himself to Tim. "Heard a lot about you," he said.

"Well, there's a lot to tell," said Tim, looking Jeb Gleason up and down. "Has Jane been regaling you with stories of her wonderful husband, Charley, and perfect son, Nick, as well as tales of Terrible Tim?"

"Why aren't we screaming here?" asked Jane.

Jeb smiled at her and pointed to his phone.

"She's going to be all right," said Jeb. "Isn't she?" he turned and asked Tim.

"Were you there?" asked Jane. "What happened?"

Tim nodded. "I was in the next aisle. She opened some kind of a wooden box and there was a popping sound. I know everyone's saying explosion, but it was a quiet one. Some glass flew around and she was hit in the head with some small pieces of metal. Her arm was cut up pretty badly."

Tim told them the studio emergency medical staff was there fast to administer first aid and the ambulance arrived shortly after. Wren would have to stay in the hospital overnight for observation, but apparently the stories of her death were greatly exaggerated.

"Probably started by a rival producer," said Jeb, trying to make his voice sound light, but the effort showed. Jane thought he looked more worried than ever.

"What was the box?" asked Jane. "Does anyone know why . . . ?"

Cynda came in, still carrying a cordless phone. "I was just on with Gary. He says they think the box might have been an old chemistry set or maybe a magic set with flash powder or something and maybe something had spilled or someone messed with it last time someone looked at it. He said something about chemicals that have to stay in water or oil and if someone pours it off, they can ignite or something. They'll try to track down what it was and why it was on that shelf."

"Who's Gary?" asked Jane.

"Gary Check . . . assistant head of props."

Wren's phone rang again and Tim, not missing a beat, picked it up. "Bix Pix Flix, Wren Bixby's office."

"Anyone see Lou today?" asked Jeb. "Has Lou Piccolo deigned to come into the office?"

"Did Gary say anything more about the chemistry set?" asked Jane. "Doesn't really sound like something that would happen spontaneously. I mean, the chemicals are usually sealed and if it's a vintage Chemcraft or something—"

"I don't know, okay? I've answered a million phone calls today and Bix is in the hospital, and I just don't . . ." Cynda put one perfectly manicured hand up to her eyes and brushed away a tear so perfectly formed that one might think it had been genetically engineered. "Sorry." She shook her head. "It's been a terrible day."

Cynda walked out of Bix's office and they heard a drawer open and close before they heard the door slam.

Jeb smiled. "Not a terrible exit. Trite and a bit overwrought, but she's got a meeting with the casting agent for some new hospital show tonight. Saw it on her calendar."

Jane opened her mouth to speak, then stopped and shook her head.

"Lesson one, honey," Jeb said. "Everyone you meet out here is someone else. The receptionist is an actress, the waiter is a director, the valet is a writer . . ."

Jeb, holding his own cell phone to his ear, frowned when he heard a ringing phone go unanswered in Lou Piccolo's office. "Doesn't that idiot even bother coming in anymore? I guess I have to do everything myself." Jeb walked into Lou's office and closed the door. Jane heard him answer the phone with a surly hello.

As soon as he heard Jeb become immersed in a conversation, Tim motioned for Jane to come closer to the desk. "We've got to get over to the hospital. That was Bix who called here before. She wants to see you."

"Jeb could drive us," said Jane.

Tim shook his head. "I've got a rental. I had it delivered an hour ago. We need to leave now," he whispered. "And don't tell Harry Handsome where we're going."

Jane and Tim stood in front of Jeb, who was swearing softly on the phone. When he looked up at them, he changed expression—his eyes and mouth went from night to day and he smiled brightly at Jane.

"All's well and all that, huh, babe? Shall we continue reminiscing over dinner?"

Jane explained that she and Tim had another meeting about another project entirely. "T & T, our estate sale business, is bidding on a big sale out here. We're expanding, going national, and cracking L.A. would be fantastic," Jane said in order to hold off Jeb's protest. "Call me later at the hotel."

"If I wasn't on hold with this son of a— Hey, Paco, sure, no problem." Jeb waved them off and turned back to the phone.

Jane, following Tim into the little front foyer of the bungalow, gave a good-bye look to the shakers displayed in the window. She noticed a few saltcellars, some tiny pink cut-glass dishes, that she hadn't seen before. In one lay two small keys. They were old enough and tiny enough to fit the lock on the secret gate. Jane picked up the saltcellar and ran a finger around its rim. "Hey, Timmy, this is the real thing. Little fleabites from the silver spoon they used."

"Look at you, Ms. Pro Picker," Tim said. "You need a set of those salts to make them worth anything, honey."

Jane knew all about the relatively small value of the saltcellars, but she didn't answer. It was the little key she had wanted to examine. Jane was a sucker for old keys and locks and hidden gates and secret gardens. Why had Jeb wanted to use the hidden entrance? She clutched the key so tightly that her nails dug into her palm. She would just borrow this key for a few days, she thought, until . . . when? Until she found out why Jeb Gleason used a secret entrance . . . why he anticipated chaos, the police . . . She could hear Bruce Oh's voice in her head, tutoring her on how to be a detective. *Refine your question, Mrs. Wheel. Learn to ask the question that hovers over the obvious.* Right. Jane would borrow the key until she found out why Jeb Gleason, when he thought his friend had been killed, wanted to *avoid* the police.

5

As soon as someone refers to you as hot—as in the hot writer/producer/director—cover your ears and do not, I repeat, do not listen. Make sure you have some money in the bank and a full tank of gas. If you're not careful, you will be heading out of town and into a new career within a month.

—FROM *Hollywood Diary* BY BELINDA ST. GERMAINE

Tim loved driving in L.A. He had picked it up quickly, loved the expensive cars he saw whizzing by, loved the beautiful girls and boys he saw driving the expensive cars, and he adored the *Thomas Guide*.

"It's a bible out here, you know," Tim said, patting it where it sat next to them on the front seat. "I studied it this afternoon while I waited for the car to be delivered."

Thankfully, it wasn't a Mini. Tim had ordered a sensible car for them to drive to Pasadena the next day. A Volvo station wagon.

"Way too soccer mom for my taste," said Tim, "but it was the best they could do for safety and storage and I figured it this way: If we brought a van, we'd feel cocky and shop too large. Anything we can fit into this, I can figure out how to get easily home. Not that we couldn't ship something larger, mind you—"

"Hey," Jane stopped him. "Why are we going to the hospital? What's the secret stuff going on here?"

"Didn't you get my message?"

Jane always answered her cell phone. It was her deal with her son. She had promised Nick that she would always answer and she always did. Even if it meant she would miss bidding on a Heisey punch bowl or a souvenir Rhode Island tablecloth, she would pick up the phone when it rang. Nick, and Tim, for that matter, both tested her by changing the rings, but she had never missed a call from her son . . . except for the time when she hadn't heard it because it didn't ring because she was on the phone already. . . .

"What time did you call exactly?"

Jane calculated that she had been on the phone with Nellie when Tim had called and left a message. She had heard a click or two on the line, but that was usually Nellie tapping a fork against the phone. She claimed it brought better reception to Jane's cell phone.

Yes, she had a message. She decided to listen to recorded Tim, since live Tim was talking out loud to himself, reciting the directions to the hospital that he had memorized, and, Jane observed, he was caressing the *Thomas Guide*, which he had moved to his lap, seemingly channeling information from it.

"Janie, don't be scared, but there was a little explosion in the prop room. Bix got hurt, but I think she'll be okay. Wild-eyed hysteria around here, though—they'll have her dismembered and dead when the telephone rumor game gets through with this. Keep this hush-hush, but Bix wants to talk to you about something, so . . . right, will do . . . hey, Cynda, thanks for the coffee, okay, Max, we'll talk to you later about the Biedermeier. Get back to me as soon as you can and don't tell anyone else, okay? Give me the first refusal, yes?"

Jane finished listening to the message as Tim pulled into the hospital parking lot.

"Did you think Cynda was listening in?"

"I don't know. She comes off like a bimbette one minute, then she's all Ms. Efficiency and number cruncher on the phone.

I wouldn't trust your old boyfriend as far as I could imagine throwing him, but I do think he was right about everyone out here being someone else. I've always prided myself on having an A-1 bullshit detector, but I couldn't tell whether Cynda's a good little actress, trying to be whatever she's supposed to be to whomever she's talking to . . . or if she's a flake."

At Wren's door, Jane hesitated. It was partially closed.

"She wanted us to come, right?" Jane asked.

"Jane? Yes. Come in," Wren called out. "And close the door all the way behind you."

Jane smiled when she saw that almost all of Wren Bixby's braids were still intact. It was comforting in the face of her other injuries. Some of her hair had been singed closer to her face. Her right cheek was bandaged and her right arm was wrapped from shoulder to wrist. When Jane met her that morning, Wren had appeared to be thirtysomething. Without makeup, her skin pale against the hospital-white pillowcase, and lit by overhead fluorescents rather than the low-wattage lamps in the rosy-walled office, Wren looked every bit of forty. A scared and tired forty, at that.

"Wren, I'm—"

"Since you're about to hear my confession, I think you'd better call me Bix. It's my real name. Mary Bixby. So I've always been Bix. Please."

Jane nodded and sat in the chair Bix pointed to and Tim pulled up an extra from across the room.

"Can you find out who tried to kill me?"

Jane tried to maintain a neutral expression. Even though she was semiofficially part of Bruce Oh's consulting service, which was, in fact, a detective agency, she wasn't at all confident in the title. She hadn't received her Illinois license yet, but she guessed that didn't mean she couldn't ask a few questions in California. It was just that she had never been asked such a by-the-book-right-out-of-Miss-Marple question.

Jane tried to remember every mystery movie and television program she had ever watched. Leaning forward and trying very hard not to stumble over her lines, she said, as seriously as the situation warranted, "What makes you think someone is trying to kill you?"

Bix pointed to a script on the bedside table.

"Flip to the middle."

Tim was closest. He picked up the script and fanned the pages. A heavy cardboard tag fell out. It had a piece of twisted wire looped through the grommeted hole. He handed it to Bix.

"Tags like these are used on props in the shop by designers who walk through and want to claim pieces for movies and shows. Remember, Tim, I showed you?"

"Yeah, all the ornate silver . . . candelabras and tankards, vases, and that kind of kitschy bling were tagged for the sequel to *Pirates of the* whatever. All the loot-worthy pieces that could pass for swag had big green tags on them with the movie logo and a *reserved for* message on them," Tim explained to Jane.

"Sometimes people use plain index cards to mark property, sometimes there are cards with a distinguishable color or picture to identify the project or the designer," said Bix, adjusting her arm, allowing Jane to plump the pillow that was supporting it. "When I saw the wooden box with this tag on it, my first thought was to get the tag off before Tim saw it and told you, so I ripped it off and put it in my pocket. Then I opened the box. . . ." Bix closed her eyes.

Jane looked at the tag. *BIXPIXFLIXBIXPIXFLIX* was written as a continuous frieze around the top of the card in a font that mimicked old typewriter letters. Written in purple ink was *Save for SCARECROW MURDERS/JANE WHEEL*.

Bix had seemed plenty confident in her office that morning, but Jane figured that was how people in her business had to act. Sure they could get Teri Hatcher or, hey, why not Julia Roberts to play Jane Wheel, then Jane signs on the dotted line and suddenly, instead of going with a star, it's going to be a breakout role for someone who's been doing cartoon voice-overs. Jane had been in advertising long enough to recognize the bravado. But to go ahead and tag props for a movie not optioned? Script not written?

"Who could have tagged the box?" Jane asked.

"Access to the tags wouldn't be a problem. The front desk in the bungalow is open and Cynda's running off to auditions and meetings herself half the time, so anyone could take out stationery. Our tags might even be in the office at the prop shop. To get into the warehouse, you need to sign in. Authorization and identification . . . all that. But . . ." Bix paused. "People have gotten in who shouldn't be there. It happens. People on studio tours have been known to sneak in. If furniture's being moved out and the side doors are open, someone could walk in, I guess."

"You kidding? Someone could live undetected up on the third floor," said Tim. "Once you've gotten in, with or without credentials, who notices when you leave? If you leave?"

"You're supposed to sign out with the time. There's a book . . . someone must check it," said Bix.

"Is someone sitting with the book?" asked Jane.

"Yes. Well, not always. I mean, they don't necessarily watch you sign or anything," said Bix.

"Honey, there was no attendant when you and I walked in and signed today," said Tim. "You called out hello to someone and they answered from another office where they were on the phone."

"Yeah . . . but they know me."

"So, if they know me, I could just sign in and mark a time out for fifteen minutes later while I'm signing in, then disappear upstairs without anyone knowing I was there past the time I wrote in," said Jane.

"Hardly has to be that complicated," said Tim. "I saw people returning a dining room set through a side door and it was just a bunch of workmen carrying things in. Someone could have walked in right behind them carrying that box, already tagged, set it down, and left the lot altogether."

This was where Jane needed the Bruce Oh side of her brain to kick in. Without him by her side, she felt herself drifting into the land of infinite questions. She hadn't found a tangent yet that she didn't want to explore. She was already jealous that Tim had seen the props warehouse and she hadn't. Aisles and aisles of Hollywood stuff, movie props, set dressing, and one of those pieces literally had her name on it. Until it blew up.

"What was the box anyway? An old chemistry set like they said?" Jane asked.

Bix shook her head. She didn't think so. "It was an unmarked oak box. It could have held a silver service or maybe compartments for type—"

"Okay," said Jane. "We don't know exactly what the box was and we know that anybody could have put it in the prop shop."

"Whoa, slow down, Nancy Drew, you are solving this case way too fast for me to keep up," said Tim. "How do you do it?"

"Go ahead, mock. It is important that anyone could have gotten into the prop shop. Not just someone from Bix Pix Flix. Think about it. Before you knew all that today, would you have thought it possible to get in there and tag something like that? You didn't even know the system existed. So it was somebody familiar with the lot and the system of marking props," said Jane. "Somebody who could get a tag from the Bix Pix Flix office . . . which you said, Bix, is easy enough. So . . . who knew about *The Scarecrow Murder*? I mean, who knew that you were trying to get the rights to this story?"

Bix sighed. "There aren't any secrets. I talked to my agent, who had already shown the treatment around to some actresses, and then there are all the rumor bloggers who announce what everybody's doing all the time even before people decide to do it."

"Teri Hatcher?" Jane asked with a smile. "Was she really getting a look?"

Bix shrugged. "We hoped, but . . . you know . . . maybe."

Jane looked around the hospital room. It was a typical room, forgettable in its antiseptic straightforward layout. There was a bulletin board opposite the bed with the only spot of color in the room—a tacked-up laminated sheet of yellow paper. Drawn and illustrated on the page was the Pain Rating Scale. A vertical line marked 1 to 10 with corresponding faces next to the number. Number 10 was a crying face, four tears. Number 9, still crying, but only two tears. As the faces went down in number, the crudely drawn expressions of discomfort lessened until the illustration of number 1 was the internationally recognized symbol of feeling good, the smiley face.

Jane went over and took it off the bulletin board. Looking at number 5, a face with a quizzical upside-down smile, she inadvertently pulled the corners of her own mouth down. She turned to Bix, who was pouring herself a glass of water with her left hand. Jane wondered if it was too painful to move her right arm or if Bix was left-handed. She hadn't noticed this morning.

"Why do you think someone was trying to kill you?" asked Jane, still frowning.

"Someone is trying to kill everyone—"

"Oh, you already have visitors, Bix? I didn't know, doll. Poor child, I heard you lost your arm, but that's not as bad as poor old Jeb got it. He heard you were dead." The breathless blonde who burst through the door without knocking stopped for a short breath before plowing on with her special brand of comfort. "You want Tressie to send the caterer with some menus? I hear the food is dreadful here. I've got the name of a hand surgeon. The best. De Niro's hand surgeon. Might as well have him on your speed dial, you know, just in case." Blondie stopped and stuck out her own perfectly groomed hand first to Jane, then to Tim. "I am Skye." She paused for a moment, as if she were giving them a moment for the name to sink in. "I am Wren Bixby's best friend." She paused again. It seemed to be a speech pattern. She was either giving her thoughts time to take effect or holding for applause.

Jane and Tim introduced themselves. Bix, looking more than exhausted, didn't say a word.

"Why did De Niro need a hand surgeon?" Tim asked.

"Great question," said Skye. She leaned forward as if sharing a secret. "No one knows because no one's talking. Not De Niro, not the surgeon, no one."

"Then how do you know—" Tim started to ask Skye at the same time Jane directed the question to Bix.

"How do you know—" Jane began, wanting to know if, before Skye entered the room, Bix was commenting on life in Hollywood where everyone was trying to kill everyone or whether she had some specific everyones in mind, but Bix interrupted.

"Skye, I'm pretty tired, but I have to finish some business with Jane and Tim. We flew them out here for a meeting and I feel—"

"Where's Lou, precious?"

"Lou went up to Ojai for a few days, so I—"

"Everybody's going to be here in a few minutes, so I could step out and wait for them in the hall and you could—"

"Oh no," said Bix. "The whole B Room? I'm too tired, honey. Get rid of—"

Jane was always amused when a concept, a description from a book came true and happened in her life. So often, a room was described as *suddenly full of people*, which of course sounds like an exaggeration, but that's exactly what this was. A before-and-after come to life. The door opened and in the same breathless manner that Skye had arrived, four more people came in, all talking at once, to each other and across each other.

Where there had been quiet conversation, there was now party banter mixed with loud expressions of concern that quickly turned into a contest of who had been the most frightened by the news of Bix's accident.

Jane was reminded of a children's story, a kind of *Not I, said the cat / Not I, said the goose* rhythm, that developed as they all spoke up, introduced themselves, and professed their horror at the news.

"I heard Bix lost her arm," said Rick Stewart, shaking hands with Jane and Tim. "I was the first story editor hired on *S and L*."

"You all wrote for *Saturday Night Live?*" asked Tim.

Greg Thale, who said he heard Bix had been decapitated, hooted and hollered and high-fived Rick, who nodded and grinned.

"*Southpaw and Lefty*," Bix said quietly. "We all worked on *Southpaw and Lefty . . . S and L*, not *SNL*. Rick gets a lot of mileage out of implying the latter instead of admitting the former."

"And a lot of improv babes," said Rick, who had to be at least fiftysomething. He was trim and perfectly tanned, but definitely had the look of the godfather of this group. "Those BU conservatory grads who come out here for pilot season . . . hmm, hmm."

"Ah, Ricky, you smack your lips like the Big Bad Wolf, but we know you only want to mentor. . . . I'm Louise Dietz." She shook Jane's hand and nodded across the room at Tim. "And we are the B Room."

"Together again," said Jeb Gleason from the doorway.

Jane turned around and saw that Jeb still posed when he entered a room. When all eyes had turned to him, he sauntered in. Presenting Bix with a perfectly tied and tissue-wrapped bouquet of long-stemmed roses, he said, with no discernible emotion, "I heard that you died."

"Decapitated sort of implies the same thing, don't you think?" asked Greg.

"We were devastated, babe," added Rick.

"The B Room," Louise continued, as if she were used to interruptions from the people in the room, "was the conference room where we all worked on *Southpaw*. There was Conference Room A and Conference Room B. Sandy Pritikin, the star of the show, took over A with his entourage, so we all hung out in B twelve hours a day."

"More like twenty hours a day. Someone wanted a snappier joke at the end of a scene, a better line somewhere, he came to the B Room, and we were there. On call," said Rick.

"We became very close," said Skye, who looked from face to face. "Greg and Rick haven't been apart since Day One. Jeb and Bix wrote screenplays together afterwards. Louise worked with Jeb on *Gal Pals* for three years—"

"You're Celie!" said Tim. "It's been driving me crazy. You played Lefty's daughter."

Skye blushed a studied shade of pink and nodded.

"The last season, when Celie was written out of most episodes, away at college, Skye started writing and we did two of her stories," said Bix.

"Yes, I only had one year in the B Room, but it changed my life," said Skye. "I'd been around actors since I was four and I didn't realize there were any good and normal people in the world until I found writers."

Jeb laughed loudly when Skye pronounced them good and normal. "All relative, baby. Only next to Sandy and those egomaniac actors would we have passed for normal. Next to them, we were the Sunday choir."

Jane looked at the people crowded into the hospital room. These were the creative minds behind *Southpaw and Lefty*? She remembered the actors—Sandy Pritikin, Denise DeMill, Larry Diamond, and, of course, Skye Miller, the child actress who had literally grown up in her six seasons as Celie—

who made up the regular cast of the show, but except for Jeb's name, Jane had never paid any attention to the writing credits.

Southpaw and Lefty was a show-within-a-show format about two writers who really didn't like each other, but each needed the other to produce successful television scripts. They were both left-handed, so one of the stars on the fictional series they wrote had nicknamed them, giving the show its catchy, if meaningless, title. Jane and Charley didn't watch that much television, but usually caught this one. It was serious drama off the studio lot, but when the writers got together, the comedy was brilliant. No laugh track except when the fictional show-within-a-show was being taped.

"I missed it in your bio . . . that you wrote for *S and L,*" Jane said to Bix.

"I don't list it anymore." Bix spoke softly and Jane could see that she was bone-tired. Exhausted. Skye noticed, too, and met Jane's eyes.

"Everybody out for tonight," said Skye. "Bix has to rest."

Her visitors gathered around Bix and began fussing with her covers, patting her feet, kissing her cheek. Louise Dietz, the first to give her a quick kiss, left her side and came over to stand in front of Jane.

"You're the detective who Bix wants to do a movie about," she said.

"Nothing's been decided," said Jane, "and now—"

"Now you've got a new case."

Jane thought about lodging a protest. Not only did she want to keep Bix's conversation with her private, she also wanted to break her habit of immediately demurring. Detective Oh maintained that silence was strength.

When Jane didn't say anything, Louise continued.

"Maybe you can find out who wants to knock us all—"

"Louise, I'll drop at you home," said Rick. "Greg and I have to go back to the office and it's on my way."

Louise nodded.

Jeb was the last to leave Bix's bedside. He shepherded the crowd of writers out the door, including Jane and Tim in his sweep. "I want you two to stay with me for the weekend. I have a guesthouse that makes the W look like a Holiday Inn Express. Bix asked me to take care of you two for her. If you'll stay through the weekend, at least until Monday, she'll be ready to talk business again before you leave."

"I forgot my bag," said Jane. It was the oldest trick in the book, but she knew if she was going to get a minute alone with Bix, it would have to be while everyone else was heading for the elevator.

Bix had her eyes closed, but opened them when Jane came in and picked up the bag she had stashed between bed and nightstand so no one would see it and retrieve it for her as they all made their way out.

"Whoever rigged that box tagged it for Bix Pix and knew I would open it," said Bix. "There have been other accidents. . . . I said somebody was trying to hurt us, but Jeb thinks I'm being silly. Today I got this."

Bix had been holding the note she now passed to Jane under the covers. It was the size of a phone message sheet.

One little, two little, three little writers, four little, five little, six little writers, seven little, eight little, nine little writers, ten little TV hacks. And then there were nine. You've got five days to come up with it. If you don't give me back what's mine, you'll all go to hell. Oops, writing for network. Heck.

"This was with the phone message I got from Jeb when you were in the office. Cynda didn't know who took it down or where it came from. I was going to ask you, when you got back from lunch, if you'd consider . . ." Bix hesitated and took a deep breath. "Look, I've already had a sleeping pill and a pain pill and maybe that's why I can talk like this, you know, without the bullshit. I knew you didn't want to sell your rights. But I thought maybe, if you came out here, maybe you could take this case . . . maybe Jeb would be okay if it was you doing the detective work . . . I mean, it was his—"

"What does Jeb have to do with it?" asked Jane. "More important, I guess, what is *it*? The *it* that the writer of the note wants?"

"I don't know. Nobody knows. If I hadn't opened that box . . . but they knew I'd open it, with the tag and . . ." Bix was fighting to keep her eyes open.

"Bix Pix," repeated Jane. "*Pix*. Lou Piccolo might have opened it, too. I should talk to Lou, don't you think?"

Bix was asleep.

6

Go for producing credit, people. Everyone knows that as soon as studios can figure out how to eliminate writers altogether, they will. Writers will be dead and buried. My prediction? Actors and directors are next.

—FROM *Hollywood Diary* BY BELINDA ST. GERMAINE

"Okay, pal, I know you are on a case," said Tim, already comfortable behind the wheel, "but let's not get our priorities screwed up, okay? Tomorrow morning we are leaving for Pasadena at 5:50 A.M. I checked at the nurses' station, using my considerable charm with head nurse Ratchet, and found out that Bix is scheduled to go into surgery at seven A.M. to have a few glass fragments removed from her arm. She won't be able to talk, let alone have any visitors, until at least two P.M. So until that time, you are my partner in T & T Sales and we are on a separate mission. *Capiche?*"

"It isn't just Bix who thinks somebody wants to kill her," said Jane. "Louise thinks somebody is after them, too. She said *us . . . why does someone want to knock us—*"

"Are you listening to me? California pottery, midcentury modern furniture, boatloads of costume jewelry, deco out the ass . . . honey, we've arrived at flea market heaven," said Tim, navigating his way through Los Angeles traffic as if he had been born with a leather-wrapped steering wheel of a café-au-lait Porsche in his hands. Never mind that the rental in which they were speeding toward Westwood was the soccer-mom-special Volvo.

"I could get used to this, Janie, I really could."

"What? Living out here?" Jane asked. "You'd never leave the good old Midwest, Tim. Four distinct seasons, honest hardworking people, and a sensible time zone where you can watch the news at ten and see Letterman's first bit before falling asleep."

"Darling, I am an antique-dealing florist who loathes shoveling snow, hates holier-than-thou hardworking people who act all superior because they graduated from the damn school of hard knocks. And, in case you've forgotten, I'm a single gay man who isn't getting any younger. I may look fabulous next to you, sweetheart, but I'm ready to settle down before these crow's-feet start wearing boots."

Jane had no idea what that meant. It did make sense that Tim was enamored of L.A. So many beautiful people, so many who were ready to pay top dollar for the kind of unique objects that Tim knew how to find. For the first time ever, Jane felt no urge to offer up her night-before-sale prayers for all the right stuff. Her silent litany of let-there-be-pottery-Bakelite-beads-and-buttons-ironwork-planters-oak picture frames-Heisey glass-cigar boxes-vintage linen-yardsticks-and-old-sewing-gadgets would not be recited tonight. Jane hoped tomorrow's flea market would be dull—worse than dull, full of Beanie Babies and tube socks. If Tim found beautiful weather, beautiful people, and beautiful objects all in one place, she could lose him.

"What would Kankakee do without you? You're the mover and shaker of that place, Tim, and they need your energy and your creativity—"

Jane's phone, still proclaiming itself by an angelic choir, sang out loud and clear.

Jane smiled in relief when she saw the number.

"Hello, Charley."

She asked for an update on Nick and their site activities

and waited for Charley to ask her if she had found any bodies that week.

"Nope," she said, "but there was an accident that I've been asked—"

Jane stopped, hearing shouting on the other end of the line. Someone, with a thick French accent, was calling Charley, her sweet smart husband, a vile name. It sounded even worse with the vowels drawn and elongated.

"Nothing serious," said Charley. "There's another team down here and they think we're trying to steal all their results and pass them off as ours. They try to pick fights with us when they see us in town, call us thieves and liars. I've never seen anything like it. A local paper, I think it was from some school, actually, did a story about the interest in digging here and they got mixed up. When they introduced us at the symposium, the moderator gave our guys credit for excavating this turtle, which was the other group's big find, and nobody can make them understand that it wasn't us trying to steal their thunder, just a mistake on paper."

"Nick? Do they yell at Nick?" Jane asked.

"Nah. You know him. He's the peacemaker. Friend of the common man and all. He's over at the town's only restaurant right now eating rice and beans with half the population of this place. We're staying here in town for the weekend. We're fine, Jane. Just one of those academic pissing matches. Always amazes me how petty these things are when there's no money or power involved."

Jane gave Charley the details of her movie-deal mystery, at least as much as she knew, mentioning at the end of the story that Jeb Gleason—did Charley remember her ever mentioning her college beau, Jeb Gleason?—had been Bix's writing partner and that she and Tim had been invited to stay at his place for the weekend. After what seemed to Jane a beat too long, Charley responded with, "Small world."

Weekly phone calls were killers. Jane thought they might be better off without cell phones. If they were writing letters, they could control the communication so much better. Best of all, they could respond to the words rather than the spaces between them.

"You know I'm crazy about you, Charley," said Jane.

Another beat, where Jane tried hard to hear whether or not he was smiling.

"I know you're crazy."

Back at the hotel, Jane took out her Lucky Five notebook where she kept her picking lists of current objects of desire, and began making notes while Tim ordered room service. He struggled with the fact that the bartender in the lobby was a ringer for Brad Pitt, but ultimately decided that the minibar would be indulgence enough for tonight.

Jane wrote down the names of the B Room. Bix. Greg and Rick. Louise. Jeb. Skye. Lou. Was Lou Piccolo an *S and L* writer? A member of the B Room? Jane wrote that as her first question. She also noted that no one at the studio had suggested calling the police. Everyone Jane encountered had dramatically re-created the moment of the explosion—at least how the moment had affected them. No one seemed to be interested in having the incident investigated. As far as Jane could tell, no one had even called the fire department. There was a quick response team on the lot that came over and sprayed down the smoking box, cordoned off the area where two aisles of glass vases had been shattered so no one got hurt before the cleanup. Did everyone really accept the explanation that an old chemistry set had exploded? If that were truly the case, all those old boxed Mr. Wizard sets that were prized for their cool graphics and sold on eBay as MIB—mint in box—condition were accidents waiting to happen. Surely nothing as volatile as what caused this box to go off when opened was normally present in a toy science kit. Jane made a mental note to ask Charley.

If Bix had shown anyone the tag that identified the box as a prop for *The Scarecrow Murder*—and explained that she hadn't been the one to tag it—the police would have been called. The box would have been saved and examined. Instead it was cleaned up and swept away by the maintenance staff on the studio lot.

This meant that Bix chose not to get the police involved even though she knew the importance of the tag. If she hadn't torn it off and looked at it, if she hadn't put it into her left hand when she opened the box with her right, it probably would have been destroyed along with whatever was in the box. Why bring it to the hospital to show Jane when she could have asked for the police then and there? *She was right*, thought Jane, *and she knew she was right*. Someone had certainly rigged the box. But Bix was a producer, so why would . . . ? Jane leafed through her copy of *Hollywood Diary* that lay open on the bed.

According to Belinda St. Germaine, the producer made the deal. Raised the money. Hired the writer, the director. Producers made the budget, oversaw the operation. Producers were at the top of the food chain. On any given project, there were probably dozens of people who would want to kill the producer, but rigging a box to explode when the producer found it in the prop shop? Producers didn't scout props.

"Tim, did Bix call anybody and tell them she was bringing you over to the prop warehouse?" asked Jane.

"I don't think so. She told the assistants where she was going as we were leaving," said Tim, handing her a glass of ice and a mini bottle of Grey Goose. He was leafing through his own notebook, preparing for the flea market. "It was all set up."

"What do you mean, all set up?" asked Jane.

"She didn't have to call Gary because she had called him before. There were passes with our names on them waiting for us, so she must have arranged it in advance."

"Where were the passes? Did someone pull them out of a drawer when you came in?"

"They were lying out on a table. There were four or five badges with different names on them," said Tim, opening a jar of olives, ignoring Jane's protest as she picked up the minibar price list. "Mine said VIP." Tim fished the plastic-covered badge out of his pocket and tossed it to Jane.

Anyone who walked by the table could see who might be coming in with a guest that day. If the box bomber wanted Bix—Jane noted that she was now starting to sound like the alliterative showbiz headlines in *Variety*—he or she could note Bix's name tag on the table, go off and rig the box, tag it, and place it where Bix would see it.

Dinner arrived. Tim was delighted to note that the room service waiter also looked like Brad Pitt and if there were this many look-alikes in one hotel, how many must there be in the whole city?

Jane picked up the tiny bottle of ketchup that accompanied her club sandwich and french fries. She attributed her love of miniature anything to her own small stature. Tiny boxes and bottles made her feel like a giant in a world where she usually had to ask for help getting Cheerios down from the high shelf in the supermarket.

"Isn't it funny how wonderful condiments look when they're tiny?" she asked, then picked up the saltshaker. "I mean, this little individual saltshaker makes you want to—"

"Slip it in your purse, dear?" asked Tim, cutting into his filet while inhaling the aroma of melted butter that accompanied the "surf" half of his dinner.

"Wait, Tim, isn't the props warehouse enormous? Didn't you say it was—"

"Huge," said Tim, spreading a bathroom towel over his Armani slacks before attacking his lobster.

"Where was Bix when she opened the box?" asked Jane, turning the saltshaker in her hand.

"I was two aisles over, I think, and we were both surrounded by table-setting pieces, so she was . . . I guess she was in the middle of the Depression glass. Lots of small cruets and salt and peppers . . . oh," said Tim. "Bix collects Depression glass salt and pepper shakers and the box was there, in the middle of them."

"Right where Bix was sure to go whenever she took a VIP visitor to the prop warehouse," said Jane. "Bix's box bomber bided his time, then planted it—"

"Say that five times fast."

"She needs police protection. She's a sitting duck in that hospital."

"Bix didn't want the police called. She made that clear to me when it happened. She wanted you. What's the code of ethics on this, Nancy Drew?"

Jane was already dialing, glancing down at her notes from the hospital.

A woman's voice answered, a perky healthy voice that didn't sound like Bix, who had been unable to keep her eyes open when Jane left her earlier.

"It's Skye," she answered when Jane asked to whom she was speaking.

"I was worried," Jane began, "about Bix being there alone all night."

"Aren't you sweet? Me, too. She was so shaken up. I've never seen Bix like that. She's always such a rock. I'm spending the night with her. Got a cot and everything. Turns out that the night nurse was a huge fan of *S and L*, particularly my character. They've got me all fixed up here. They'll wake me first if anyone comes in wanting to see Bix." Skye took a deep breath. "They said it was impossible to get up here after visiting hours and I reminded them that I had come back and walked right up, so they get it."

"Can you persuade her to call the police, Skye?"

"The only one who can talk Bix into anything is Jeb," said Skye. Jane thought she heard disapproval in Skye's voice. "And he thinks calling the police would be bad pub and a bad move all around."

Jeb and the B Room had left Bix's hospital room when Jane and Tim left. Jane asked Skye when Bix and Jeb had discussed calling the police.

"Oh, Jeb came back up for a minute after you all had left. He wanted to know if Bix wanted him to call her sister or something. Kind of a made-up excuse, if you ask me. Jeb just always wants the last word. Bix told him she was scared and maybe it wasn't an accident and he just cut her off and patted her arm and shushed her. I was listening right outside the door," Skye said. "I always try to keep an eye on things when Jeb's around.

"Told Bix she'd lose her office at the studio while some investigation dragged on. He said it'd give the prankster just what he wants. What?" Sky responded to someone in the room. "Dolly, the nurse, said the phone has to be shut off now. I'll be here until they take her into surgery in the morning. Don't you worry, I've got it covered."

It was hard for Jane to imagine Skye as a bodyguard. Although she realized that Skye was all grown up, only eight or nine years younger than Jane herself, she would always think of her as the little girl on the show. Celie was a resourceful, spunky girl, the kind of wise and funny daughter that every parent on television spawned. Since Jane watched the show long before Nick was born, she had no idea what it would be like to have a smart-ass-TV-worthy-wisecracking kid. Now that she knew, she'd have to cut Sandy Pritikin's character a little more slack. No wonder he always seemed so hapless and defensive. Having

Nick, who could outthink her in almost every subject, made her head hurt. As much as she adored her son, his steady assurance made her feel all the more wobbly. What if there was only so much self-confidence allotted per household? Charley was totally comfortable in his own skin and Nick was almost uncrackable—except when his mother talked about his soccer prowess on television—so were those two using up the household's ration of confidence? Better grab some while they were out of the country.

"I know you do, Skye," said Jane, taking a deep breath, "but if Bix wakes up in the night, I want you to use all your power of persuasion to get her to call the police. Tell her I called and I'll do anything for her I can. But the police need to be there to protect her. Do you—"

The line clicked off. Jane redialed the hospital to make sure it was the switchboard shutting off the phone. She listened to the first sentence of the recorded message about patients' room phones being silent until seven A.M. tomorrow and hung up.

Jane dialed Jeb Gleason's number and got a businesslike message—no jokes or cutesy patter—but didn't leave a message. She would call back in the morning and accept his invitation. She had been ready to refuse his offer of an extra few days at his place, but now she thought it might be a good idea. If Jeb was the only one who could persuade Bix that she needed more help than Jane could give, Jane needed to persuade Jeb. The B Room group was an odd little cabal. Since Jeb seemed to be the leader of the pack, his house was as good a place to start as any. And according to the note Bix had received, they only had five days to figure it all out.

Jane Wheel had come all the way to L.A. for what Tim had assured her was a well-deserved vacation. As she prepared for tomorrow's adventure—laid out her tan fisherman's vest and loaded the pockets with sunscreen, a small notebook, and a camera—she realized that she had flown across the country to do exactly what she would be doing back in Evanston. At six A.M., she would stuff her hair up under Nick's old Little League baseball cap, put her sunglasses on a neck chain so she could whip them off in a hurry to check colors on a vintage tablecloth and read the markings on the bottom of a flowerpot, and wear thick, cushioned socks with her most comfortable running shoes. Armed with cash in one pocket, tools of the trade in all of the others, she and Tim would walk every inch of the vast parking lot, sweep every table with their eyes, and lift and scratch and smell every object that whispered their names at the Pasadena City College Flea Market.

Jane and Tim would scold and laugh with their imaginary children, Patina and Veneer, who had accompainied them on all their jaunts since they had invented them out of boredom during a few ho-hum lots of new pots and pans at a Kankakee auction. They would relentlessly comb every aisle for the most precious treasure of all, the one which, when glimpsed, would set their hearts racing, take their breath away, stop them in their tracks, infuse them with the I-found-it-and-you-didn't power that is a picker's potent drug—that object which they wouldn't know until they spied it, wanted it, had to have it, couldn't explain how they had lived without it before that moment. That's what Jane would be doing in Pasadena in the morning . . . all the things she did every weekend morning of her life. And, just as she did every market morning in Evanston, she hoped she wouldn't find a dead body in the middle of it all.

7

If you mention a hot gossip item to an actress, be prepared for a quizzical know-it-all glance. It's not that she's already heard it, it's just that she can't move her eyebrows out of that position. And that actor who doesn't seem to be concentrating on the question you just asked him? Honey, no one's been able to furrow their brow out there since an in-the-know hostess served mohitos at her botox party.

—FROM *Hollywood Diary* BY BELINDA ST. GERMAINE

Tim needed no help navigating the freeways. Jane held a map in her hand for the first five minutes until she realized that her directional skills, praiseworthy as they may be, were not necessary. Tim had either crammed for this trip by studying maps and charts, pulling an all-nighter to become an A+ student of greater Los Angeles, or he was telling the truth when he said simply, "I was born to live in this place."

Since Tim was happily listing the pros and cons of the various neighborhoods he had decided he might be able to live in and Jane did not want to listen to any of it, she shushed him and dialed Detective Bruce Oh's cell phone number.

"Oh," he answered.

"My," said Jane, trying yet another counter to his stubborn habit of answering the phone with his confusing last name.

"Mrs. Wheel," he said. "I was just about to call you. I have been called away on a personal matter and was unable to reach you before I left."

"Me, too. I had to leave town and tried to call."

"Interesting that we have so many devices for keeping in touch and yet somehow we still miss giving each other our vital information. How do you suppose one would document whether or not communication has really improved?"

"I won't be able to stop by the office to pick up messages on Monday. I'm in California with Tim. I think I've taken a case." Even as Jane said it, she felt ridiculous. Taken a cold, maybe. Taken a fever, certainly. But taken a case? What was she thinking? Just because Bix was sure Jane could help her didn't mean Jane actually could.

"Congratulations, Mrs. Wheel."

"Thanks. I sort of fell into it because the producer I was talking to out here was involved in an explosion and she thinks someone is trying to kill her. It wasn't a large explosion, but—"

"I would like to take you out to celebrate. It is in your wallet at all times, yes?" said Oh.

"I'm sorry . . ." said Jane.

"Your license. You received your private investigator's license. We will celebrate when we return from California. My wife is parking our car now. I should make myself available if she requests guidance."

Jane heard Claire Oh's voice in the background. It did not sound as if she were asking for help. Maybe she was just commenting on Oh's use of the royal *we*. Had Oh told Jane where he was?

"I will call you later."

Ah, sweet missed communication. Jane now wished they had continued the game of phone tag. Talking to each other was not exactly communication in its purest form. In order to obtain her private investigator's license, Jane had promised she would take the required state of Illinois examination. She had studied all of the material Oh had brought to her home—the handbooks on criminal code and procedures, the government statutes, every mind-numbingly boring piece of professional literature he had thrown her way. Nick and Charley had quizzed her from the sample test. Piece of cake. She knew the information. She was also a good test-taker. She loved nothing more than sharpening a handful of No. 2 pencils and strutting her stuff. It was just that the test was scheduled on the same date as the first day of the Canton farm sale in Crete, Illinois. Jane and Tim had planned their strategy for months. There was to be an auction of large items out in the yard, a conducted house sale inside the rambling fifteen-room main house, and a barn full of *all the rest*, as the bill of sale described it. The Cantons had lived on the property for over a hundred years, hoarding and gathering and saving and mending, and when the last grandchild agreed to let it all go, mouths began watering in five states.

So, while Jane should have been acing her exam, busily answering which amendment guaranteed the right to bear arms and other questions equally pertinent to the day-to-day life of being a private investigator, she was wrapping up twenty place settings of antique china in bubble wrap after beating out three dealers to the barrel in the barn where they were stored. Detective Bruce Oh, former police investigator, now her partner in criminal investigation, was never sarcastic. He sincerely believed she had received her license in the mail. He believed it because, Jane now realized, she had forgotten to tell him she did not take the exam.

He hadn't said how long he would be gone. Maybe she could get home, take the exam, and pass it before she saw him again. Yeah, and maybe they were handing out a free carved Bakelite bracelet with every flea market admission today.

Tim parked the rental in the covered garage structure as if he had reserved this spot for every first weekend of the month. Jane looked her friend up and down as they got out of the car.

With her hair stuffed under her cap and her vest pockets bulging with her flea market essentials, she was dressed like an illustration from *Picker's Digest*, if such a magazine existed, and she fervently wished it did. Tim, as usual in linen shirt and pressed trousers, was modeling for *GQ*. Tim had always looked handsome, but he had never looked so . . . alive. When had he gotten so tan?

The market was laid out inside the parking garage as well as in the parking lot outside. Most friends who attended flea markets for their own entertainment strolled the aisles together chatting and holding up the teapots that were just like Grandma's and the old pot holders that their mothers had thrown away, but Tim and Jane had a more professional approach. Tim was a speed scanner—looking over a table quickly and only honing in on the valuables on his own list. He was open to finding the unexpected, but only if it began beeping on his radar screen during that initial methodical scan.

Jane, on the other hand, was a feeler. She had to touch every object possible, turning over pots and vases to check marks, yes, and feel Depression glass for chips and cracks, of course, but more than that she had to feel the texture of cloth, hold a candlestick in her hand, turn the pages of an autograph book. She had to touch it all. She knew what she had to have by how quickly it warmed her hand.

The plan was for each of them to go at their best pace and reconnect every hour. Tim pointed to the spot where they'd meet after the first hour. A blue truck with yellow lettering and four I BRAKE FOR JUNK bumper stickers plastered across the tailgate.

Jane walked to the first table, called over by the green McCoy flowerpot with saucer. She had two of them already, but needed to check prices out here to see how they compared to Chicago. That was another essential when easing into a new market. Check out the familiar objects right away to see how prices compared. Often, what was dear in one region might be plentiful in another. Of course, with the television shows on collectibles and treasures multiplying exponentially, the playing fields were being leveled all over the country.

First, it was Martha Stewart jacking up the price of jadeite dishes everywhere by featuring it in her magazine and on television. Activities related to insider trading were the least of her crimes. How about price-fixing? As soon as she featured crocheted pot holders in the magazine, Jane saw the price jump from twenty-five cents to five dollars each. And the *Antiques Roadshow?* As much as Jane pined for the Keno twins to appraise her with half the excitement they lavished on a Philadelphia highboy, she knew that the show did more harm than good. Everyone believed that they just might have a treasure and raised prices accordingly.

Jane picked up a box from under the table and sifted through the heavy cardboard rectangles. Great graphics. Primary colors on light brown card stock. Illustrated alphabet flash cards. Large classroom-sized and, best of all, bilingual. C is for *cake* and *T* is for *Torta*. Too cool. *Muy bueno*. Jane bought the whole box, practically stole it for five dollars. The dealer showed her another box of classroom flotsam and jetsam. Science experiments, art project ideas on heavy square cards with bold illustrations from the 1950s. The group of blond curly-haired girls and clean-cut rosy-cheeked boys cavorting on these cards were even more fun than the unbiquitous Dick and Jane illustrations. Jane bought the whole box.

At the next table, there was a huge suitcase filled with keys. Old, rusty, and corroded. Jane's heart pounded. Need, desire, greed inflamed her. She wanted them all. She wanted to be able to fill a suitcase with keys—with all of their potential. That many keys had to provide answers to almost everything. Jane reached in and fished out a stainless steel ring five inches in diameter, filled almost entirely with keys. It weighed at least three pounds, She needed to own it. Jane didn't like the look in the dealer's eyes. A wizened old scalper she could handle, but a young girl with long brown hair was going to mean trouble. She was there because she still saw the stuff instead of the dollar signs. Jane could tell she was afraid to sell any of her keys. She needed them, too.

"I didn't even know that ring was in there," she said, hesitating. "I'm not sure . . ." she began fingering each key. "I hadn't meant to—"

"How much?" Jane repeated, trying to seem casual.

"Thirty dollars?" the girl said, hoping that the ridiculous price would send Jane away so she could hide these keys.

"Twenty?" asked Jane, hoping the girl wouldn't notice the hope and fear in her voice.

"Well, maybe I could do twenty-five."

Jane had the money out before the girl could change her mind and dropped the keys into her bag, knowing that her back would be killing her tomorrow. Big heavy purchases could usually be paid for and left at the dealers' tables, but this ring of keys would disappear if Jane didn't keep possession. Jane walked away, automatically putting her hand in her pocket to make sure the tiny gate key she had borrowed from Wren Bixby's office was still there. What would she do with all these keys? She could already hear Tim's questions, see Charley's quizzical look.

"I'll unlock doors," Jane said softly to herself.

"Hey, hi! Sorry, are you on the phone?" Louise Dietz, wearing a wide-brimmed sun hat and carrying a straw shopping bag, waved a plate in front of her. "Bluebird china," she said, unable to hide how much she wanted the plate from the dealer, who Jane could see out of one eye had already decided he wouldn't have to lower the price on that piece.

Jane shook her head—no, she hadn't yet stuck the phone wire into her ear that would make her look like even more of a bag lady.

"Should have known you'd be here," said Louise, peeling off a twenty from a roll Jane thought was too carelessly replaced in her shirt pocket. "Bix loved the collecting angle. We're all into this. . . ." Louise waved her free hand to encompass the market. She tucked the carefully wrapped plate into her bag and began walking next to Jane.

"Except for Jeb. He says he comes to these places to study characters. Claims not to want to own anything that wasn't his first." Louise took Jane's elbow and steered her away from the next table. "Down at the end, there's some great jewelry. You'll love it."

Jane's nightmare. Shopping *with* someone. *Someone talking to her.* Expecting her to answer, to pay attention. And now Louise was steering her away from a table that might hold exactly what Jane wanted. Needed. Damn it—here she was at a flea market across the damn country and she still could run into someone who could throw her off. How far did you have to go to shop in lustful peace?

"I told Bix you wouldn't sign away your rights. I could tell when I heard your story," said Louise.

Great. Not only someone who could push her off course literally, but someone who could actually put her off balance figuratively.

"I mean, here you are, from the Midwest, suspicious as hell of anyone out here anyway. You know we're all glitter and bluff," said Louise, looking closely at an ornate rhinestone sunflower brooch. Not Jane's style, but whenever Jane saw someone look at something that closely, she started thinking maybe she did want it after all.

"And," Louise continued, "you have a family and a life and when I saw that tape of you at Jeb's, I told everyone it would be a coup just to get you out here, but you'd never sign."

"Tape? At Jeb's?" Sure, it was just a few minutes of her babbling away about her life, not exactly the Paris Hilton video, but she still felt violated. What were they doing? The entire B Room crowd having a pajama party and making fun of her, planning on making her wacky life fodder for their dirty business?

"Yeah. We always have meetings there. Best screening room. Best cook." Louise paid for her pin. Jane noticed she didn't even attempt bargaining. These were the people who drove prices up all over.

Louise shrugged. "It's *Joseff—Hollywood* with the 1938 trademark and they only had three dollars on it. I don't know how they missed it. It's worth a lot more. Wouldn't have been right to bargain on that one, would it?" she asked Jane.

Okay, so perhaps Jane had underestimated Louise.

"I'm not sure I understand. Does the B Room get together to vote on everyone's individual projects?" asked Jane.

"It's not a vote. We're just close as writers and as friends and we got used to running things by each other. Then after Heck died . . . Can you sit for a minute?" Louise motioned to a couple of benches. "Sorry, but I get too distracted looking at the stuff."

Jane nodded. She was beginning to feel like she was getting a fair trade for missing some of the stuff. Louise talked as if Jane knew a lot of what she was saying already and Jane, remembering Detective Oh's admonition that silence brought more answers than questions, smiled encouragingly but didn't say anything as they got comfortable on the bench, their bags between them.

"Did Jeb tell you about Heck?" Louise continued when Jane shook her head. "Henry Rule. We called him Heck because he wouldn't swear. I mean, he wouldn't say . . . well, you know . . . if he had a mouthful. That was out loud. But he *wrote* the foulest stuff. I mean, he would parody some of the scripts we wrote for S and L, you know, write the X-rated version, and it would be so bad. No one believed that sweet little Heck had it in him. We had to make him stop when Skye started coming to meetings.

She was grown up and everything, but still, it didn't seem right since we had been writing for her when she was just a kid.

"Anyway, when *S and L* ended, we all started different projects. Heck was writing movie scripts, but none of them got made. He had invested all his money, hadn't bought a thing, still lived in a little cottage in Los Feliz, so he wasn't anxious to sign up for another series. He liked working alone. We all got together a couple times a month, but after six months or so, Heck started canceling on us. We should have gone over there, you know, checked on him more. We had always said we'd take care of each other."

"What happened to him?" Jane asked.

"About six months ago, he called Bix and told her he was frightened. Thought somebody was out to get him. She went over there and said his place was really scary. Piled-up newspapers, garbage, wrappers from food, a giant ball of twist ties. Stacks of unopened mail. He told Bix he was afraid there was anthrax in it. Bix tried to contact his family, but she could only find one cousin. He lived out here, but didn't want to get involved. Heck told Bix to make Jeb come and see him alone. Two days later, after Jeb told us Heck thought someone was trying to kill him, I got a call. There was an added second story on Heck's little house. And the person before him had built an observation platform, up another story. It was a goofy little structure, but safe enough, I guess. Heck had climbed up on the roof of the observation tower and fallen off. Not really that high, two-and-a-half, three stories, but he landed facedown on the brick patio and broke his neck. Police called me because inside his house, taped up by the phone, was a list of phone numbers to call if anything happened to him. Jeb was first and Bix was second. They weren't around and I was lucky number three. The cousin and I had to go identify the body." Louise stopped talking for a moment. When she started again, her voice was lower and she spoke each word deliberately.

"The cousin said he hadn't seen him in twenty years and had no idea what he looked like, so he would be no good at identifying the body. They made me go in. Later, after signing some papers, I left with the cousin, who asked me how he looked. I asked him what did he care since he was too busy to see him when he was alive, and this creep says, 'I saw him last Wednesday. We had dinner once a week.' The weasel just couldn't make himself go in there."

"Were the police satisfied that Heck's death was an accident?" asked Jane.

"Sure. He was paranoid, his place was a death trap. He had almost stopped eating entirely because he thought his food was being poisoned. The cousin told me he changed his carry-out place every day so 'they' couldn't find a pattern."

"Anybody figure out why he was on the roof? I mean, if he was scared to come out of the house and all?" asked Jane, digging out a power bar from one of her vest pockets and breaking it in half. She gave half to Louise, wishing she had something more substantial to offer.

"A detective said they figured he thought someone was in the house trying to get him. He had climbed on stacks of newspapers to get out the attic window. They said there was no sign of foul play, but . . ." Louise studied the wrapper and read the carb count out loud. Then she shrugged and bit into it anyway. "If you ask me, the whole house reeked of foul play. Jeb is the main executor of the estate. Heck left everything to us. Every bit of garbage in that place belongs to the B Room."

"Did you find anything of value there? Was there any reason to believe someone had broken in looking for something and frightened him out on the roof?"

"We haven't gone through the house yet. Most of us haven't been past the entryway. We're supposed to do it next week, before we sell it. . . . I don't know if I can. . . . Look, all I know about mental illness is what I've learned from television and researched for scripts. I'm no expert. Heck was ill, no doubt about it, but he was also believable. Maybe I just want to believe this because he was part of the B Room, but I think something real was eating away at him."

Jane asked Louise if the rest of the group agreed with her.

"You're here, aren't you?"

Jane shook her head.

"At first no one agreed with me, but then Bix got a letter that said she'd be next. She might be able to help herself and save the rest of us, but she'd have to wait for instructions. Said if she called the police, she wouldn't have a chance.

"She showed us the letter at Jeb's. It was the same day you were on TV, I think. Jeb had recorded it. Played it for us. Bix said she thought your story would make a good movie."

"And thought that if I was here, I might be able to figure out who sent the letter?" asked Jane. She hoped she didn't sound as incredulous as she felt. These people had lived in a fantasy world so long it had addled their brains.

Louise nodded. "And who made Heck jump off the roof."

"*If* someone made him jump," said Jane, and Louise nodded. But Jane was only being careful. She had already decided that there was something fishy about Heck's death. It was a tragic illustration of one of her core beliefs. Just because you're paranoid doesn't mean there isn't somebody out to get you. And then there was Bix's note from yesterday that Jane had in her pocket. Someone had threatened that they all would go to hell. Or heck.

Jane was a few minutes late for her rendezvous with Tim. Louise had gone off in search of more costume jewelry and with a promise to find Jane later. Jane tried to fill him in on her conversation as fast as she could, but knew he was only half listening. He grabbed her bag filled with keys and flash cards and volunteered to make the first run to the car. He was carrying two small lamp bases, metal, maybe brass, accented with a deep orange ring, maybe Bakelite. He waved another bag—pointed out their next meeting place—and sprinted off.

She started down the next aisle, pausing at a table with old autograph books. Jane picked up one with a heavy blue cardboard cover, dated 1928, and paged through it, trying to focus on the rhymes and spidery signatures that usually delighted her.

> *May your cheeks retain their dimple,*
> *May your heart be just as gay,*
> *Until some manly voice shall whisper,*
> *Dearest, will you name the day?*

Manly voice? Why hadn't Jeb just called her and asked her, point-blank, to come out to L.A. and work on this?

> *Once upon a time,*
> *A chicken found a dime,*
> *She gave it to the rooster*
> *And the rooster said, "It's mine."*

Isn't that just like a rooster? Of course Jeb couldn't ask for her help. He couldn't even ask her why she walked out on him all those years ago. He had shrugged it off and acted all manly and roostery about it. So this was a perfect plan—let Bix ask Jane and Tim to come out here under the pretense of the movie deal, and while they were here, rope them into whatever was going on with the B Room. When Jane dated Jeb in college, he rarely said anything directly. *Do you know how to make grits?* he had asked her one night and she had answered, *No, how?* He told her it wasn't a riddle, he just liked grits with eggs in the morning and he could handle scrambling the eggs. At the time, his convoluted proposal that she spend the night at his place seemed charming.

"Passive-aggressive bullshit," she said out loud, recognizing it for what it was.

"Now are you talking on the phone?" asked Louise, who had once again come up behind her.

Jane sighed and handed over three dollars for the autograph book without blinking. Its wisdom was priceless. And if Louise was back to chat, Jane figured this might be her last opportunity for a purchase. When she turned around, she was even more certain that she was done for the day. Rick and Greg were standing with Louise, who apparently had gone to gather them. She pointed to a group of tables and chairs near a refreshment stand.

"Jeb said he'd meet us over there," she said.

"Cock-a-doodle-do," Jane muttered under her breath.

Jane dropped the blue autograph book into her bag and spotted a table that looked like it had more of the small volumes. She said she'd be right over to the snack area and zigzagged across the aisle. She picked up a zippered brown leatherette journal with a fifteen-dollar price tag on it. Without even looking through it, she replaced it on the table and saw some battered cardboard-covered books in a small case on top of a trunk a few feet back. Stepping over to the shelves, she pulled out the stack of autograph books and found herself staring at a face. At first she thought it was someone looking at the same books from the other side; then she noticed that the eyes were not studying book titles. In fact, these eyes were not searching for any flea market treasures, since these eyes belonged to the face of a man no longer browsing, bargaining, or buying. This was the face of a dead man.

Jane opened her mouth, hoping she would be able to scream, when she felt a hand on her shoulder. Just behind her, the B Room had gathered with their leader, Jeb Gleason. Jeb was so close behind her that Jane heard his statement as a low whisper in her ear.

"Look, gang, Lou Piccolo's back from Ojai."

Jane, realizing, if only for one lucid second, that this must be the "Pix" of Bix Pix Flix, Lou Piccolo, studied the face, her open mouth still poised for a scream. Lou Piccolo had brown straight hair, a bit shaggy, and what had been, she felt sure, a handsome tanned face, with perhaps just a touch of cosmetic work. Although features and faces might grow rigid without life, Lou's eyes were stretched a bit more than even death called for. In that second of reflection, Jane was ashamed to admit that she was judging a dead man, but she couldn't stop herself from thinking, *How vain.*

In the next second, the scream escaped and Jane yelled loud and louder. Even though Jane was familiar with the bodies that cropped up around her when bargain-hunting, she still felt woozy enough to turn and take Jeb's arm for a moment. But there was no arm. No Jeb. Across the garage she could see the B Room scurrying away, cutting against the crowd coming in answer to Jane's call for help, with Jeb following behind them, his arms outstretched, hurrying them along. Back, Jane guessed, to the henhouse.

It's not that everyone's dishonest. Really. It's more like they've lived their own version of the truth so long that they now believe it *is* the truth. I mean, I'm guessing that most Hollywood showbiz types would pass a lie detector test. Until somebody invents a bona fide, fool-proof bullshit detector, the people in the "entertainment industry" are safe.

—FROM *Hollywood Diary* BY BELINDA ST. GERMAINE

Jane was given a chair and a bottle of water and a cold towel and, from a kind anonymous soul, a vending machine package of cookies. In turn, she gave a police detective her name and address and described how she had pulled out the stack of autograph books and discovered the dead man. A few feet to her left, Jane could see the proprietor of this particular table, wringing her hands, answering another set of questions from another police officer, and, most probably, wondering if Jane was still interested in those autograph books and if she was going to be allowed to sell them.

Because a policeman reporting to the superior officer who was taking Jane's statement announced he had found his wallet and ID, but not spoken Lou Piccolo's name out loud, the police officer did not ask Jane if she had any connection to the dead man. He merely asked her if she had ever seen him before.

"No," she answered honestly.

If the officer had asked her if she knew Lou Piccolo, she

would have to explain who she was and how she happened to be in L.A. and how she was connected to the dead man in front of her. However, as long as the name was not spoken, she rationalized that she had no obligation to bring up any confusing and problematic connection to the man who, it now became sickeningly clear, had been stabbed to death with a classic daggerlike letter opener, flea market price tag still attached. Police had been dispatched throughout the flea market with elaborate descriptions of the weapon to see if any vendor recognized the dagger as one he or she had sold, and, if so, did they remember the purchaser well enough to give a description?

Jane was rather pleased to note that she was now being ignored. Had this been Kankakee, Illinois, where she was quite well recognized as someone with a penchant for uncovering bodies rolled up in Oriental rugs or walking into crime scenes littered with garage sale detritus, or had it been Evanston, Illinois, where she was known to walk into more than one murder plot, she might have garnered unwanted attention. Here in sunny Pasadena, she was just another hapless tourist at the flea market, who instead of cool bargains found the stuff of which nightmares are made.

The market was a tricky place to close down. Although the police had spread out through the perimeter of the flea market area and set up checkpoints at the exits to the parking garage, so many shoppers had strolled through and come and gone throughout the morning, the giant roster of names and addresses and phone numbers seemed like so much make-work to Jane. It had to be done. Of course. But Jane thought she ought to at least try to make their work a bit more efficient.

"Officer?" Jane asked.

"It's Detective Dooley, Mrs. Wheel," he said, not looking up from his notepad.

"I believe the dagger is actually a letter opener," said Jane. "It's hand-crafted sterling, arts and crafts, early twentieth century, looks like it might have been made by Kalo, although I'd have to check to see if they made such a piece. There'd be a signature." Jane stopped as she realized the mark, if there was one, was probably covered in Lou Piccolo's blood.

"Mrs. Wheel, whoa," said Dooley, who was trying to smile, although Jane knew he was the type who never did, had never known how. He forced the corners of his mouth upward as if he had studied the steps in a how-to manual. "We're looking for a killer here, who probably grabbed the closest weapon from a nearby junk stall. Smart, too, since there'd be no connection to the murderer. Got it here and left it here."

"Yes, of course," said Jane, practicing her own version of condescension for those who didn't appreciate the history of the objects in their lives. "But there are two things," she began. "First, since this is a very fine and expensive piece, it probably would have been kept by the dealer in a locked case. It couldn't have been easily grabbed without notice. It was probably purchased. And if the murderer didn't know he or she was going to run into this person, it might have just been a purchase, you know, by a collector. So you know that the murderer had a lot of cash on hand to pay for it, and might be a collector of Kalo or Kalo-style silver."

Dooley had looked up from his pad and was staring at Jane, but she wasn't sure she was making herself clear.

"Look, for example, I collect vintage sewing items—knitting things, too, as a matter of fact. If I came across a really great pair of vintage sterling silver scissors here, I might buy them and put them in my purse. Then, if I ran into someone I got angry at or that I just wanted to kill, I would just have those scissors handy. Of course, then I'd have to leave them. But when I purchased them, I would have assumed I was going to be taking them home. If I wanted to kill someone, there are any number of rusty old letter openers and scissors and knives here."

Dooley didn't bother to put on his paint-by-number smile. He just continued to stare at Jane.

"It means it probably wasn't premeditated," Jane explained. "No one would buy a Kalo letter opener and plan to leave it in someone's back."

"You said two things, Mrs. Wheel. What's number two?"

"The tag on the dagger. Looked to me like it had a small stamp of a four-leaf clover on it. There's a dealer table in the next aisle called Lucky Finds and I noticed their tags had four-leaf clovers on them, so . . ."

"News I can use, Mrs. Wheel," said Dooley. He sent an officer in the direction Jane had pointed.

"You're an extremely observant person. Not a licensed PI working security for the market, are you?" Dooley asked, his tone clearly indicating that he was straining to make a joke.

"Nope," said Jane. "Not a licensed anything, I'm afraid." She rarely got a chance to behave in such a scrupulously honest fashion. She had never seen the dead man. She wasn't a licensed PI. It made her giddy. When she heard a noise like a Swiss bell-ringers' choir, she wondered if her giddiness had fast-forwarded into delusion, then she traced the sound to her bag. How had Tim gotten to it to change the ring this morning? It hadn't been out of her possession, had it?

"May I answer my phone?"

Dooley nodded. He was looking over his shoulder at the young officer he had dispatched to Lucky Finds, now sprinting back toward them.

"Four or five people were looking at the opener, passing it around and oohing and ahing, and one of them bought it. No description. Said he'd had a busy morning and he couldn't even say if it was a man or woman who ended up buying the thing. Didn't think the group who had been looking at stuff in the case were even together. Buyer paid cash." The officer lowered his voice and nodded in Jane's direction. "She was right about it being a pricey blade. Five hundred bucks. The dealer said the purchaser told him to take the price tag off because it was a gift, and he did, but he left the Lucky store tag on it when he wrapped it up for them."

Jane tried to listen to Dooley and his officer discuss their own lucky find, but it was difficult, since Tim was describing the items he was surrounded by, trapped by police officers on the west side of the parking lot.

"Unfriggingbelievable. Across the aisle, there's an entire table full of hotel silver. I could have gone over it and given the guy pocket change, since he's dying to sell something, anything, since the whole day is a bust for him. I can see it in his eyes from here. And where do I get trapped? I wander in here because I think I see an old Steiff bear, one of those tiny brown ones with the articulated limbs? In a pile of sock monkeys, I see this thing peeking out, but it turns out to be a piece of crap when I get close up, and what else is in this booth? Beanie Babies out the ass. I am trapped in Beanie Baby world. Who thought this crap up? *Weenie the Dachsund? Cheesy the Mouse? Nutsy the Squirrel?* Holy shit! Did you know there's a Princess Diana bear? Who knew? I was the only florist in Illinois to refuse to carry them in the shop. Could have made a bundle, sure, but I had my pride, oh shit, here's—"

"Timmy, calm down. I can't talk. I'm with the police. I was looking at some autograph books when I—"

"You found the dead guy? Of course. What was I thinking, bringing you to a perfectly fine flea market? What is it with you? Ask the cop how soon I'll be released from the Cuddle Town Jail," said Tim. "Are you okay?" he added, almost sincerely.

"I'm okay. Be productive while you're there. There's a blue elephant that's worth a lot of money. Look for that one."

"Yeah, right. Oh look, here's *Lymey the Tick*—"

Jane clicked off her phone, hoping to hear more news about the group who purchased the letter opener. Since she couldn't ask a question without arousing Detective Dooley's suspicions about what questions she herself might be able to answer, she tried to conjure up Detective Oh. He would advise her to listen, as she was doing, but he also had told her once that occasionally drawing a random conclusion might prove irresistible to someone who always thought himself to be right. If she was wrong, he would have to correct her, and that would give her the information she sought.

"When I browsed the Lucky Finds booth, I didn't see any Kalo or look-alike pieces in the display case, and that was probably around eight A.M., so she must have purchased it first thing when the market opened."

The young detective nodded. "Yup, first thing when he opened this morning. At first he said it was a guy, then he changed his mind to a woman, then back to a guy," he said. "Then he said he just couldn't say for sure." The policeman looked like he wanted to continue hashing out the time with Jane, who had, after all, given him his lead, which made him forget that she was a nonlicensed nobody who just happened to find a dead man.

Dooley held up his hand and told him to go back to the dealer, where he would join them both in a minute. "We're going to allow people to leave, Mrs. Wheel, and you're free to go as well. We have your hotel information, yes?"

Jane nodded. "I'm not sure how long we'll be at the W. We might relocate to a friend's . . . do you want me to . . . ?"

"We have your cell phone. We would like it if—"

A female uniformed officer came over to Dooley and apologized for interrupting. "There's a man over there with his wife. Out-of-towners, wife's a dealer on a buying trip. Guy's bored and starts roaming. He says he saw two pickpockets working the market. Following people who were buying high-end stuff and plucking it right out of their bags. He was looking for someone on duty to call in a detail for the collar. Guy in a baseball cap, jeans, and a T-shirt and a woman with silvery gray hair and glasses . . . a pair that blended right into the crowd. Probably had a third or fourth that they were handing off merch to. He saw the two actives work this aisle and one over." She pointed in the direction of Lucky Finds. "Might not mean anything, but somebody could have set up another layer of smoke between them and their victim if they stole the weapon and used it on our boy here."

"But a pickpocket?" said Jane, immediately wishing she had said this silently, to herself. Had she? Maybe she had. . . .

No. Dooley turned back, surprised to see that she was still standing there, more surprised to hear her offer a comment.

"We'll call you, Mrs. Wheel, if we need to speak with you again."

Dooley's dismissal of Mrs. Jane Wheel, duty-performing citizen, did not stop Detective Jane Wheel from finishing her thought. Pickpockets are thieves. Whoever stabbed Lou Piccolo in the back with a handcrafted letter opener was a murderer. Jane could hear Detective Oh's voice in her head. Why would a formal operation like a pickpocket ring spoil their plans with a murder? Suppose one of the thieves had been spotted and in a panic wanted to get rid of the witness? Even then, he or she would never use such an expensive prize to do the deed.

Jane noted that the autograph books she had taken from the shelf had been bagged, tagged, and placed next to a case holding evidence-collection paraphernalia. She gave a sympathetic nod to the dealer, who knew that Jane would have been good for the sale. Jane knew that she knew and they waved a sad I-would-have-bought-it-I-know-you-wanted-it good-bye.

The market was officially closed for the day. Sellers were being allowed to pack up their wares and shoppers were heading for their cars after allowing police to take their names and addresses and check their bags. Jane noticed that the dealer from Lucky Finds was surrounded by three uniformed officers and Detective Dooley. Another person, dressed in jeans and a T-shirt, had what looked like a drawing tablet and, Jane figured, was asking for remembered details for a composite sketch of the purchaser of the letter opener.

Jane found her way to the stall where Tim waited, a pained expression on his face. She bailed him out of Beanie Baby jail and together they headed for their rental car.

Looking back in the direction of the table where Jane found the dead man, whom Jeb Gleason had identified as Lou Piccolo, Jane figured that Jeb and the B Room were able to get to their car and pull out of the parking garage at least three minutes ahead of the time her screams brought attention, police, and any kind of checkpoints or blocks at the entrances and exits.

As soon as they were in the car, Jane phoned the hospital to check on Bix. Still in surgery. Jane imagined the entire B Room assembled in her room when she came back. How long would they wait before they told her that her partner, Lou Piccolo, was dead? Would it be Jeb who delivered the news? Jane was sure. He was the leader of this little cult. He had always been charismatic. In college, Jane had been thoroughly charmed by his cool confidence, his mysterious demeanor, and just as thoroughly disgusted when she discovered his dishonesty. But they were college kids and he was a handsome guy at whose feet girls—especially equally cool girls like Linda Fabien—threw themselves. He wasn't a bad guy then. He wasn't evil or sinister. Jane remembered hearing Jeb's voice behind her when she found the body—*Lou Piccolo's back from Ojai*. Was it the whisper of a murderer?

Jane knelt facing backward on the front seat, rearranging packages in the rear. She almost fell headfirst onto the backseat reaching for the *Thomas Guide* under a stack of colorful souvenir metal trays.

"These aren't your thing, Timmy. Kitschy-kitschy-koo kind of stuff," said Jane.

"I know. Definitely low-end. Much more you. But I loved the colors and the photographs reproduced on them. Seemed so Southern California and, you know, if I had a little bungalow here, I could see those on a kitchen wall above the door and—"

"Tim, what do I look up to guide you back to the studio? I've got to stop in at Bix's office for a minute."

Tim had the instincts of a bloodhound who carried a driver's license. He maneuvered through traffic, sniffed out the fastest lanes, and calmly sensed the exits and turns just before their signs appeared. He was slowing their Volvo down in front of the studio gates in what must have been record time. Jane told him to drive past and turn the corner, directing him to the auxiliary parking lot Jeb had parked in the day before.

"There's a visitor's lot across the street that's closer," said Tim.

Jane smiled and held up her little key.

"This is a direct route."

Jane led the way through the maze of shrubbery both outside the gate and inside the gate into what was the postage-stamp backyard of the Bix Pix Flix bungalow.

Although they saw a few people walking on the lot, the pace was definitely that of the weekend. Most offices looked empty, few cars were in the reserved spaces scattered between the buildings. Jane and Tim had walked around to the front of the office to see if anyone was at the front desk. The front door was locked. They walked back to the rear entrance and tried that door. Open. Why not? The gate into the backyard had been locked from the inside, so no one could get to the back door unless they came through the hidden gate or were allowed in by someone already in the backyard.

"I figure we might have as much as a twenty-minute head start on the police," said Jane. "They'll send someone to Piccolo's house, but they'll come here, too, if the address is on any business cards in his wallet."

Jane handed Tim a vintage handkerchief, one of a few she always kept in her bag.

"Use this if you touch anything, hon, but don't wipe anything clean. We were here yesterday, so our fingerprints should logically be here," said Jane.

"What's with the criminal mind? You sound like we're the bad guys instead of the crime solvers," said Tim.

"Nonsense. I just want to look around Lou Piccolo's office before the police get here."

"I didn't say there was anything wrong with the criminal mind. He has a signed first edition of *A is for Alibi* out there in the bookcase that might just go to waste if I don't take it," said Tim.

"You will not steal, Tim Lowry," said Jane. "Especially from a dead man."

"Dead men don't press charges," said Tim.

Jane was sure that Tim was teasing, but just the same, she made a mental note to check the bookshelves before they left. The last thing she needed was to lose her PI license. It would be particularly galling if it happened before she had gotten her PI license.

Jane had little need for the handkerchief. The door to Lou's office was open. She remembered that Jeb had walked into it yesterday when they had rushed over from lunch. Was it just yesterday that Jane had been lulled by Jeb's voice, feeling that she understood his appeal, his magnetism? No, couldn't have been. Jane was not the naïve young girl she had been in college and Jeb had grown into what college playboys became . . . sad middle-aged loners looking ahead to seedy old age. It was a harsh judgment. Not as harsh as another conclusion that Jane was fighting against reaching.

On Lou Piccolo's vintage oak desk—it looked like something right out of the newsroom of *The Front Page*—he had carefully lined up a collection of metal paperweights. The Eiffel Tower, the Empire State Building, a few California bank buildings, a baseball stadium. In a row just in front of the paper-weights, another collection was lined up. Vintage letter openers. Brass, Bakelite, silver and gold. Lou might be meticulous in the way he placed objects on his desk, but he wasn't a perfect house-keeper. A thin layer of dust covered the desk. If Jane had been browsing in an antique shop, she would have succumbed to her impulse to use her handkerchief to wipe off the surface—all the better to display these exquisite pieces. In this case though, she only clutched her handkerchief, now wadded up in a tight ball, harder in her closed fist. The dusty film showed a definite outline of what was not on the desk. An object had recently been removed from between two hand-hammered silver exam-ples. And although Jane was no expert in gauging exact length and width, she would have bet her last collectible silver dime that what she was gazing at on the desk was the chalk outline of the letter opener she had seen sticking out of Lou Piccolo's back.

9

Backstabbing and air-kissing? In Hollywood, those are two gestures that signify exactly the same thing.
— FROM *Hollywood Diary* BY BELINDA ST. GERMAINE

As Jane was locking the gate behind them, she asked Tim
for the third time if he was sure he hadn't touched anything he
shouldn't have. She knew he hadn't lifted any of Lou Piccolo's
first editions. Tim wasn't a thief. Besides, he hadn't carried in
a bag and none of the books would fit in his pockets.

"You act pretty holier-than-thou for someone who hasn't
explained how she got a key to a hidden back entrance to a major studio. I just can't imagine that those are handed out as party
favors—even to people whose rights someone is dying to get."

Jane tried to freeze him with a look.

"Oops. I didn't mean that, sweetie. Even I am not that
crass."

Jane looked around the parking lot before they came out
of the shrubbery and quickly walked to their car. The lot was
far from full. It was a weekend and after all, this lot was a two-
block walk to the entrance while two other parking lots were
directly across the street from the main gate. As Jane was about
to express her disapproval of the studio head who obviously
had arranged a pretty sweet setup for himself all those years
ago when the trees and bushes were first planted to cover up
the perimeter of the lot, a tall young man dressed in black jeans

and a black T-shirt came walking in through the street entrance.

He seemed to be heading right for them, but veered off toward another row of a few cars, where he set a large bag on the hood of a red Mustang convertible and pulled a key from his pocket.

He opened the trunk and Jane could see that it was almost full of bags and boxes. He adjusted a few things, and carefully wedged the bag in. Tim looked up at the slam of the trunk's lid and called over to him.

"Gary, hey," said Tim, waving.

The man had been so lost in thought, he started at hearing his name. When he looked up, his face was completely blank.

"Tim Lowry. Bix was taking me through the prop warehouse yesterday."

"Oh man, sorry I didn't recognize you." The man in black walked over, his hand extended. He was smiling, but still looked a million miles away. "How's Bix?"

Tim told him she would be in the hospital until after the arm surgery, but as far as he knew she would recover.

"Yeah, I called last night and talked to Skye. Sounded like she's stepped up. Probably nice for her to be able to pay back and all."

Jane was amazed that everyone who was involved with the studio assumed that everyone knew everything about everyone. She liked it.

"You think Skye feels she has to . . . you know . . . pay back?" Jane said, trying to sound casual and knowing at the same time.

"Bix has been taking care of Skye for fifteen years or so. Don't you remember all those stories about Skye when she was on *S and L?* Sandy Pritikin tried to dump her from the show every season. When she was twelve and starting out, she was just a brat, but every year there was something else. She gained weight—you know puberty." He lowered his voice. "Sandy pitched a fit about her eating her way out of show business and Bix convinced Sandy that they could handle it in a story line and be heroes for embracing real family problems and concerns in a comedy. Show won two Emmys that year. Writing and acting. Sandy's portrayal as a sensitive and loving father won it for him. Well deserved, too. That jerk playing a nice guy was the acting feat of the century."

Tim introduced Jane to Gary Check, the head of props for the studio.

"Yeah, Jane Wheel," said Gary, nodding. "I've heard of you, right?"

Jane started to shake her head, but stopped herself, considering what Belinda St. Germaine might advise. Not to mention Detective Oh. *Agree with everyone*, Belinda had advised. *Your agent can demand the change later.*

"Maybe," she said with a smile. *If you listen more than you talk, you will hear more*, is what Oh might advise in this situation.

"Yeah, you're in a movie, or no . . . Bix is doing a movie about you . . . yeah. It's not on the board yet, but I think I've seen some tags. You must have a go-getter for a designer."

Jane squeezed Tim's arm, hoping that he interpreted it as a warning not to mention that a bogus tag was what led Bix to opening the box

"What kind of stuff have they found for it?" asked Jane, trying to look like she might be a rising star or at least the kind of person a rising star might want to play. "Remember where you've seen the tags?"

"I see hundreds of those a day," he said, shaking his head, then he laughed. "I do remember seeing a few of yours that cracked me up, though. We're doing an inventory." He sighed and ran his hand across his face. "We're always doing an inventory. Too much stuff, not enough space . . . you know the routine. I've got some of my people weeding out a lot of the trash.

They filled three boxes with junk—lamp parts, broken glasses, scratched-up plastic dishes . . . just crap, you know. And the boxes were all by the door to be taken to the trash. Has to be disposed of properly, you know?"

Tim and Jane shook their heads. "Recycled, you mean?" asked Jane.

"Studio name is printed on the bottom of everything. *Property of . . .* you know. Nobody's allowed to go through the dumpster and take stuff."

"What a shame," said Tim. "What a treasure trove . . . movie and TV props . . . from the set of . . ."

"Exactly. Can you imagine the market for that stuff on eBay? People'd be running off to Target, buying up cheap candleholders, stamping the studio name on them, and passing them off as *Gilmore Girls* props. They probably do it already anyway."

"You found a Jane Wheel tag in the boxes of junk?" asked Jane.

"Not *in* . . . Jane Wheel tags were *on* the boxes of junk. Somebody thought the throwaways were just right for your movie. What's it about? Landfill?"

"Pretty much," said Tim, nodding.

"What happened to the boxes?" asked Jane. Gary didn't know about the tag on the box that exploded. These boxes could have been rigged, too. Jane looked at Tim. They would have to warn him. It didn't matter how adamantly Jeb had warned Bix and the other members of the B Room off calling in the police, Jane couldn't allow the risk of another explosion or fire at the studio.

"I went through them thoroughly, thinking one of the kids had missed something in there. Called Bix and Lou, and Lou sent a message back that we could go ahead and toss the stuff. Said the tagging was premature anyway. If they needed junk for a rummage sale, they could find it. You can always find junk, you know?"

They nodded. They knew. Back in their car, Jane watched Gary Check drive away.

"What do you think he was putting in his trunk?" asked Jane.

"Remains of his lunch," Tim said, "or a bit of rejected inventory being disposed of into Gary's house?"

"That's what I was thinking, too," said Jane. "Could you imagine letting any of that stuff go to the dump?"

"No. But we don't really know. He's in the middle of it all day. That's the thing. If you work in the ice-cream store all summer, by August you don't want any more ice cream," said Tim.

"Whoever started that rumor?" asked Jane. One summer, between her freshman and sophomore years in college, her father, Don, had pulled a few strings and gotten her a job at an ice-cream factory in Kankakee, where she packed Popsicles and ice-cream bars eight hours a day. The old-timers had trained her and she had finally gotten fast enough to be ahead of the machine that delivered the frozen confections to be packed. She could grab a bar, tear off the wrapper and bite off half, throw the rest away, and be ready to scoop the next handful and stuff them into the box. All day long, scoop, stuff, eat, scoop, stuff, eat. At night when Jane returned home, exhausted and numb, Nellie treated her with grudging respect and the closest words to praise that Nellie had ever spoken to her.

"At least now you know what work is," she'd say. "You're not sitting around reading like a lazy bum."

And what did Jane do each night after being nurtured by Nellie's version of maternal concern? She ate ice-cream bars. If the work hadn't been so physically demanding and if it hadn't been the hottest summer on record so that her appetite for anything besides something cold vanished, she would have gained fifty pounds. Just thinking about it now gave her a taste for an Eskimo Pie.

"I don't get why somebody tagged the boxes of junk. I mean, the box that got Bix was placed in the aisle of Depression glass . . . where she would look if she was in the prop shop. And anybody who saw the passes for the day would know that Bix was going to bring a guest through," said Tim.

"Wait a second," said Jane. She found the phone number of Bix's hospital room and dialed. "I want to find out if Lou Piccolo was a writer in the B Room. Nobody's mentioned him as a . . . No answer. Skye is probably in the family waiting room, but I don't want to call and ask her and end up telling her about Lou over the phone."

Jane told Tim to drive directly to the hospital.

"We won't beat the B Room there, I'm sure they've already set up camp. It's odd, isn't it, how they move as a pack?" asked Jane.

"More than odd. Spooky. How did you ever date that guy Jeb Gleason? He's one step away from telling everybody to drink the Kool-Aid."

Jane would have liked to defend Jeb, but right now she couldn't think of anything about him that was defensible. In college, he was handsome and charismatic. He gave off a kind of smoky cool—dry ice. Steamy, but cold. All irresistible qualities to a girl from Kankakee, Illinois, in a twentysomething campuswide world.

That was it. It was still college here in L.A. Jane realized what irritated her about Jeb and the crowd surrounding Bix was that, in a very short time, she could see them as a clique . . . a campus or sorority or a fraternity clique. They all buzzed around Jeb as the leader, and they all stuck together. Last night, in Bix's hospital room, they were all pairing off to go home, watching over each other. Or just watching each other. Didn't they have families or other lives? They had worked together on a successful show years ago. Why were they still going to the Pasadena flea market together on weekends? No spouses? No children? No real-world commitments? Did working in Hollywood mean you never had to grow up?

Tim drove to the hospital and on the way, since she wasn't needed for navigation, Jane tried to put together the pieces to the puzzle in front of her. Someone rigged a box in the prop shop that was baited for Bix with a Jane Wheel tag. A gaggle of television writers, joined at their hips, were being threatened by someone. Someone connected to them was murdered at the Pasadena City College Flea Market.

"Who would target a group of television writers?" she asked Tim.

"Disgruntled television watchers?" said Tim.

"If that were the case, we could cut the population of this town in half. Gosh, my dad would have killed the writers who killed off Edith Bunker if he'd had a weapon and if he'd ever bothered to read the credits and find out their names."

Jane tried to play Detective Oh and ask the next level of question. If she could figure out *why*, she would know *who*. Bix and Lou . . . and maybe, if everything Louise had told her was true, Heck, too, had been the targets so far.

"Tim, you said your name tag was ready for you at the prop warehouse, right?"

Tim nodded and made a left turn onto a one-way street which led to the hospital parking lot.

"Did Bix have a name tag?"

"No, I don't think so. I had something like a visitor's pass. There was a sheet out on the table that said I was the guest of Bix Pix Flix."

"Not just Bix?"

"It was the whole company name."

"Why have we been assuming that the box was intended for Bix? Could have been Lou who opened that lid. We know now somebody was out to get him," said Jane.

"The Depression glass. All the shakers in the office. Bix would go down that aisle where the box was planted," Tim said, swinging the Volvo into a parking spot.

"How do we know the shakers belong to Bix? The first editions are Lou's. In his office, he had paperweights and letter openers. He was a pack rat. We assumed the glass was Bix's, but why? Men collect Depression glass, don't they?"

"Of course," said Tim. "A client of mine, this guy Sheldon who used to be a dealer? He and his wife have the most extensive collection of green glass I've ever seen."

Jane took a deep breath. She had been viewing all of this through only one lens. She had made the assumption that Bix was a target, but what if it was Lou all along? Jeb's reaction upon confronting the late Lou Piccolo was hardly that of a grief-stricken friend. Perhaps the whole B Room cabal wanted Lou dead for some reason and Bix was at the wrong place at the wrong time.

Jane hoped they would get to see Bix before everyone else arrived. She didn't relish being the one to tell her about Lou Piccolo, but that would be a small trade-off for getting the answers to a few questions without the entire B Room as the audience and bodyguards. And if Bix was still groggy, Jane would talk to Skye. It was clear to Jane that Skye's loyalty was to Bix more than to the group. And if she had been pacing all morning in the family waiting room, she would be ready for some company.

Jane and Tim stopped outside Bix's room and listened. There were voices, low and solicitous. Of course the group would be there. They had probably raced over directly from the flea market. Jane tapped lightly on the door and opened it. Skye looked up from where she was sitting in the chair next to the empty bed. She had a knitting project sitting in her lap, something loopy and soft in lavender and pale yellow. The person to whom she had been speaking was just behind the door. Jane turned and saw a man with black curly hair wearing a Yankees baseball cap. He looked from Skye to Jane to Tim, who had walked in behind her, and then back to Skye.

"It's Jane Wheel and Tim Lowry, so you can put that silly thing away now," said Skye, shaking her blond hair and wagging a finger at the man.

Jane looked back and saw that the man, who was now looking back and forth from Jane to Tim, looked even more nervous. His hands were shaking. Particularly the one that was holding the gun pointed first at Jane, then at Tim.

"I told you to put that thing away. Jane's going to help all of us, so you don't have to shoot your foot off proving you're a macho guy who can protect us all."

"Shut up, Skye, I know how to use this if I have to," said the man in a low raspy whisper.

"Oh, Lou, you couldn't shoot your way out of a Gucci shopping bag," said Skye, with that ringing laugh that was her trademark as Celie on *Southpaw and Lefty*.

"Who?" asked Jane and Tim at the same time.

"Meet Lou Piccolo. The man who wants to buy your story rights," said Skye. Looking at the gun and once again laughing, she added, "Or else."

"Okay, I'm officially confused," said Tim. "I thought you told me that Lou Piccolo—"

"Had red hair? I don't know where I got that idea," Jane said, laughing her best okay-I'm-confused-too-but-I'm-trying-something-here-don't-ask-questions-old-pal sort of laugh. Jane stuck her hand out to shake Lou's hand, then dropped it when she remembered that people holding guns don't usually extend themselves for the meet-and-greet.

"Put it away, Lou," said Skye, "and talk to Jane. She isn't going to help a crazy man. And you are definitely acting like a crazy man."

Or a frightened one. Jane could see that his hands, with gun and without, were still trembling. "Maybe I can help, but like all those cliché private eyes in mystery novels, I think a lot better when there isn't a gun pointed at me."

Lou put the gun on the floor next to his leather briefcase and took a deep breath. He almost smiled.

"That's a cliché? I must have used that line a hundred times in *He's for Hire* and nobody ever told me that."

Lou took off his cap and rubbed his head. He looked like someone who hadn't been sleeping. "Hell of a way to meet someone," he said, looking at both Tim and Jane. "Sorry. I heard some news that scared the . . . that scared me . . . and I guess, according to Skye, getting hold of a gun was an overreaction."

"The news you heard," said Jane. "Was it about Bix getting hurt?"

"No," said Lou. "I mean, that's terrible, but that was an accident, right?"

Bix must still be in surgery. Or the recovery room. Although Jane didn't know what kind of personal relationship Bix had with Lou, she felt that he couldn't have seen her yet. Even if he wasn't part of the B Room, Bix couldn't have hidden her own fears about the prop department incident. She looked too vulnerable lying in that hospital.

"Wasn't it?" Lou looked at Skye. "Why didn't you tell me?"

"Oh heavens, Lou, you come in here like a cowboy, showing off your new toy and acting like you're Clint Eastwood or something—when am I supposed to tell you what's really going on?" Skye tossed her head and used her hands to accent the question, and Jane realized a real dilemma for successful television actresses. Everything Skye did was a gesture she had perfected in front of the camera. Every pout and laugh and smile and flip of her hair reminded Jane of Celie on *Southpaw and Lefty*. It was bad enough that an actress probably couldn't get away from a popular character she had played in order to get more work; what about finding some kind of real balance in her personal life? Because everything about her was associated with a fictional character, how could she ever appear genuine?

"Where is Bix?" asked Tim. "It's after three. Shouldn't she be back from surgery?"

Skye shook her head. "Late start," she said. "I got a different surgeon to come in. Did they really think they were going to get away with any old cutter on Bix?"

Lou patted Skye on the shoulder and nodded, clearly grateful to her that she had taken care of business.

"De Niro's?" asked Tim.

"Better," said Skye. "I found the guy who—"

Before she could elaborate on the doctor she had brought in, one of the floor nurses entered and motioned for Skye to come with her.

Lou watched her go, waited for the door to close, then moved closer to Jane and Tim.

"I got to talk fast, Jane, and I'm sorry to lay all of this on you. I just don't want Skye to hear it. Bix is practically a mom to her. You know about the B Room stuff? The one-for-all-and-all-for-one crap?"

"They obviously take care of each other," said Jane.

"More than that," said Lou. "First show Bix and I did together, she could never work late on Tuesdays because it was the night the B Room met—like a frigging secret society or something. Jeb ran meetings and they all kept each other in business. If one of them was on a show that went down, somebody else folded them in, partnered up with them on a script until they got work again. I mean, in some ways it was cool, you know? In this town, you're as good as your last project, and since we're all getting older . . . I mean, we're of the age that we're priced right out of the business. Young guys come into town every day willing to start at minimum and we're all in a different bracket, so we don't get hired. We're like ballplayers, you know? Rookies are ready and willing to come in and take our spots. We're the creaky old-timers."

"How did you and Bix team up?" asked Tim.

"Did you ever have a job on *S and L*?" asked Jane.

"I was kicking around town as a stuntman, believe it or not, and my uncle was one of the directors on the last season of *S and L*. I banged up my knees pretty bad and needed to find something else to do. At an *S and L* party, I hit it off with Bix and we ended up writing a couple things together and one of our scripts made it into development. Bix and I had a thing for a while, but then we realized we were much better friends than we were parts of a couple," Lou said, looking toward the door.

He leaned forward to continue. "Listen, bottom line here. I'm a hack. Bix gets the ideas, I pound things out with her, and I do a hell of a pitch, but she's the story person. But even story people, good story people, get dry, you know? A year ago, we start getting letters with story ideas in them. Whoever's sending us the letters says we can write them up as treatments, have them for free, do what we want with them. Someday he might want to get into the business, but not now. Maybe we'll help when he's ready. In the meantime, anything we like, we can use. Crazy, right? We're throwing the letters away, but they keep coming, and one day we're desperate to come up with something for this actress we got a deal with. Bix fishes out the last letter and reads the thing. It's got everything—a whole pitch for a series, pages of character descriptions, story ideas for two seasons. Incredible. I mean, it's a lot of work. And it's great."

"So you pitched it," said Jane, "as your own."

"Yes and no," said Lou. "Bix thought we were going into the meeting with the one lame idea we had, and after we pitched it and the exec shook her head and said, 'Got anything else?,'

Bix started to say no and I shushed her and brought out the mystery pages. I gave the pitch of my life on this show. It was easy because it was all laid out for me. I put our names on it with a Mr. X as the third writer. I told Bix that the guy'd come out of the woodwork if the thing sold, so we better be prepared."

"You sold it?" asked Tim.

"Yup, went into development. Two other series, too. Then we started getting other kinds of letters. Crazy stuff the person wanted to get on the air. Wanted us to support certain causes, just random stuff, but oddball. Letters started getting more and more threatening. Bix wanted to go to Jeb and that B Room coven with it and I said no. Told her she didn't need to give them one more thing to tie her to them. She didn't like that and we had a big fight. She went to Jeb, of course, and I went to the Tuesday meeting, too, and I could see how this was going to go down. Jeb started saying that it was clear that I was the dead weight in the partnership, I had insisted that we *borrow* these story ideas and pass them off as our own. He was planning for me to bow out of Bix Pix, taking a kind of artistic dive and allowing Bix to keep her golden reputation.

"And you know what? That was fine with me. I'd land on my feet. I didn't care one way or another about my *writerly integrity* or any of that crap. This was television, for Christ's sake. Then we got a letter that said it was time to give credit where credit was due. And I was okay with that, too. But the writer started accusing us of not wanting to have anything to do with him. We wrote back to this post office box all the time and I started trying to watch it, you know, see if I could put a real face on the guy."

"How do you know it's a guy?" asked Jane. "You keep saying it's a man, but the writer never gave a name or an identity, right?"

"Referred to himself as a guy in one of the early letters, so we just started picturing a him. Never saw anybody at the post office box, but I only went a couple of times. Anyway, the guy said he was tired of giving us everything and it was time for payback. We offered to pay, hell, we had set aside a third of the money on everything for him. My agent thought we were nuts— he had an account for what he called the phantom writer. We told him we'd take him on as a partner, anything . . . but it was like he was arguing with somebody who we didn't know—his own voices. We sure as hell weren't arguing, but the last letter said somebody was going to have to be killed off if the series were to continue."

"And you don't have a series on air right now. . . ."

"I was almost back when I got a phone message that somebody was found murdered at the Pasadena Flea Market today and Jeb told the B Room that I must have found my ghostwriter and killed him."

"How would Jeb know who the guy was or that you had—"

"There was this guy who did accuse me of stealing a story . . . he came around the office all the time. Everybody knew him, knew about his claim. Novelist. Different thing altogether. His novel came out around the same time I sold a script . . . first one I had written on my own. Not that good, but you know . . . good for me. Stories were similar, but because mine was out there, nobody wanted to touch movie rights for his novel. There was no way I knew his book. I collect *first editions*, for God's sake, I don't read *books*. Besides, my script was written way ahead of his book and it wasn't all that original to begin with. Two brothers have a fight and one murders the other. Hello? Genesis anyone? Bible was way ahead of both of us on that one. He keeps coming into the office and demanding credit for my script. Hell, there isn't even a movie yet."

"Lou Piccolo's back from Ojai . . ." said Jane, recalling the words that Jeb had whispered. That was what had made her think she was looking at the murdered Lou Piccolo.

"So Skye doesn't know any of this?" asked Tim, peeking

out the door. Jane and Lou both looked toward Tim and the door. "Don't worry, she's still at the nurses' station. Looks like they have a bunch of people who want her autograph. Apparently everyone wants a picture, too, and every cell phone is also a camera out there . . . poor kid."

"She's a sport. Skye's not really a part of those B Room drones. She just hangs with Bix. Good kid. She'd do anything for Bix and Bix has helped her plenty. She started acting when she was eight or something and her family tried to take all her money . . . just squeezed her dry. I think Bix is the only person who ever gave a damn about her."

"I've got three quick questions," said Jane.

Lou nodded.

"Were you in Ojai?"

"Yeah, I got a place there," said Lou.

"Were you alone there? When did you get back, and can anyone vouch for your whereabouts this morning?"

"I was alone. Hung out at a used bookstore yesterday and maybe the guy'd remember me, but I don't know. When I go there to work, I kind of tune out. I was supposed to be back for the meeting with you guys yesterday, but when Bix and I talked, she said to stay and work out the kinks in this other script, she could handle the initial meeting. Tell you the truth, I think she thinks I come on too strong. I'm impatient in meetings and sometimes I sound angry or something. She said you'd take some convincing and it might be better if she worked alone on this. I'm the pitch guy for networks, but not necessarily for people who are skittish about this business."

"I guess I have more than three questions," said Jane. "One more, at least. Do—"

"Anything. Look, I love Bix. Somebody's trying to hurt her because of this stupid thing I did . . . I'm an idiot. Jeb Gleason's right about me: I'm an idiot hack. But I didn't kill anybody. And Bix didn't do anything to deserve this."

"I think the nurses are letting Skye escape," said Tim. "She's headed back this way."

"Do you collect Depression glass?" asked Jane.

Skye walked in, still laughing her famous Celie laugh, assuring the LPN who accompanied her that it was no problem to sign autographs, she loved talking about the old days.

Lou smiled for the first time since Jane had met him. "Yeah, I do. Real men can collect Depression glass, you know," he said. "My mom was a huge collector and I caught the bug." Lou looked over at Tim, who had shot a look when he made the "real men" reference. "Hey, no offense, I mean . . . shit . . . you see why Bix didn't want me at the first meeting? I have to grow on people."

Tim shook his head. "I'm gay, I'm not thin-skinned. Besides, if you collect Depression glass, well, hell . . ."

"What?" asked Lou, anxious again.

"It's only a matter of time," said Tim.

10

Out here, East Coast–style flattery will get you in the door, it can get you past one gatekeeper receptionist, it might even get you an invitation to a B-list party, but in order to actually make a Hollywood omelette, you have to crack open the rotten egg of ass-kissing, California style. And you'll be surprised how quickly you can learn it.

—FROM *Hollywood Diary* BY BELINDA ST. GERMAINE

Jane excused herself after Skye returned. She wanted to find a glass of water and a moment to collect her thoughts. If Lou Piccolo collected Depression glass, he would have been just as likely as Bix to walk down that aisle in the prop warehouse and open the rigged box. And if Lou was as abrasive as he claimed to be, if he had borrowed a few story ideas—freely given or not—he was the half of Bix Pix more likely to have made a few enemies.

Jane walked down the hospital corridor, stopping to study a framed poster. So much of the art in public spaces was institutional—ordinary and forgettable—but this was different. It was a photograph of a hand holding a yellow No. 2 pencil over what looked like a three-dimensional scribble rising from a blank page.

Jane leaned toward the print, trying to see what the material was or how the photographic trick, if that's what it was, had been accomplished.

"Some kind of wire?" a polite male voice queried from behind her. "Tungsten filament, perhaps?"

"Tungsten filament certainly," said a voice behind the voice. "That's a Shotwell. My client, Dr. Bouchard, wants nothing but eighteenth-century French furniture in his house and nothing but Charles Shotwell photographs on his walls. Strange mix, but I've seen—"

"So it wasn't a *royal we*," said Jane, turning around to face former Evanston police detective Bruce Oh and his wife, Claire.

Bruce Oh raised an eyebrow slightly, which for him was a thoroughly out-of-character display of expression. Jane did not know, however, whether he was surprised to see her or had no idea what she meant by the reference to the *royal we*.

"When we spoke on the phone," said Jane, "you said *when we return from California*, but I didn't know you were in California, so I thought you were just—"

"I apologize, Mrs. Wheel," said Oh. "I dislike being unclear." Bruce Oh turned to his wife, who was standing beside him. "You phoned Mrs. Wheel to tell her we were visiting your relative in California?" Claire, rubbing a piece of dust off the photograph, nodded impatiently. He turned back to Jane. "I thought you had received the message that we, too, were in Los Angeles. My wife's aunt is ill and we came here to visit. So the *royal we* you speak of was, in fact, a . . ." Oh hesitated, searching for the correct word. "A *plebeian we*, after all."

Jane hated that falling-down-the-rabbit-hole feeling she experienced whenever she realized she had forgotten something. Worse was the feeling of not realizing . . . not remembering the forgetting. When had Claire Oh called her? Charley was supposed to be the absentminded professor in the family. Jane, easily distracted by a piece of pottery or a souvenir tablecloth, was still the one who was supposed to process the information she was told.

"I called to tell her we were going to California, but there was no one at home and when the answering machine picked up, I decided to phone back later and speak with her in person," said Claire.

Should Jane remind Claire that she was standing right here?

"Ah," said Oh, "and then you were unable to make the second call?"

Claire nodded and, with no further explanation or apology, went back to polishing the glass covering the photograph.

Jane noted that her partner and his wife always did this—spoke to each other directly, no matter how many other people were in the room. Jane liked to think it had something to do with their unique relationship, which she puzzled over every time she watched the two of them interact. Such an odd couple. Claire, tall and imperious, meticulously dressed in designer clothes of the very season they were designed for—unlike Jane's own clothes, which occasionally carried all the right tags but were purchased just a season or two after their prime—and Bruce Oh, so quiet and still that he became invisible wherever he stood. The only remarkable aspect to his outward appearance was his daily neckwear. Claire found the most fantastic vintage ties and insisted that her husband wear one from the collection daily.

Were Bruce and Claire Oh odder than any other married couple, though? Jane could remember being twentysomething—she could conjure that mad rush of passion that overtook her back then when Charley smiled at her from across the room. Now did people wonder what Charley saw in his pack rat, almost-detective wife? Growing old with someone, after all, was only one letter away from growing odd with someone, and maybe that's what they were all in the process of doing.

Claire explained to Jane that her great-aunt was at death's door and that she and Bruce came out to be with the family and say their good-byes.

"She's a horrid woman, but we're all grateful to her for her genes. Living to one hundred and six, she gives us all hope, you know, that we've got what it takes to become our own antiques."

"She's here in the hospital?" asked Jane, somewhat surprised that someone that age wouldn't prefer to be taken care of at home.

"Her son and his wife are in their eighties now, healthy, but not able to care for her, really, so they needed her to come to the hospice here at the hospital. Aunt Violet refuses to go quietly."

"You perhaps mean quickly," said Bruce Oh. "She has been quiet."

Claire, to relieve her boredom, had been touring the hospital art. Discovering a Shotwell she hadn't yet seen was a satisfying distraction from the vigil at her aunt's bedside. She announced that it was time to go back to the hospice wing and check in with the family. Claire insisted that Bruce remain with Jane.

"Jane is so good at finding adventure . . . I think she should catch you up," said Claire. "Aunt Violet will wait for you to return."

Jane proceeded with the catching up.

"A body at the flea market?" said Oh, shaking his head slightly. "At a house sale, in an antique store, in the midst of his own trash . . . but a flea market . . ." He paused. "This would be a first for you?"

Jane, as quickly and efficiently as possible, explained the events that had let up to the body in Pasadena. She omitted that she'd had a romantic history with Jeb Gleason, just mentioned him as a college friend. It had no bearing on the case, she reasoned, so why bring it up? She did tell Oh, however, that she had felt slightly guilty about playing dumb and not telling the police detective on the scene at the market that the body belonged to Lou Piccolo.

"But it did not belong to Mr. Piccolo," said Oh.

"Yes, but I didn't know that then," said Jane. "I mean, it turned out to be okay for me to *not* say what I thought I maybe *should* have said, but it might have gotten pretty confusing with the police later if the victim *had* been Piccolo and we had been questioned again after the investigators checked his office records and found out Tim and I just flew in for a meeting with the man."

Oh nodded. "Confusing," he said.

"I mean, is it less of a lie if you think you're lying about something, but it turns out you were telling the truth because you were misinformed?" Jane asked, feeling as if she were performing some kind of corkscrew dance that was driving her to the center of the earth.

"Whoa, baby, does the ER have an ethicist on call?" said Tim, who had come out of Bix's room to find Jane. He shook hands with Oh, accepting the fact the man was going to show up wherever Jane happened to be discovering a dead body or two.

"I'm just saying that if the dead man *had* been Lou Piccolo, I realize I took a chance when I parsed words over whether I knew the victim," Jane said, adding under her breath, feeling that whirling dervish thing all over again, "even though it turned out that I didn't know him after all."

"Sometimes silence is the greater truth," said Oh.

"Dumb luck," Jane agreed.

Jane was ready for Oh's next question, since she had been asking it herself after her conversation with Lou Piccolo. She answered Oh the same way she had answered herself.

"I don't know why Jeb looked at the dead man and said that Lou Piccolo was back from Ojai. He had to have recognized the victim and known that there was a connection to Lou. Since no one knows who the phantom writer was . . ." Jane stopped and looked up at Oh, who had the good grace to look pleasantly expectant and puzzled at the same time rather than confused and irritated that Jane Wheel was carrying on an investigative meditation with herself. "I'll explain all of this, but the most important thing is that Jeb recognized the body as someone Lou had a connection to and, I guess, might have wanted dead.

"But why that cool acceptance of the fact?" she continued. "I mean, if Jeb really believed that Lou could murder someone, why did the B Room disappear en masse instead of telling the police who the victim was and who they might want to start looking for?"

"Mrs. Wheel, you of all people should know what can happen if you claim knowledge of a victim," said Oh. "There are those in law enforcement who are so happy to have information handed to them, it doesn't matter that the information should have them up and running in a different direction. They will keep the person with something to say talking and retelling what he or she knows until the good citizen begins feeling very much like an ill-used citizen."

"Now that everyone is filled in on everything," said Tim, "can you come back in and help referee between Lou and Skye? They're in some kind of pissing match over who cares more about Bix and her well-being and who is going to take better care of—"

"Moot," said Jane. "Listen."

The conversation among the B Room members grew louder as they approached from the elevator. They were arguing over which route they should have taken from some restaurant in Pasadena, where, apparently, they had stopped for brunch even though they had all just encountered a man murdered by someone who at least one of them had believed to be their associate. Rick was insisting that they should have anticipated the traffic jam they encountered. He added that the stops at everyone's houses and offices had been totally unnecessary. Greg agreed with his partner, but insisted that the stop they made at their office had been a necessary one. He managed to sound both belligerent and apologetic at the same time. Louise was doing a blah-blah-blah-I can't-hear-you counterpoint.

Jane, Tim, and Oh stood facing them as the group rounded the corner at the nurses' station and Jeb held up his hand like a crossing guard to stop the bickering.

"Bix has been in good hands, so stop the noise," said Jeb, reaching both hands out to Jane. "You came here right after the flea market? What a friend you're being to Bix. She's going to up the option money, I can feel it."

Jane dodged his hands and began to introduce Jeb to Bruce Oh. She started to call Oh her partner, but hesitated, remembering that Oh had kept himself out of the newspaper stories that had been written about their last case at Fuzzy Neilson's farm in Kankakee and had asked her not to mention him when she had appeared on the television newsmagazine that had started this whole Hollywood mess. Why not allow him to remain a silent partner?

In the beat in which all of this ran through Jane's mind, Oh picked up the signal.

"I am a colleague of Mrs. Wheel's husband, Charley," he said, stretching out his hand toward Jeb Gleason. "Adjunct professor only," he added, which Jane realized was absolutely true. Bruce Oh did teach classes at Northwestern University, where Charley was a faculty member. Using the truth to perpetuate a lie was incredibly convenient.

"The coincidence of us both having loved ones in the hospital so many miles from our homes is fascinating," said Bruce Oh, bobbing and weaving around Jane, putting himself between her and the B Room. It allowed him to look over all of the individuals and memorize their faces at the same time as he set a screen for Jane as she gathered herself behind the cover he was providing. She marveled at how he used his foreign appearance to such wide-eyed innocent advantage when he wanted to re-main anonymous.

"Coincidence?" asked Jeb, and for a moment Jane panicked. Had she mentioned Oh to Jeb in their lunch conversation?

"No such thing as a coincidence, Professor Oh. The way I see it, everything is ordered for a reason. We are meeting be-cause we need to meet," said Jeb, shaking Oh's hand and smiling.

It sounded almost conversational. In equal measure, al-most creepy.

11

My mother used to tell me to believe none of what I heard and half of what I saw. She was way ahead of the curve when it comes to living in a town like Hollywood.

—FROM *Hollywood Diary* BY BELINDA ST. GERMAINE

"That's what Nellie always says," said Jane, breaking the silence in the lounge.

Tim looked up from *People,* mildly curious, wildly bored. "So you're actually reading the Belinda St. Germaine book? I bought it for you as a joke," said Tim.

"That's how desperate I am," said Jane. "How do they expect anyone to want to get well in a hospital if all they provide to read are these dreadful gossip magazines? Why would you want to get out and reenter the world if the breaking news is whether or not some middle-aged actor will marry some teenage actress?"

"Why would you want to get out of here if the breaking news was the actual breaking news?" asked Tim.

Jeb looked up from a script he was reading and smiled at Jane. He seemed not to hear what she and Tim had said, just to be aware that someone was talking. Greg and Rick had gone off in search of a corner to work on something that they said was already overdue. Louise had left to make a phone call, promising to find and bring back decent coffee for all of them.

It might have been a scene out of any day at the hospital where friends and family gathered to wait for their loved one to emerge from a medical procedure—an operation, a serious test, or even labor and delivery. Jane and Tim, though, felt oddly stuck in place, being neither real friends nor family to the patient or those waiting. On the other hand, Jane, watching Jeb redline a script with a disgusted air, thought she might end up being Bix's best friend in the world if she could figure out what made Jeb Gleason and the B Room tick and get to the bottom of the threatening letters and exploding props.

Oh had left Jane and Tim to rejoin Claire with a promise to call later. Jane and Tim had then followed Jeb and company into Bix's hospital room, where Tim had left Skye arguing with Lou only a few minutes before. The room was empty. Jane had asked at the nurses' station if there was any word on Bix and the nurse, after looking Jane up and down to see if she might be anyone famous, shook her head. She also shook her head when Jane asked if she had any idea where Skye Miller and the man she had been talking to had gone.

"No," she said, smiling, "but the light sure goes out on this floor when she leaves, doesn't it? Having her here is the most excitement we've had since you-know-who had the face-lift."

Jane nodded, not even realizing that she made an enemy for life when she didn't ask the follow-up, and returned to the lounge, where they now sat killing time until someone came to tell them how Bix had fared in surgery.

"You know, I thought I might find Lou Piccolo here," said Jeb, putting the script he had been reading back into a brown leather messenger bag. "Thought he might be back from Ojai."

"So you said before you ran off with everyone at the flea market," said Jane.

"Did I say that out loud? Sorry to leave you standing there, but I did not want to get involved in that mess. You see," Jeb said, dropping his voice, "I recognized the poor guy."

Jane had learned many lessons from Oh, the most important one being patience. Oh, a serious student of baseball, had told her many times that a walk was as good as a hit, and after her son, Nick, explained the reference to her, she got it. Instead of flailing away at every pitch, she could hold out for the one she wanted. This time, she waited for Jeb to continue, to frame his own speech without benefit of her question.

"It was a writer who had a connection to Lou Piccolo. In fact, I think the guy, Patrick Dryer, is—I mean *was*—suing Lou. Something about Lou stealing his novel for a screenplay."

"Did he?" asked Tim, who had not learned to wait on the curveball, and began swinging away. "Did Lou steal the story?"

Jeb shrugged. "Lou says no. Claims the story's an old standard, biblical in nature." Jeb rolled his eyes. "He actually said that."

Jane looked at her watch. Even if Bix's surgery had started as late as Skye said, surely she must be in recovery by now. She felt as if they had been there for hours.

"Do you go to the flea market together every weekend?" asked Jane. She was interested in what Jeb had to say about Lou, but she realized she was more interested in the coincidence of the B Room being right behind her when she discovered the body.

"Often," said Jeb. "We started going when we worked on *S and L*. It was a first job for most of us and we were just starting to make money, buy houses, and stuff, and Louise suggested one Friday that we all get together and go. Became a habit for us," said Jeb. "A ritual, of sorts."

"What do you collect?" asked Jane.

"I tell everyone that I don't collect anything. But I like a few things. Smoking paraphernalia—old cigarette cases and lighters. I admire vintage watches. Paintings of racehorses. Old religious tracts," said Jeb.

"That's a new one. For example . . . ?" asked Tim.

"Oh, you know, pamphlets on Lourdes, Our Lady of Fatima . . . Catholica. And all kinds of handouts from the sixties when street-corner preachers were handing out cards and booklets with *The End Is Near* kind of rhetoric."

"What's the attraction?" asked Jane, her curiosity about why people collected what they did overcoming her for the moment. Before Jeb could answer, they were distracted by Skye's voice, Skye's loud and disturbed Celie-at-age-sixteen voice, at the nurses' station.

"I don't understand how this could be, how this could have been allowed to happen."

"There was nothing unusual about it, Ms. Miller. The surgery was done under a local. I just talked to Billie in recovery and she said when the doctor was satisfied she understood the aftercare, Ms. Bixby was free to leave."

"But her things?" Skye asked, gesturing toward Bix's hospital room. "Didn't anyone think it might be unusual for her to just leave without her belongings?"

"Her nurse packed everything for her early this morning when you went down for breakfast. Ms. Bixby had a change of clothes sent over by her secretary. Have you tried her at home?" asked the nurse, getting more and more upset when she realized how distraught her new celebrity friend was becoming. She looked down at a sheet of paper on a clipboard. "She was discharged just over an hour ago and said she had a ride home. One of the nurses thought she might have left in a taxi."

Skye turned away and walked directly to Jane. "I've lost her," she said, struggling with tears. "I said I could watch her and take care of her, but I've lost her."

"We haven't lost her, Skye," said Jeb in a low voice. "Keep your voice down and stop acting like a fool. No cameras are rolling. Bix got fed up with all of this hovering and went home, that's all."

"Shut up," said Skye, all trace of Celie or any innocent in-genue gone from her voice. "Lou Piccolo was here."

"So? I expected that. Why wouldn't he come here when he heard about Bix?"

"He hadn't heard about Bix. He'd gotten a call this morn-ing that said Patrick would be taken care of for him. Then the caller said all Lou would have to do was to return the favor sometime. Then whoever it was told him to visit his friend in the hospital and gave him Bix's room number."

Jeb's expression didn't change, although Jane thought his perfect L.A. tan grew one shade paler.

"Lou showed up here," said Skye, "carrying a gun, for Christ's sake. We had a fight about where the safest place for Bix to go recuperate was. I said I was going down to recovery to see what was taking so long and he said he was going to make a call. When I got down there, they gave me the bullshit about Bix taking off on her own and Lou Piccolo was nowhere."

"Has anyone tried calling Lou?" asked Jane.

Skye and Jeb turned to face her.

"Maybe he took her home in a cab," said Jane. When she saw Skye's eyes fill with tears, she added, "Or maybe he heard she went home and just left by himself."

"Has anyone called Bix?" asked Tim. "Since there were no complications after the procedure, maybe she just wanted to get out of the hospital and back to her house."

"Why didn't she say anything to me, then?" asked Skye. "I would have packed her things up and taken her. She knew I was here to take care of her." They had been standing directly outside of Bix's former room and Skye now walked into it and looked at the empty bed as if she expected to see Bix material-ize there. "I'll bet they didn't even find all the stuff I had brought in and unpacked for her."

Jane noted that the plastic basins, hand cream, tissues, and cheap hospital-provided toothbrush were all still wrapped and sitting on the deep windowsill next to a plastic-wrapped tracheotomy tray. Something didn't look right about the small hospital still life, but Jane couldn't quite put her finger on what it was that bothered her.

Tim suggested that they check the drawers and closets for anything left behind, then call Bix to see if she needed anyone to bring anything to her home. Although it sounded like a logical course of action, Skye continued to look distraught.

"This is not how it was supposed to be," she said. "I told Bix I would take care of all the discharge details. I know what I'm doing. I'm not a child, you know, I can do this. But no, Lou comes along and she listens to him just like she listens to you," Skye said, turning on Jeb. "And look where that's gotten her."

"Calm down, Skye," said Jeb. He kept his voice low, but there was steel in the tone of his delivery. "It's like Tim here said. She just went home. We'll head over there and make sure she's okay."

"Did she have stuff in here?" asked Jane, opening the small useless drawers of the nightstand. Jane found only an extra hospital gown—nothing belonging to the stylish Bix.

Skye walked over to the door and peered down the hall. They all heard Louise and Rick discussing some award nomination as they returned from their errands.

"What do we tell everyone?" she asked Jeb, sounding more like herself again . . . or more like Celie. Jane was still not sure which mood or voice was the real Miller. "I mean, I don't want everyone to be upset or worried."

Jane walked over to the closet. She was listening for Jeb's answer, but she wanted to keep busy. Although Skye's reaction bordered on the theatrical, Jane wasn't so sure how off the mark it was. Bix had been pretty out of it last night and after a two-hour surgery on her arm—no matter that the nurse was now describing it as a procedure to reduce scarring, primarily cosmetic—it seemed unlikely that Bix would feel like hopping into a cab and going home alone. Bix was frightened when she talked to Jane. She believed the threatening note she had received. Lou had confessed to some disturbing behaviors. And then there was Louise's story at the market. Her revelations had been the most interesting. The story of the missing member of the B Room . . . Heck. Was there a story behind his breakdown that related to Bix's accident? The note certainly seemed to refer to Henry "Heck" Rule.

Oh yes. And there was a dead man at the flea market. Why was it that in the midst of all the angst and noise of the living, the true victim often came last into Jane's thoughts? The dead are so quiet, she guessed. So undemanding compared to the living.

Jeb had dismissed Skye's question about the others with a head shake. Louise arrived in the doorway holding a cardboard tray of coffees and looked from face to face. She started to ask if anyone knew what was taking so long and Skye began to answer before she got the question out.

Jane, listening for Skye's answer but not wanting to appear overly curious, opened the closet door to make sure none of Bix's belongings had been left behind. She wondered if the startled *oh* she heard herself make was as loud in the room as it sounded in her own head.

Tied around the globe light fixture that turned on automatically as the door opened was a piece of fine string. Tied to the end of the string was part of what appeared to be a coat hanger and three other pieces of string. Attached to the pieces were two folded origami swans and one piece of card stock advertising a book and an upcoming signing at a bookstore in Pasadena. The author pictured on the mini-poster was Patrick Dryer, the man Jane had seen stabbed to death at the flea market. So much for the silence of the dead.

Louise and Skye both screamed at the sight of the grotesque mobile. Jane held out her arm, stopping Jeb from touching it as he came forward. She tilted her head to look at the folded bird tied to the string. The paper from which the origami swan was created looked like a page from a script. Jane could see the character names and dialogue format. A red marker had been scribbled over some of the typescript.

Jeb followed Jane's lead and tilted his head to try to read the pages without touching them. Pointing, holding a finger an inch from the paper, he read some of the fragmented lines.

"It's a shooting script from *Southpaw and Lefty*."

Jane turned to look at the reaction of the others in the room and as she moved her body, Jeb darted in front and pulled the entire mobile down.

"Jeb. That's evidence," said Jane.

"What's the crime?" he asked. "Bad writing?"

"Which episode?" asked Greg. He and Rick had been lured by the coffee and were haggling with Louise over the last one in the tray.

"Eighteen," said Jeb.

"When Celie and her friends steal the car to go to the rock concert," said Louise, nodding.

"That one did criminally suck," said Rick.

"Hey!" said Jane. "Can we get back on track here? There is a picture of a murdered man here. This is some kind of threat or warning," said Jane. "Or—"

"Yeah," said Tim. "The origami death threat . . . too bad old Stephen King never thought of that one. You know, the paper that folds itself into a party hat, then kills you with a thousand tiny cuts . . . I can see it now."

"Okay, smart guy," said Jane. "Less of a threat . . . more of a . . . signature."

"So the guy who stabbed Patrick at the flea market makes origami?" asked Louise. "Is that what this means?"

"Yeah, we find a guy who carries a bone paper folder in his pocket and we've got our murderer," said Greg.

Everyone in the room turned to stare.

"What? My first wife did paper arts . . . origami and stuff. You use something called a bone folder," said Greg, his cheeks flushed.

"Whatever you say, crafty," said Louise.

"The only thing it means for sure," said Jane, "is that someone visited this room who is handy with dental floss and . . ." Jane walked over to the windowsill where the tracheotomy tray and washbasin sat. She saw that the plastic was broken on each at one corner, then it was tucked neatly back around. In the basin, the container for the dental floss, used as the string on the mobile, was now unsealed. "And a scalpel," said Jane, recognizing what was missing from the tray. "I'm not sure why that tray was placed here unless they thought Bix was in some danger of choking, but someone took the small—"

"I told the nurse that Bix had a lot of allergies and I was worried about her in the night," said Skye. "I didn't know if she'd react to the medication they were giving her. I told them to take every precaution. . . . Maybe they—"

Jane stepped outside into the corridor and looked down to the lounge where she and Tim and Jeb had been sitting. Unless one really leaned over or craned his or her neck, none of them would see someone go in or out of Bix's room.

"How long was this room open? I mean open and vacant?" asked Jane. "I was in the hall by the nurses' station, talking to"—Jane hesitated for just a beat—"Professor Oh when Tim came out and asked me to come back in because you and Lou were having a disagreement over who could take better care of Bix. Jeb and the others arrived then, so we came here together. The room was empty."

Skye gathered up her purse and a loose-knit green sweater she had draped over a chair to ward off the hospital air-conditioning. "I have no idea how many minutes transpired between the time your friend Tim came to tattle on Lou and me and when we went downstairs. I know that I was outside of that recovery room arguing for at least twenty minutes, since I couldn't even get anyone to tell me anything for the first fifteen. And now, if you're done with your little grill session or whatever you call it, I am leaving."

"Honey, I'll drive you over to Bix's if you want," said Louise.

Jane looked over just in time to see Jeb give Louise a slight head shake. Jane wasn't sure whether or not Louise noticed it.

"Thank you, but it won't be necessary," said Skye. Jane could tell that although she was truly upset, something that crossed her mind almost made her smile. Watching Detective Oh for the slightest trace of an expression had given Jane a keen eye for the almost smile and the minimal frown. Jane could see that Skye's expression carried a trace element of pride.

"No longer necessary ever again," she said, jangling a key ring in front of them and walking out the door.

They listened to her steps in the hall, then heard the hum and thud of the elevator door.

"Attention all drivers, buckle up and batten down," said Rick.

"Good for her, I say," said Louise.

"About time, isn't it? Hasn't she had her thirtieth birthday?" asked Greg.

"At least twice," said Jeb.

In Kankakee, Illinois, the primary driving force behind growing up was getting to be old enough to drive out of town, so Jane and Tim, like everyone else they knew, had been ready and able to pass their road tests on their sixteenth birthday. Jane figured that Skye, who was having a busy year as one of the stars of *Southpaw and Lefty* around the time of her sweet sixteen, probably never had the time to take driver's education, let alone take the test to get her license.

Jeb told Greg and Rick to go gather up their work. He asked Louise if she had her briefcase and was ready to go. His cell phone rang just as he began to say something to Jane and Tim.

Jane had been a cell-phone watchdog earlier, explaining to Tim why cell phones weren't allowed in the hospital. Twice she had snatched Tim's trusty BlackBerry away. Tim gestured toward Jeb, but Jane shook him off. While Jeb was engaged with the call, Jane began scanning the room. She moved Jeb's messenger bag off the bed and place it on the floor next to her large tote. Bending down next to them, she disappeared from sight for a moment while she looked under the bed, then shook out the blankets.

"Where's the mobile, Jeb? The police should have it."

"Skye must have taken it," said Jeb, signing off from his call. "I'll get it from her."

Jane nodded. She closed her eyes and took a deep breath.

Jeb came over and put his hand on her shoulder. "You're exhausted, Jane. You've had a terrible day, finding Patrick and all, and now this bit of the bizarre. Why don't you and Tim head over to my place like I suggested? I can call the W and have your things sent over to my guesthouse. I'll be there after I make sure Bix is okay at her place and we can hash this thing out."

Tim shook his head violently behind Jeb's back. Mouthing *no* and waving his hands like windshield wipers, he made it clear he wanted no part of Jeb's hospitality.

"We'd love to," said Jane. "But we'll go back to the hotel, pack our stuff, and meet you later."

"Good girl," he said. He picked up his bag and promised to meet them back at his place in a few hours.

"What in the hell was that all about?" asked Tim.

Jane picked up her giant purse and took Tim's arm. She hustled him out of the room and down the corridor in the opposite direction of the elevator that all of Bix's guests had been using.

"I don't want to run into anyone from the B Room on our way to the parking lot," said Jane.

"Oh no, you'll have us stay with that warlock in his cave of shrunken heads, but we wouldn't want to run into him in the elevator, oh no," said Tim. "Have you lost your mind?"

Jane shook her head. As soon as the doors of elevator D, a full city block away from elevator B in Bix's corridor, closed behind them, Jane turned to Tim.

"First of all, Timmy, did you notice that Skye carries a darling little blue Kate Spade bag?"

"You picked a fine time to discover your inner *InStyle* girl," said Tim.

"So she would have no place to stash that weird arts-and-crafts project we found in Bix's room, right?" Jane asked. "But Jeb, who carries that nice big eight-hundred-dollar leather messenger, he had plenty of time and room to take it when Skye was dangling that key ring in front of us. Have you noticed that every one of them puts on a show every chance they get?"

"So if you thought he took it, why didn't you say something?"

"When he got on the phone, I checked his bag," said Jane. She reached into her own shopping-bag-sized purse and pulled out the photo of Patrick Dryer attached to the origami swans. "And I took it back."

"Excellent, Nancy Drew. Now what? I mean, I don't mean to be unimpressed, but . . ."

"I also grabbed this." Jane held up the small sharp blade that had been missing from the tracheotomy tray.

"Good. You set us up to stay at Jeb's place because not only is he creepy, but now we have the extra added feature that he might be the dangerous phantom origami folder. You are a thinker, Nancy. You were so busy during Skye's little rant. Lucky for you she distracted them all by waving her keys around," said Tim.

"That's another thing," said Jane. "Did you notice that key ring?" Despite the fact that they took the least convenient elevator, they found themselves almost as close to the parking lot entrance on the first floor. Jane slipped into the front seat, tossing Tim's *Thomas Guide* onto the floor.

Tim started the car and headed toward the hotel, but Jane suggested they make one stop on the way back.

"On her key ring, Skye had a car key and what was probably a house key and one more thing. . . ."

"Yeah?"

"A teeny tiny key just like this one," said Jane, pulling the key to the secret gate behind Bix's office from her pocket. "Want to go see if she's using it?"

12

He asked you out and you are thrilled! Why wouldn't you be?
He's got a steady gig on a weekly series. Now ask yourself . . . is
he a sincere actor or is he acting sincere?
—FROM *Hollywood Diary* BY BELINDA ST. GERMAINE

There would be no sneaking in through anyone's back
door this Sunday night. The street that led to the parking lot
annex that led to the hidden gate that led to Bix Pix Flix was
closed. Large sawhorses blocked access and uniformed police
stood around enforcing the roadblock, looking stern, official,
and bored all at the same time.

"While you turn the car around, I'll just hop out for a second," said Jane. Before Tim could ask any questions, she had
opened the door and was heading toward the men in blue.

"Excuse me, Officer, is there a problem here? I left something in my car in that parking lot and . . ." Jane asked one of
the sleepy on-duty cops.

"The street closing was clearly marked in advance, ma'am,"
he said. Now wide awake and up to full speed, he added, "That
lot has been closed for hours. Your car must have been already
towed . . . right, Len?"

"Yup."

"Oh no," Jane said, trying to sound suitably distraught,
hoping they wouldn't ask for any details about her phantom car.

"Yup," said Len again, "and towing is plenty expensive around here. Course, if you want to slip us a buck or two, maybe we can fix it up for you."

Jane's jaw dropped. How could a uniformed police officer on a city street be so openly crooked? She searched for a number on his badge, deciding then and there that she would call Oh and see how best to approach cleaning up the bad cop situation in Los Angeles.

The first cop, Len's partner, started giggling.

"That was pretty good," he said. "You played a cop before?"

"Just about all I do," Len said. "Usually I play a Chicago cop, but I find the emotional work pretty much the same for most urban law enforcement roles."

The two actors became engaged in shop talk, forgetting all about the citizen they had fooled with their expertise.

"So you're actors? This is a movie set?"

"Yup," said Len. "We just got set up. I don't think any cars really got towed from the lot, but they surely won't let you in there."

Jane nodded, looking at her watch. "How long would you say the street's been blocked?"

Len and his partner told her that the street had been impassable for at least two hours.

"Gosh, I wonder if my husband and his secretary know about the street closing," said Jane, pulling rabbits out of her hat. "I mean, they might have tried to get in and get my shopping bag for me. Jane described Lou Piccolo and Skye Miller and asked the two actor cops if they had seen anyone who looked like them trying to gain access to the parking lot.

"I saw a car with two people in the front seat come down the street and read the signs and turn their car around, but I couldn't tell what they looked like," said Len.

"Was it a BMW?" asked Jane. Although she didn't know the make of any cars belonging to the B Room, she did remember that Jeb's car was black and expensive-looking. BMW was her default expensive car model. Might as well go fishing with it.

Len shrugged. "I'm not a real cop, lady. I don't waste my time eyeballing cars or memorizing license plates."

"It was a vanity plate, though," said the other actor. "I can't remember what it said, but I remember it being a word."

Len looked approvingly at his acting partner. "You get into the part, don't you, pal?"

So Jane might not get back into Bix's office via the annex parking lot, but neither would Skye or anyone else who held a back-door key. Not tonight anyway. The sign that Jane now noticed for the first time said the street would be closed until midnight.

When she got back into the car with Tim, Jane explained the street situation. They headed back to the hotel, with Jane recapping what she knew so far and filling Tim in on what she had learned from Louise about Heck and all that she had and hadn't learned from talking to the seemingly open Lou Piccolo.

"He seemed so forthcoming," said Jane, "about confessing to accepting the ghostwritten scripts and all, but there's something weird about it. He was so self-effacing. So ready to say he was a hack and didn't mind ghosting scripts. Not sure any of that modesty rings true around here. Then his fight with Skye, leaving without saying anything to anyone . . . I don't know, it's all so damn theatrical."

Walking into the hotel, Tim suggested they eat something before deciding what they were really going to do. In his own self-conducted poll, he voted against moving to Jeb's place.

"I don't really want to do it, either, but I think that it's the place to discover more about the whole group and why someone is trying to hurt them. I mean, at first it might have been some sort of threat, but Patrick Dryer's murder puts . . ." Jane stopped talking when she couldn't make her key card work in the door. Tim stepped in front of her, brandishing his own card. His, too, failed to trigger the flashing green light that signaled admittance to their suite.

At the desk, they learned that Mr. Gleason had been by, paid their bill, and checked them out of their room. He had someone pack up their suite and transport their things to his guesthouse and he had left an address and a driver.

"You allowed someone to come into our room like that?" Jane asked, shocked. She couldn't cash a check for fifty bucks at her hometown bank without a picture ID and a major credit card.

The clerk excused himself and came back talking to someone on the phone. He covered the mouthpiece and explained to Tim that the lady had authorized it, signed her name.

"That lady?" Tim asked, pointing to Jane.

"A Mrs. Jane Wheel," answered the clerk, checking the paper he was holding.

"Me?" asked Jane.

"Mrs. Wheel accompanied Mr. Gleason and they checked out of the room together."

"I am Mrs. Wheel and I did not authorize—"

"I am very sorry, Mrs. Wheel, but I was not on duty. The clerk who was here," the man said, nodding to the phone he was holding, "says he thought he recognized the woman as Jane Wheel, who was a guest of the hotel. He didn't formally ask for ID because they didn't ask for a key or any help with access to the room. They simply paid the bill and left the address and driver for Mr. Lowry. He wants to know if it was perhaps a friend of yours who had a key and was surprising you by doing your packing."

The person on the other end of the line, apparently, was the clerk from the earlier shift and Jane and Tim could both hear him talking loudly. He seemed to alternate between being defensive and apologetic.

"He says he is very sorry for any inconvenience, but he's

sure that it was just a friend planning a wonderful surprise. The two people were quite enthusiastic and . . ." The clerk standing nervously in front of them seemed to hesitate as if deciding whether he should be interpreting and/or editing for his colleague on the phone. "He says to tell you that he's quite certain that the lovely woman who had Mrs. Wheel's key could not mean any harm."

He hung up the phone and looked as if he might cry. "I am so sorry. I'll report the idiot to my supervisor and call the police immediately, Mrs. Wheel. What a fool!"

Jane held up a hand and asked him to hold off on phoning the police. She dialed Jeb Gleason's cell phone.

"I know it was presumptuous of me, Janie. I tried to call you, but you weren't getting service. I did leave a message, though. The clerk assumed that Louise was Jane Wheel and we didn't disabuse him of the notion. A maid let us in and we thought we could just save you some trouble. You've had enough since you arrived. Please come over and we'll work all of this out. My driver is waiting there for you," said Jeb. He sounded like he was close to apologetic, but not quite there.

Since Jane had turned off the sound on her phone, it had been easy to ignore the blinking light signaling a message—Jeb offering to save them a trip back to the hotel. He said Bix would want them to salvage their trip by spending a few days of R and R, where, perhaps, Bix herself would be recuperating.

After accepting the apologies of the hotel—Tim tried to get them to throw in a bathrobe, but apologies were the only offer on the table since Jane had refused to call the police about the matter—Jane suggested to Tim that they accept Jeb's hospitality for the time being.

"I have a feeling we'll know a lot more about the B Room if we actually visit the secret clubhouse," said Jane.

"I'm not giving up my car," said Tim, "and getting into a limo with some driver owned by that creep Gleason. Tell me again about how he was once your boyfriend. . . . I knew it was a mistake to let you go off to a different college for four years. Something bad happens every damn time I let you out of my sight."

"We'll keep the rental car. We'll get the address or follow the driver, whichever is easier. He's been paid to take us there anyway. Besides, we've got all our flea market stuff in the back," said Jane. "And about college, my friend, remember I met Charley there, too. Besides, Jeb was different then."

Jane's defense of Jeb was rote by now. She felt required to protest Tim's assessment of Jeb as a lifelong creep, but she was not so sure he was wrong. Jeb had behaved badly with her. Maybe he truly was a creep, not just a college-age scoundrel-nudge-nudge-wink-wink with a wandering eye. Why had she always needed to file him away under one of her mistakes rather than just dismiss him for the liar he had been?

The packing and moving of Jane and Tim and all of their belongings from the hotel to Jeb's house was, at best, a grand gesture. And as high-handed and controlling as it might seem, the aspect that most troubled Jane was the thought of someone, anyone, going through her things, packing them up. No one could really believe that a violation of privacy was a kindly gesture. Jeb and Louise were looking for something they believed Jane and Tim had in their possession.

Jane had stolen the mobile from Bix's hospital room back from Jeb, but even if he discovered that it was missing and suspected that she had taken it, he couldn't think she'd managed to stash it in her room already. Jeb and Louise had to have come there directly from the hospital, one step, or so they had thought, ahead of Jane and Tim, if Jane and Tim hadn't detoured toward the studio.

"Whoo doggies," said Tim, after they turned down a private lane. "Look, Elly May, at the size of that there cement pond!"

Tim had driven their Volvo around a circle drive, following the driver provided by Jeb, then he had branched off toward a six-car garage in the rear of a large Spanish-style house. An Olympic-sized pool shimmered to the east of the garage. An art deco mosaic-tiled half wall on one end of the pool added to its glamour and provided a backdrop for six midcentury modern turquoise chaises. Jane felt her jaw drop and was not sure she would ever be able to close her mouth again. Among her stacks of postcards, she had several that were accordion books of photos of the stars' homes. Lucille Ball and Desi Arnaz, Ozzie and Harriet, James Stewart, Harpo Marx—a souvenir album from the fifties was the one she recalled now. She'd swear that this house had been one of those pictured.

What was most surprising about the house was how unexpected it was. This was an old and beautiful neighborhood, for sure, but most of the houses were more modest. Jeb's place, if it hadn't been so well hidden at the base of that circle drive, would have been the showplace of any neighborhood. As it was, it commanded most of the block but sat well away from the street. A well-maintained and stunning secret of a house.

Parked in front of the garage were two other cars. The license plates read, as the cars were lined up, Lou7 and Ric7. Jane saw Louise sitting by the pool and figured Rick and Greg were huddled up somewhere working on the never-ending script that was perpetually late.

Jeb spoke with the limo driver and pointed toward a house on the other side of the pool that looked like a miniature of the main house. Jane nudged Tim to note where their bags were being taken.

"We're in the mini-mansion, Timmy boy," said Jane, as they watched the middle-aged driver struggle with their two large suitcases.

"Doesn't he have oompa-loompas for that?" asked Tim, nodding toward Jeb. "I expect a flock of servants to come out for inspection."

Jane nodded. "Wrong movie, though. I like the way the help sings and dances in to that big entry hall for Annie's inspection."

"Yeah? Well, in our version, Daddy Warbucks has left capitalism for the Moonies."

Jane followed Tim's eyes and watched Jeb walk away from the limo. When Jane had lunch yesterday with Jeb, he had dressed in what Jane had assumed was normal everyday wear for a successful Hollywood type. He had worn appropriately fitted and name-branded blue jeans with a coffee-colored woven shirt and an earthy tweed sport coat, unstructured and casually elegant—the kind of jacket that was supposed to look like something from the back of the closet, but had cost a cool few thousand when purchased from a runway show in Manhattan or Paris. It was expensive in the most expensive way—made to look old school, casual and already comfortably worn.

Jeb apparently cultivated a different look for entertaining at home. Here, he wore a long, capelike maroon robe. Jane desperately hoped it was because he had just been swimming. If that wasn't the explanation, it was troubling to think of this old boyfriend running around as a middle-aged Superman wannabe. Not quite ready for takeoff, he glided toward them, arms outstretched.

"So sorry I behaved so impetuously. I just pictured the scene—you two arriving back at the hotel and being overwhelmed at the thought of packing up and moving, so you'd say no to my invitation out of that travelers' ennui," said Jeb.

"Because we wouldn't be refusing the invitation because we didn't want to come," Tim hissed through clenched teeth and a fake smile. "Because you scare the bejesus out of me," he added.

"Thanks for having us," Tim said out loud.

"I know you'll be comfortable. There are bathing suits and robes in the guesthouse if you didn't pack yours and you want to relax by the pool. We'll serve dinner shortly. There are drinks and snacks. Ask for whatever you need."

"Thanks," said Jane. "I hadn't expected such . . . opulence."

Jeb shrugged. "*S and L* was very good to all of us. I didn't spend a dime in those days. I didn't even spend money on rent. I boarded with this old Hollywood couple and helped them out around their place, saved all my money, and invested wisely. Continuing to work in the business, I made some good choices and was lucky. The past few years, I decided it was time to enjoy my life here, accept it as my earthly reward . . . for the time being, that's the reward we have, right?"

Jeb excused himself, saying he needed to check on dinner preparations. He suggested that Jane and Tim check out the pool house and see if there was anything else they required for their comfort. Watching him glide off, Jane was struck by her complete lack of knowledge of this man. The Jeb Jane lunched with yesterday was recognizable as the Jeb she knew in college. At-home-in-Hollywood Jeb was a horse of a different color.

"Does he seemed rehearsed to you?" asked Jane.

"Rehearsed? I feel like we just got a paragraph from his *People* magazine interview," said Tim.

Tim went off to check out the guesthouse, promising to find something wrong with it so they could go back to the hotel.

"I am allergic to faux marbling," said Tim, "and I have picked up on this creep's decorating style."

Jane walked over to the pool, hoping that Louise would be as open in her conversation as she was at the flea market. She jumped up from the chaise and apologized for her part in spiriting Jane and Tim away from the hotel. Jane waved it away and told her it was all for the best.

"We probably would have been too tired to pack up and we would have missed staying in this lovely place," said Jane. She noticed that Louise was wearing a different pair of sunglasses. These were larger and covered more of her face. Since Jane sat to the side of Louise, she could look behind the dark lenses. The glasses, from that angle, could not conceal the fact that her eyes were red-rimmed from crying. Detective Oh would advise Jane to wait, to sit it out and allow Louise to answer the unasked question, but Jane's heart rose above her head.

"Is everything okay?" Jane paused. "Are you okay?"

"I miss Heck," said Louise.

Jane counted the empty glasses on the side table. So far, all she knew about Heck besides the story of his illness and death was that he could write funny and he could write blue. Maybe Louise, in a margarita-infused moment of truth, would reveal something substantive.

"Would you like some iced tea? I'm obsessed with this orange ginger mint," said Louise.

So much for an uncensored monologue.

"Have you talked to Bix yet? Is she home?"

"She left a message for Jeb. She said she's on some pain medication that has her all doped up and she just wants to stay home by herself for now. Jeb sent one of his housekeepers over there with food."

"Did she say how she got home?" asked Jane, considering the great Skye-Lou showdown over who was going to get to protect their wounded pal.

"Don't know that. I'm guessing she just bypassed her room where she knew we'd all be hovering and took a cab," said Louise. "Sometimes I wonder if we've done each other any favors by being so—"

"Jane," Jeb called from the door of the house.

"So . . . ?" asked Jane, hoping at last for an unrehearsed word.

"Protective?" said Louise. But it was a question, not a definitive statement.

Jane remained seated, holding up a hand to Jeb to indicate she'd be with him in a minute. Jane decided to give a little to get something back.

"I don't have a large circle of friends. I've just got Tim, but I don't know what I'd do without him. Unconditional support . . . isn't that what we all want from our husbands and wives, but what we really get from our friends?" asked Jane, feeling like a traitor to Charley, who gave her enough rope to hang herself on a daily basis.

"Maybe," agreed Louise, "but Heck needed more from us. He gave us everything he had. And I mean everything. Too much. And we didn't know how to give him what he needed."

"It's always hard to lose someone. Especially hard to be the one to have to identify him," said Jane.

"Truth is I barely looked at him," said Louise. "When he jumped, he was wearing the robe he practically lived in that last year and these goofy dog slippers. I went into that room, when his idiot cousin wouldn't go in, and they pulled down the sheet and I couldn't focus on his face, I just wanted to see his feet, to look for the slippers. And of course they weren't on his feet. I asked the technician where his bathrobe and dog slippers were and she looked at me like I was nuts, then I started babbling about how I didn't want them or anything, it was just that I wanted to say good-bye to Heck when he looked like Heck and she just hustled me out of there. A few days later, a box was sent to the house, and it had the . . ." Louise stopped.

"They sent the slippers home," said Jane.

Louise nodded.

Greg, carrying a notebook, and Rick, carrying a laptop, came out of the house. They nodded at Louise, and Rick gave Jane a vague smile. Greg looked at her like he had never seen her before.

"We're going to work out here for a little while before the meeting," said Rick, the taller of the pair. Greg sat down and began writing immediately in the notebook. There were single pages stuffed into the notebook and a few came loose and floated to the ground under the table as he set his material down on one of the wrought-iron tables next to Louise and Jane.

"Greg, what exactly are you working on now?" asked Jane.

"Movie script. Cable."

"Is it appropriate to ask what it's about?" asked Jane.

Greg shrugged. Rick sat down opposite his writing partner and opened the laptop.

"It's not inappropriate at all," said Rick. "It's just exhausting to talk about. We've been through the initial meetings where we hashed it all out, then the pitch where we sold them on the idea, then we wrote the first draft, now we're working on the second, and, I don't know, it gets hard to describe, because it's been through—"

"—the fucking wringer," said Greg. "And I, for one, am sick of the whole thing. I'm telling Jeb that I've had it with this one. I'm out. He can—"

"Yeah, yeah," said Rick, "you quit. He can take that job and shove it." Rick turned to Jane. "Greg quits every project during the second draft. Then I finish writing it and he's so appalled at what I do that he rejoins the team before I can hand it in."

"Get bent," said Greg, standing and walking quickly into the house.

Jane bent over to pick up the napkins she had knocked to the ground while talking to Louise. Not seeing a trash receptacle, she stuffed them into her bag and stood up.

"Who is the show for?" asked Jane.

"Pilot for a cable network," said Rick, standing and looking off to where Greg had disappeared inside.

"Didn't you say it was a movie?" asked Jane.

"Back-door pilot," said Rick. "I mean, it's a movie, but if the response is good, they'll pick it up as a series."

"If it gets made," said Louise.

"Yeah," said Rick. "If."

"Why is Greg going to tell Jeb he's quitting?" asked Jane. "I mean, what does Jeb—"

"I've got to go make a call. Please excuse me," said Rick. "I'll probably see you at dinner."

Rick did not seem to be in any special hurry. Jane noticed that everyone from the B Room had a California languor, a mellowness that cried out sunshine and palm trees. But he did keep his eyes on the door where his partner had disappeared as he picked up his own drink and laptop and headed toward the stairs that led to a coach house over the multicar garage.

Louise watched him go, then stood up herself.

"Later," she said to Jane without any explanation, and followed Rick to the coach house.

They hadn't seemed terribly worried about Greg's angry departure. They all acted out their little dramas for each other so frequently that it wouldn't surprise Jane to know that they took each other's fits and pouts for granted. But Jane wasn't sure she was supposed to be privy to this one. She took some papers out of her bag. Along with the napkins she had picked up from the ground, she had picked up a stray page that Greg had knocked loose from his manuscript. Jane had folded it and sandwiched it between the napkins to get a look at what Greg and Rick were working on.

Page eight of a script. Few stage directions—some quick give-and-take between a father and daughter. Jane couldn't tell very much from the content of the scene. She noticed two things about the page itself, though. It appeared to be typewritten, not printed from a computer printer. The paper felt different. It had the heft and weight and texture of typing paper, heavy bond, rather than a multipurpose office megastore sheet of printer paper. And the name in the corner was neither Greg's nor Rick's. The shorthand identifier typed in the corner read: "*Your Pal, Pete*" / *first draft*/ *H. Rule.*

H. Rule. That would be Henry Rule. Heck. Why were Greg and Rick working from a first draft of a script written by a dead man?

13

"Dinner in a half hour? Okay with you and Tim?" Jeb called out to the pool from the doorway. He seemed to have given up on Jane coming into the house before the meal was served. Or he had just gotten too busy with Greg coming in to tattle on Rick or whatever was going on among the members of the B Room.

Jane went to check on Tim to see if he had made his peace with the guesthouse. It adjoined two small rooms that were the changing rooms for the pool. There was a separate entrance with a mailbox, a doorbell, and a welcome mat. Jane opened the door and surveyed the entire first floor, which was visible from the entryway. It was laid out like a one-level loft with a large open area surrounding a kitchen with a round table in its center. There were seating areas and reading nooks situated all around the edges of the house, but basically it was one open room. A stairway led to what Jane guessed were the bedrooms, and there was one enclosed room behind the kitchen which Jane assumed was a powder room. The house was bright and comfortable and cozy without being crowded.

"Tim, are you upstairs?" Jane called, opening the refrigerator, which was stocked with champagne, bottles of tonic, olives, some expensive cheese, and a few lemons.

"Where there's tonic, there's vodka," said Jane. "How about a drink, Timmy?"

When Jane turned to face Tim, whom she'd heard come down the stairs, she was prepared for him to pepper her with more questions about why they were staying at Jeb's and how could she agree to this, and so on, but she was not prepared to see her friend, serious and worried, holding up the large tote bag she carried as a purse.

"I brought this up to your room and the mobile fell out," said Tim.

"I showed it to you. You knew I took it," said Jane, pouring vodka for both of them and, not finding any toothpicks in the drawer, throwing olives into the glass. "Sink or swim, boys. What's the deal?"

"Look at this thing," said Tim.

Jane had only glanced at the mobile before Jeb had taken it and she had retrieved it. Both origami swans, well folded, made from pages of S and L scripts, were attached to the coat hanger with what appeared to be dental floss. A faint smell of mint came from the piece. The picture of Patrick had a crude hole punched in the top, probably made with the little scalpel, and the floss was poked through. Jane turned the picture over and saw that it had quotations, blurbs on the back. It was a postcard announcing the publication of the novel.

"What?" asked Jane, scanning the card. Then she saw what had turned Tim so serious. Patrick's picture was on one side of his publisher's publicity department postcard, superimposed over the book's title, now unreadable, and the cover. On the other side, there were two blurbs on the top half of the card. Beneath the manufactured raves for the novel, someone had hand-printed in very tiny letters an additional quotation.

"Not since *And Then There Were None* by Agatha Christie have you read such a horrific tale! Ten Little Indies! Screenwriters who think they can make it on their own without a major studio! Who will be next? Jeb Gleason, Louise Dietz, Greg Thale, Rick Stewart, Wren Bixby, Henry Rule, Skye Miller, Lou Piccolo? Or will it be special guest star Jane Wheel?"

"Time to call the police, Nancy Drew?" asked Tim, draining his glass of Grey Goose.

"Almost," said Jane, taking out her cell phone.

As she dialed, she pointed out what intrigued her about the postcard. Yes, the hand-printed quotation that Tim had found so chilling was . . . chilling. Even more intriguing was something printed above the blurbs for the book.

Publication Date, December 1.

"This book isn't out yet," said Jane.

Tim took the card from her and turned it over to look at the author's face.

"Poor bastard isn't going to do many signings, is he?" asked Tim.

At dinner, Jeb kept the conversation going. It was an uphill task. Jane would have found it more surprising that a group of good friends, writing partners, and all-around show business funny people could be so quiet and surly, but as Tim kept reminding her by kicking her under the table and covertly pantomiming calling the cops, a cloud hung over the B Room.

Wren Bixby's accident—or attack, depending on who was doing the spin—then the murder of Patrick Dryer at the flea market, had cast a pall. Even by the high Hollywood dramatic standards of this group, it had been an extraordinary few days.

"If Bix isn't up to it tomorrow, someone ought to take Jane and Tim on a tour," said Jeb. "I'd do it, but I've got that meeting. . . . They should see something besides a hospital room."

"We've been to the flea market," said Jane, "although that was cut a bit short."

Jane tried to get a member of the group to look at her when she brought up the flea market. Louise poured water for herself, keeping a careful watch on her glass. Rick pushed sushi around on his plate and refused to make eye contact. Greg had not come to the table, although Jane could hear someone she assumed was Greg bumping into things in the kitchen and arguing with the housekeeper.

"Did you all know Patrick Dryer?" asked Jane. "Or was it just you who recognized him, Jeb?"

Jane might have asked the question, but the diners all looked at Jeb as if he had posed it.

"I had met him before, but I didn't know him well," said Jeb. "Rick, you knew him, didn't you? From the gym or something?"

"No," said Rick. "I met him at the health club once, but he was there as the guest of someone I didn't know very well. He recognized my name when we were introduced and asked me about the B Room, said he knew all about our group. Passed himself off as a friend of Lou Piccolo's. I didn't know he was trying to sue Lou at the time. I guess he was trying to see if I knew."

"I knew Patrick Dryer," said Greg, who had come in quietly from the kitchen. He was holding a tumbler full of ice and lemon slices and what Jane sensed might be vodka. He was sipping it too slowly for water and with too much relish for it to be simply tonic. "Doesn't anybody besides me remember old Patrick?"

"Drinking your dinner tonight, Greg?" asked Jeb, watching him make his way to a seat at the table.

"Patrick visited the set a couple times when we were on *S and L*," said Greg, setting his glass down hard, splashing his drink onto the linen tablecloth. "In fact, I thought he and Bix—"

"He was visiting a family member who worked on the show," said Louise. "I remember now. But he was a snob, didn't want to talk to TV writers. He introduced himself as a novelist."

"Anyone know what his latest book was about?" asked Jane.

The question got everyone's attention, although no one had any answers.

Louise and Rick both said they had no idea that there was a new book. Rick shook his head. Jeb shrugged and said it was probably some thriller with a limp. "You know, the kind that purports to be all action and plot, but when you break it down, there's no 'there' there. All a bunch of rambling thoughts in some know-it-all narrator's head," said Jeb.

"Interesting title, though," said Jane.

"What was it?" asked Jeb. "And how do you know it?" Jeb had exchanged his maroon robe for a kind of tunic, open at the throat, but he stretched his neck when he asked the question as if a collar were choking him.

"Even hack novelists don't deserve to be stabbed in the back with a—" Greg began, but was interrupted when Jeb's housekeeper came in and announced that there was a gentleman at the door to see Mrs. Wheel.

"I forgot to mention that Professor Oh was stopping by," said Jane. "He offered to drop off a manuscript of his new book for me to bring home to Charley. When he mentioned he was staying with family in the Los Feliz neighborhood, I gave him your address and he knew right where the house was, so . . ."

"No problem at all. Let's invite him to join us, shall we?"

Oh entered the room in his professorial persona, all shyness and apologies.

"Please, I can see I am interrupting your dinner," said Oh, backing out of the room.

Jeb, all host and director, pulled over a chair from under one of the massive windows and placed it next to his own.

"You must stay, Professor. We have too much food and too little to say to each other. We all know each other too well to entertain Jane and Tim here," said Jeb.

"We need fresh blood," said Louise.

"That remark is in questionable taste under the circumstances," said Greg, wagging a finger at Louise, who blushed and shook her head.

"Thoughtless. Sorry."

"We were discussing the murder victim from the Pasadena Flea Market today, Professor. Patrick Dryer. Have you heard about it?"

"My wife's family has talked of nothing else. Her brother is an antique dealer who had a booth at the market. He was complaining that his business was dramatically reduced because of the murder. Even though we reminded him that a poor man lost his life, he was adamant that the police should not have closed the market and held everyone up in such a fashion as they did," said Oh. "His complaint was that so many people were coming and going during the time of the murder, before it was discovered, that the police barricades after the fact were of no use."

Jane arched an eyebrow and studied her old friend Jeb Gleason. He had successfully avoided any direct mention to Jane of what went on at the flea market and to her surprise, he now looked openly angry.

"Your brother-in-law is absolutely right. Anyone could have gotten in and out during the window of time that the murder was committed. I didn't like the guy that much, I mean, as much as I knew about him, but no one deserves that and, according to the police, they didn't find any suspects among the bargain hunters they managed to trap inside the market after the fact. Poor bastard."

It was the worst piece of acting Jane had witnessed since she had arrived in Los Angeles.

"You knew the man who was killed?" asked Oh.

Jeb looked past Oh, fixing his eyes on some map that no one else could see. After a moment, he chose his path.

"Slightly."

Jeb stood up from the table and looked deliberately at each member of the B Room still seated. Jane knew he was trying to convey a message, something he hadn't had a chance to work out with them in advance. It was the silent communication a parent attempted with a child when someone entered the room about whom the parent had just been speaking. If Jane, for example, had just been mentioning in front of Nick that her neighbor had a big mouth and said neighbor walked in, Jane would give that look to Nick—that please-don't-repeat-what-I-just-said-even-though-what-I-said-was-right-and-I-have-nothing-to-be-ashamed-of look—half pleading, half threatening, half guilty. That's right, three halves. Jane, like every other parent, felt that two halves of any feeling, two sides to any question, were never enough to explain how one felt when faced with a child's quizzical look.

Jeb's look at his dinner guests had less pleading, more threat, but overall was a mute request for backup on whatever he was about to say.

"Patrick Dryer was a novelist who came out to Los Angeles hoping to be treated like something special. He thought he was ready for prime time immediately, couldn't understand why no one hired him to write a movie or invited him to come on staff at a television show. He didn't bother to ask anyone why things didn't work out, either—he just began whining and blaming everyone in his path."

"And suing them, as well?" asked Jane.

Jeb ignored Jane's comment.

"Patrick never wrote a script on speculation, he never bothered to talk to an agent about what he needed to do to be taken seriously, he never bothered—"

"To pay homage to Jeb Gleason and the B Room? Never handed over his pound of flesh, did he? And we don't like it when someone tries to draw from our well without asking politely for a drink. Reminds me, may I have another drink? Please?" asked Greg, cutting between the table and where Jeb was standing, making a direct beeline for the bar.

"Greg," said Louise, standing, "maybe you ought to call it a night."

Jeb shook his head and gave Jane, Tim, and Oh one of those looks that once again made him the parent, this time giving them the what-can-you-do-with-crazy-kids shrug.

"We're having a meeting in the study. The B Room, I mean, is having a meeting now. Please stay and have coffee and dessert," Jeb said, including Oh in the invitation. "Bobbette makes a wonderful chocolate mousse cake. Make yourself at home. Or if you'd rather, you can have it served in the guesthouse," he offered.

Louise, already up, was speaking quietly to Greg. Rick stood up, carrying his coffee cup. Tim, with more enthusiasm than he'd shown since they'd arrived at Jeb Gleason's house, jumped up and said he thought having dessert in the guesthouse was a wonderful idea. Jane and Oh stood up together, Oh watching Jeb as if he were waiting for him to finish his earlier story. Jane, facing a case on the opposite wall, noticed for the first time that Jeb had a large collection of books, all sheathed in the acid-free clear plastic jackets with which collectors protected their precious volumes. She would have to explore the titles later.

The sharp slam of the door to the dining room made them all, to one degree or another, start. Even Greg, whose reaction times were slowed by alcohol, gave a slow-motion head snap. Odd, Jane noted, that none of them were facing the door. Had they been looking in that direction, they might have been even more startled if the odd trio had simply walked in on them without the warning shot.

Like a bizarre tableau from a souped-up version of *The Wizard of Oz*, Bix stood in front of them. Her braids pointed in all directions, taking the place of Dorothy's tamer pigtails. She had her left arm linked through Scarecrow's arm, tonight being played by Lou Piccolo, in jeans and a plaid flannel shirt. Her other arm, heavily bandaged, rested on Skye Miller's arm. Skye was decked out in a wildly fringed, long, and loosely hand-knit gold vest. A not-so-cowardly lion, she shook her giant mane of honey-blond hair and smiled sweetly at Jeb.

"Did we scare you?" asked Skye. "At the hospital, I heard you mention there was going to be a meeting tonight."

After the first moment of silence, the group crowded around Bix, asking her about her arm, her hospital stay, her hospital exit, her pain, her pain medication.

"Any extra Vicodin for Uncle Ricky?" Rick said, pulling on one of Bix's braids.

"I'm absolutely fine. The surgery was to reduce the scarring from some jagged glass that went into my arm when the box blew. I have recovered from the shock and my arm is recovering from the cut and all is well. Skye and Lou are practically fighting over who gets to take care of me, so what's not to feel better about? If I don't recover, I won't be able to get rid of either one," she said, laughing.

"I'll amuse myself studying your bookshelf while you have your meeting," said Lou to Jeb. "Don't worry about me listening at the keyhole."

"All the books are cataloged, Lou, so don't think I don't know what I have and where it's shelved," said Jeb. He was trying for a light touch, but fell short. The remark tumbled to the ground with a thud and made him sound like a petulant child.

Instead of trying to recover by saying anything more, he put a proprietary arm around Bix and escorted her away from Lou.

Pausing at the doorway, Jeb turned back to the room, where everyone was either waiting to follow him into the meeting or, in the case of Jane, Tim, Oh, and Lou, be served Bobbette's famous chocolate mousse cake.

"So what is the title of the late Patrick Dryer's new novel?" asked Jeb.

Although Tim was upset about the quote on the author/novel postcard, Jane felt that its importance paled in contrast to the other information gleaned from the focal point of the mobile. The book cover had been obscured by the author photo, so the title of the book was not noticeable when they had first found the crude objet d'art in Bix's hospital closet. Jane, after scrutinizing the postcard in the guesthouse, could hardly contain herself when she saw the cover clearly. She'd wanted to reveal the title earlier when the group was sitting around the dinner table. Although then she thought it the perfect time, she realized now, as Bruce Oh often told her, the perfect moment presents itself to one more often than one is able to invent the perfect moment. Now, in addition to an audience made up of Jeb, Louise, Rick, and Greg, she had the complete cast of characters in view. Bix, Skye, and Lou now looked at her as expectantly as the others. Even better, she had Oh there to help Tim and her assess the reactions of the group.

"*The D Room*," said Jane.

14

As soon as you hear about a meeting to which you are not invited, fight fire with fire. Call your own meeting. And don't invite anyone from the first one. But, and this is key, make sure one of the noninvitees sees your memo.

—FROM *Hollywood Diary* BY BELINDA ST. GERMAINE

Jane knew she didn't trust Jeb Gleason, but she wasn't sure, after tasting Bobbette's chocolate mousse cake, whether she could brand him an out-and-out liar.

"This is unreal," said Tim. "It's like the cocoa bean's last request."

"Not last request," said Jane, "too grim. More like favorite place to set up housekeeping."

"Perhaps," said Oh, lifting another bite and studying it for a moment, "it is chocolate's highest calling."

The three of them sat around the table in the guesthouse with generous slices of the cake in front of them. After their first bites, they uniformly slowed down, wanting to make this incredible treat last.

Lou Piccolo had declined cake, claiming he just didn't get what the chocolate thing was about. Instead of joining them for dessert, he said he was going to go smoke a cigar by the pool.

"I pick and choose among the common vices and these babies have never let me down," said Lou, holding a monogrammed leather cigar case in front of him, Holy Grail–style.

Detective Oh put down his fork and stood up from the table. He walked to the window and made sure Lou was thoroughly involved in reading *Variety* and savoring his cigar.

"While we are alone, perhaps it would be the best time to show me this mobile you described and I can give you the package I brought," he said.

Jane had the mobile in her bag, which rested on the floor next to her, and she fished it out, carefully unwrapping the origami from the postcard. Oh studied the hand-printed quotation.

Jane unwrapped the package Oh had laid on the table. He had placed his find in a brown paper bag and taped it so it appeared to be a thick manuscript. Jane was delighted to see it was one step beyond loose manuscript pages.

"How did you manage this?" asked Jane, holding the paperbound galley of *The D Room* by Patrick Dryer. The cover was plain heather-gray card stock with the title and author's name in black. In a large circle under the title was printed, *Advance Uncorrected Proofs.* In the lower left corner was the publisher's name and logo. "These aren't available to the public."

"When you told me the title and the publisher, I phoned an old schoolmate of mine who owns a bookstore in San Francisco. I asked him if one could ever obtain a book before it was available to the public and he explained that these paperbacks, these bound galleys, are sent to booksellers in advance so they will better be able to discuss the author's book with their customers. My friend knows all the independent booksellers in the area and offered to phone them and track down who in Los Angeles might have been sent a bound galley of *The D Room*. He gave me the name of a splendid fellow at the Mystery Bookstore who goes by the curious name of Dark Bobby. Bobby offered me the store's copy. He said that neither he nor another bookseller there, Linda, predict a large success for the book. The entire staff read it, hoping it would be good, since it was set in Los Angeles. He did tell me, though, that Carol, the bookkeeper, mentioned something interesting after she finished it. She said that every time Patrick Dryer introduced a character, she felt she was supposed to know who it was, as if the book were a roman à clef, but none of the characters were famous enough to be truly recognizable."

"Ouch," said Tim.

Jane opened the book and scanned the acknowledgments. Patrick Dryer thanked his agent and his editor, which Jane assumed was predictable. He also thanked some office assistants and a few experts who advised him on copyright law.

"Listen to this," said Jane, reading aloud.

> At some point an author of fiction is supposed to note that any resemblance between real people and his characters is an accident. The author is supposed to claim that each man, woman, and child who makes an appearance in his book is purely a figment of his own imagination. Well, I won't do it. Are these characters based on real people? Yes. Are they as silly, vain, greedy, and ignorant as I make them here? Yes. And would they ever sue me over their portrayal? No. Not one of the models for the members of *The D Room* would ever do that. They are, after all, television writers. They don't read books.

"I repeat, ouch," said Tim. "You going to finish that?" he asked, pointing to Jane's cake with his fork.

Jane moved her plate out of Tim's fork's range and continued reading silently.

"The origami swan is not that difficult," said Oh, holding up the mobile, turning it slightly, and allowing the swans to move freely. "Fish base, mountain fold . . . of course, the swivel for the neck might take some practice."

"Didn't Rick say he knew something about origami? Something about a bone folder?" asked Jane.

"Or Greg. Until Greg got drunk, I couldn't see much difference between the two of them," said Tim.

"And now?" asked Oh.

"Greg's the drunk one," said Tim.

"This is one bitter man," said Jane, still reading Patrick's acknowledgments. "He won't even thank his parents without a sarcastic slam at Nurture vs. Nature. Listen to this. 'As far as my parents are concerned, I thank them for not drowning me at birth. That's all I can think of at the moment. Since they are dead now, I hurt no one by paraphrasing the poet Philip Larkin, agreeing with his poetic line, *they fuck you up, your mum and dad.*'"

"Brutal," said Tim.

"Remind me to call Nellie later," said Jane.

"Mrs. Wheel," said Oh, "at the hospital where my wife's aunt and Ms. Bixby were patients, there was a family arts and crafts room. Yesterday and today, Claire and I walked the entire hospital, keeping ourselves busy. In the family room this afternoon, a volunteer was teaching paper craft. It is possible that anyone waiting to see a loved one could have dropped in and learned to fold a simple shape such as the swan."

Jane nodded, putting down the book for a moment and taking the mobile from Oh.

"Yes, but the paper. Whoever made this just happened to have a television script in her purse," said Jane. "Or his messenger bag."

"*Southpaw and Lefty* is an old show. Only one of the writers or someone connected to it would have an old script," said Tim. "And it's hard to believe even one of the B Room would have pages just lying around like that. Haven't they all moved on to other projects?"

"Aren't they all still meeting together as if the show were never canceled?" asked Jane, looking toward the main house. "How weird is that? If you told me they slept on mattresses stuffed with old scripts, I think I'd believe it."

"I'm not sure I can stretch my visit here too much longer, Mrs. Wheel. I am, after all, simply a professor dropping off a manuscript. When I get back to Claire's relative's home, I am going to call Officer Dooley and explain the situation. There is a threat to everyone in this house, including you, written on this mobile. We cannot ignore it."

Jane nodded. She agreed that the quotation that someone had filled in on the postcard sounded like a threat. Sort of. But Jane didn't feel threatened.

"It's too cute," said Jane. "Too literary, too."

"What does that mean?" asked Tim.

"Feels like a pose, doesn't it? How many people who really want to kill someone leave him or her a note? I mean, other than in mystery books? Origami-trimmed art-project-type notes, at that?" asked Jane. "I mean, if I wanted to kill someone, wouldn't I just do it? No muss, no fuss, no additional artifacts to trace back to me?"

"I agree with you, Mrs. Wheel," said Oh, nodding. "Creating and planting this mobile is a childlike exercise."

"Yeah, well, childlike can be *childlike* . . . all innocent fun and games, or *childlike* . . . as in *The Bad Seed* or *Whatever Happened to Baby Jane*," said Tim. "I think the thing is scary as hell."

"I also agree with you, Mr. Lowry. Childlike can be quite dangerous. The police have to be alerted. After all, Patrick Dryer was murdered, and it was his picture on the mobile, so there seems to be some connection, even if the threat to you, Mrs. Wheel, is not something that you feel so strongly."

Jane placed the bound galley of *The D Room* on the butcher block next to the refrigerator and covered it with a dish towel. She didn't want any of the others to see it if they happened to wander in. Looking out the window, she saw Lou Piccolo still sitting by the pool, puffing on what she assumed must be an exceptional cigar. When he first settled in, he had opened a magazine and seemed to be engrossed. Jane had noticed, as they sat there eating cake and discussing Patrick Dryer, that Lou had never turned a page while he was in her sight. The window was open, but they had talked quietly and his chair was twenty feet from the guesthouse. Unless Lou Piccolo possessed superhuman hearing, he was not privy to their conversation. The magazine rested in his lap and he sat perfectly still and smoked. *Automatic pilot. He's smoking in a trance.*

Jane looked beyond the pool to the main house. It epitomized grand old Hollywood. The coffee-with-cream-colored stucco walls looked as if they'd feel warm to the touch. The house sprawled comfortably, curving itself around the pool, which glimmered and beckoned. The property wasn't all that showy, Jane realized, not as immense as it had seemed when they drove up earlier. It was the relationship of Jeb's house to those immediately surrounding it that gave it its imposing stature. The others that Jane could see across the lawn, their windows now warm squares of light, were attractive houses, quite desirable pieces of real estate, Jane was sure, but they were smaller, more sensibly scaled residences. Jeb's place, though a manageable size, was still the biggest house on the block.

Turning back to the main house, Jane could see that the B Room had either called its meeting to a close or its members were on a break. Jeb stood in the window, looking out toward the pool, and said something over his shoulder to Louise, who was trying to see around him. Maybe they were speculating about the normally loquacious Lou's pensiveness. Or maybe they were wondering if Jane Wheel had figured out who rigged a box to explode and who was sending malicious notes. And worrying about whether that *who* was the same *who* who killed Patrick Dryer.

"Who kills a writer?" asked Jane out loud.

Detective Oh looked at her expectantly. A man who loved questions almost as much as he loved answers, he seemed delighted that his protégée was asking an interesting one.

Tim, a man who preferred answers, his own, offered, "Critics?"

"They don't need a hammered silver letter opener. They use a pen," said Jane, "or if they really want to make their victim suffer, they probably use the silent treatment."

"How about a nightcap?" The voice was Jeb's, a bit muffled, but loud enough to make them all start, although Jane had already jumped at a clicking noise that had preceded the invitation.

Jane, Oh, and Tim looked first at each other, then each of them looked around the room, their eyes falling on the intercom speaker next to the light switch at about the same time.

"Why not?" said Tim, directing his voice to the hole in the wall.

"Fine. Come over." There was a click, then silence.

Jane approached the small speaker and pointed. "I didn't see this before. Do you suppose . . . ?"

Oh examined the speaker and the off-and-on switch underneath it. It was turned on. He switched it off, back on, then off.

"This is an old system, not sophisticated at all. We were sitting in there around the table until a few minutes ago and we clearly heard the monitor on their end turn on and off. I don't believe anyone was listening to our conversation, Mrs. Wheel."

Tim shot Jane an I-told-you-so look. He slipped his jacket on and shook his head. "If I could understand why . . . how you dated that guy . . ."

Detective Oh straightened and tilted his head slightly in Jane's direction.

Jane took it as it was intended—a direct question.

"I dated Jeb in college. When Bix saw me on the news program and mentioned the story to Jeb, he said he knew me and encouraged her to call me."

"No," said Tim.

Oh and Jane turned their attention to Tim.

"Bix called me after she talked to you and you said no, remember? She told me that a friend had shown her the tape of you on the show. Bix told me it was an old friend of yours. I remember now. She said Jeb saw you and brought the movie idea to her attention. I didn't remember that you two had dated until you told me you were nervous about seeing him. Yeah, I'm sure she said Jeb was the one who had brought the idea to her."

Jane was off balance. Literally. She rocked back and forth on the balls of her feet, trying to find level ground. Why did Jeb suggest to Bix that Jane's life as a newly minted detective would make a good movie? And why did Bix explain the project differently to Jane? She said she had seen Jane on television and mentioned it to Jeb and the coincidence of his knowing her had been just that . . . a coincidence. Jane remembered that Louise told her they had all seen the tape at Jeb's. At the time, Jane had just figured that Bix had called it to everyone's attention. Was it really Jeb who was responsible? Did any of this matter? Or were the explanations to Tim and Jane just innocent juxtapositions of events? Coincidence.

Charley told Jane once that as a scientist he believed in coincidence and it should never be counted out as a possibility when figuring out a problem. However, when you found yourself saying *coincidence* more than once, it was time to accept the fact that it probably wasn't one.

Jane found herself blushing. Something about remembering Charley's words about coincidence and standing under the scrutiny of Detective Oh, who was regarding her most intensely, was making her uncomfortable. Jane looked at Detective Oh, who seemed taller than he ever had before, and realized that she was embarrassed. She didn't want him to think that she . . . what? That she came out to L.A. because of any feelings for Jeb Gleason? Or that she hoped Jeb Gleason had any feelings for her? If Charley were staring at her right now, she would tell him he was ridiculous and laugh at the absurdity of any connection to Jeb.

Detective Oh, though, was not her husband. Husbands can be laughed off and dismissed and argued with and cried over and ignored and made up with. Mentors are another matter. It was important that Oh respect Jane, that he believe her to be honest. This was ridiculous. Jane realized that she didn't care what Charley thought from moment to moment because she had a lifetime of moments to straighten things out between them. With Charley, it was an ongoing conversation—even when he was halfway around the world, Jane continued to talk and listen to Charley's voice in her head. With Oh, however, a man for whom words were rare and carefully chosen, it mattered a great deal what he thought of her—even moment to moment.

Jane wanted, in Oh's eyes, to be pure of heart.

"Jeb was an old boyfriend who I was curious to see when I discovered he had a connection to Wren Bixby and Bix Pix Flix, but I never dreamed he had any part in actually bringing me out here. What could he possibly want from me?"

"To be the star of his creeped-out horror movie?" asked Tim.

"We could ask Mr. Gleason," said Oh. "It looks like he's coming over here."

"No, let's head him off," said Jane. "I want to ask Bix about leaving the hospital the way she did and see if Greg and Rick made peace. You know, get a feel for the group dynamic after one of their meetings."

Jane's moment—moments—of reflection passed. There was no reason for her to worry that Oh thought less of her or was disappointed in her. Because she'd had a boyfriend in college? Tish-tosh. Claire'd probably had a million of them and she'd probably made them wait on her hand and foot. Why in the world did Oh's eyes locking on hers have such a paralyzing effect? Jane shook her head and managed to lead the two men over to the main house, waving to Jeb and announcing that they were on their way.

"Careful," Jeb called out. "Don't trip. That landscape lighting is pretty worthless."

Inside the main house, it appeared that the B Room had kissed and made up. Greg and Rick were once again huddled over a script. Greg had traded his cocktail glass for a coffee mug. Jane purposefully walked behind them to see if the pages in front of them had *H. Rule* typewritten in the corner. Rick's arm was slung over the margins and Jane saw only dialogue centered on a page. She could see margin notes printed in a tiny hand in red pen.

"Do you critique each other's work in your meetings? Like an ongoing workshop?" asked Jane.

"Something like that," said Rick. "It's kind of like Al-Anon except we're not recovering, we're not related, and we drink a lot."

Bix settled herself on one of Jeb's slipcovered down sofas. The couches were so soft that one nestled rather than perched, and since Jane did not want to get pillowed in, she pulled up an ottoman and sat next to Bix, who rested her bandaged arm on a cushion provided by Skye.

"Any pain?" asked Jane.

"It's surprising, but I really feel fine," said Bix. She leaned closer to Jane. "I'm beginning to think this was all a weird mistake. An accident in the prop warehouse and some prankster writing the note."

"The note sounded pretty threatening," said Jane. "You'll all go to—"

"People out here always say crazy stuff," said Bix.

"Heck," said Jane. "The note said you'd all go to Heck. And you know what happened to Heck."

"You know about Heck? Who told you about that? About him?" asked Bix.

"I ran into the group at the flea market this morning and Louise told me about Henry Rule. She seems to think somebody is seriously threatening all of you, too."

"No, I think it's over," said Bix. "I'm sure it's over."

"Because Patrick Dryer's dead?"

Bix didn't answer. She looked up and away instead, searching the room. Jeb was heading toward them with more of that incredible cake.

Bix smiled at Jeb and continued to look at him while answering Jane. "Yes, because Patrick Dryer's dead. It's over."

Bix might be right. The threatening note could certainly have come from Patrick. The box, rigged to explode, could have been planted by Dryer, too. Jane knew he was on the studio lot yesterday—she had heard him come in and threaten to kill Lou Piccolo. Patrick had been in the office and knew Lou well enough to know he was a collector and would be drawn to the aisles of Depression glass in the props warehouse.

Jeb delivered Bix's cup of tea and patted her arm gently. He asked her if she wanted anything else, if she was tired, if she wanted to spend the night there. Bix smiled and shook her head. As an afterthought, Jeb turned to Jane.

"Everything okay in the house? You and Tim need anything?"

"No, but you might want to make sure Bobbette is happy in her work. I've never seen Tim as smitten as he is with this chocolate cake. If I know the boy, and I do, he's working her pretty hard right now."

"I have no problem with keeping people's loyalty," said Jeb. He followed Jane's eyes to where she had focused them on Tim, oozing charm, and Bobbette, blushing and giggling. "Just the same, I'll go over and give Mr. Personality a run for his money."

"Oh boy, a charm-off," said Louise, who had approached the couch in time to hear Jane's warning. "I'm going to get a front-row seat."

"I can't believe she told you about Heck," said Bix, watching her follow Jeb across the room.

"Was it something you all had decided to keep secret?" asked Jane.

"No," said Bix. "It was so painful for Louise, though. She was the one who had to be there for him when Heck . . ."

Jane stopped herself from filling in either *died, jumped,* or *was pushed.* Instead, she channeled Oh, who had become lost in Jeb's library, a wall of books on the other side of this expansive room. Jane wanted to finish Bix's sentence for her, to help her out of a painful thought, but Oh would counsel Jane never to jump in. He was right . . . if one waited for someone to come up with the word, it was often an illuminating choice.

". . . pulled that dirty trick," said Bix.

Jane waited for Bix to say more. She knew that there were those who were angered by suicides, who felt that ending one's life was a supremely selfish act. Heck, however, by Louise's account, was mentally ill. Jane wouldn't have guessed that Bix would be such a hard-liner on the subject. Maybe there was more to Heck's "alternative" writing, his X-rated spoofs. Was that what Bix might call a dirty trick?

"So you didn't suspect foul play with Heck? Louise mentioned that there might have been . . ." Jane stopped when she saw the horrified look on Bix's face.

"I forgot," she said. "Oh my God, I forgot that Heck was dead. I was thinking of another time entirely." Bix blinked hard. "How could I forget, even for a moment . . . ?"

"Bix, you've been through a traumatic experience yourself," Jane said, forgetting all about not jumping in. "It must have been terrifying when the box blew up, painful when your arm was injured. One gets disoriented in the waiting room of a hospital, let alone when one is a hospital patient."

There is that moment that occurs with a roomful of people, talking in small groups, mingling, when everyone falls silent. A break in the action, a collective intake of breath, and when the moment passes, one person usually sets the new course of action. Partners change, groups intermingle, or the person who has taken the lead makes an announcement that changes the direction entirely.

Before Bix could question her own memory further, before Jane could continue to reassure, that moment occurred. After the pause, Skye Miller yawned. A loud, dramatic, stretching yawn that reminded each and every one of them that it had been one hell of a long day.

Bruce Oh, who had planned to exit much earlier, before he became lost studying Jeb's bookshelves, approached his host and thanked him for his hospitality.

"You have the most interesting library, Mr. Gleason."

"Thanks, Professor. I've done a lot of research for television shows I've worked on and I hate relying on the Internet or the public library. I like to own the books I need to use."

"Your books on ancient weaponry and poisons are particularly interesting," said Oh. "And rare, I believe."

Jeb nodded, pulling out a volume by Sir William Osler. "This guy is the father of the history of science and medicine. I didn't really need it for the medical intuitive show I was pitching, but you know, there's something about the research that just deepens the concept, you know?"

"And you like owning first editions," said Rick, barely looking up from the script open on the table in front of him.

"Where's Lou?" asked Skye.

"I knew things had seemed too cordial tonight," said Jeb. "Maybe he got bored and left. Is that too much to hope for?"

"He was smoking out by the pool earlier," said Tim. "I stole his cake," he said to Bobbette, who looked up at him adoringly.

The wall opposite the library shelves was all glass and faced the pool. Jeb had not exaggerated when he called the landscape lighting worthless. Now that it was truly dark outside, the small metal-encased lights along the ground did nothing to illuminate the pool area. Jeb crossed the room and pushed two switches that turned on floodlights mounted on the changing rooms and one on the guesthouse. Although the light did not shine directly on the table and chair where Lou was now visible, it was now bright enough to see his silhouette.

Skye opened the sliding door to the patio that adjoined the pool.

"Lou, time to head out? Are you driving home with Bix and me?"

Lou continued to stare straight ahead, leaning forward as if he were straining to see something beyond the driveway.

"For heaven's sake, Lou, are you asleep?" asked Skye, walking out the door and crossing over to the table.

Jane and Oh both headed for the door, almost running to overtake her.

Stepping out at the same time, Jane looked at Oh. "He hasn't moved at all since we came into the house."

Oh already had his cell phone out and was dialing.

"Don't touch him, Skye," said Jane at the same time Skye Miller demonstrated years of vocal training with a scream piercing enough to cut through two nights' worth of darkness. The windows across the street that Jane so recently had imagined as warm squares of light got brighter and grew in number so that all of the houses on the block blazed.

"She could donate her services to the emergency fucking broadcast system," said Jeb, running outside. Rick and Greg jumped up, followed by Louise, led by the siren voice of Skye over to where Lou Piccolo sat, his cigar burned down to its last inch in the heavy glass ashtray.

"Should we, you know, apply the Jaws of Life?" asked Skye when she caught her breath.

"You mean CPR, honey," said Bix, who had come out last, but now bent over Lou, her bandaged arm resting on the arm of his chair. "Jaws of Life pries somebody out of a car," she continued in a soft voice, as if she were explaining a difficult concept to a young child.

"Whatever," said Skye. "Shouldn't someone do something?" She turned to Jane, who was standing in front of the table listening to Oh give the emergency operator Jeb Gleason's address. Jane watched Oh automatically lay two fingers on the side of Lou's neck as he spoke quietly on the phone.

"Shouldn't you do something, Jane Wheel?" asked Skye. "Aren't you here to do something?"

Jane didn't look at Skye. She couldn't take her eyes off the body of Lou Piccolo, unquestionably dead, staring off into the distance. She had the nauseating sense of déjà vu that was becoming too familiar, much too *déjà*, way too much *vu*. The first dead man she had seen that day, Patrick Dryer, had been staring into the distance, too. What were all of these dead people looking at?

"Did you hear me?" Skye screamed at Jane. "You're supposed to be doing something to help us!"

If this were a movie, Jane thought, *this is where I'd slap her across the face.* However, since it was poolside at Jeb Gleason's house, Jane didn't think she'd get away with the old film noir tough-guy treatment for a hysterical dame. Instead, she explained that the ambulance had been called and that they all should be careful not to touch the body or anything in Lou's vicinity.

"The fool smoked and drank himself silly," said Bix, staring straight at Lou. "No cardio, no stretch, no supplements, no stress relief. No hobbies, no family, just work, work, work. No wonder, you big idiot."

It was more loving treatment than harsh assessment. Anyone who heard it, and they all heard it, knew that. Jeb came over to Bix and put his arm around her. Louise stood next to Skye, placing her hand on the younger woman's arm. Rick and Greg actually kept their eyes averted from the notebook that Rick never set down, had carried with him from the house.

Jane understood Bix's sentiment. It was easy to get angry at people for dying. To accuse them of all the things they should have done to prevent their own deaths. After all, they were gone and those living were the ones left with the cleanup. Jane got why Bix was so upset with Lou. She just couldn't figure out why Bix had to play so fast and loose with the truth when she gave her angry farewell speech.

15

It's not that those who work in the business are insincere. They are, perhaps, some of the most sincere, heartfelt people you will ever meet. It's just the world in which they have learned to operate . . . a most insincere world. It is difficult to be a real person in a make-believe world.

—FROM *Hollywood Diary* BY BELINDA ST. GERMAINE

At first, Jane thought she knew that Lou Piccolo was dead as soon as Jeb turned on the outdoor lights. She saw that Lou hadn't moved from his spot, hadn't changed position. But Jane thought she saw something else. The attitude of Lou's body, so still, yet caught in a kind of frozen surprise. *Death? Dying? Me? Now?* Lou's body was thrust forward in the chair, as if he had scooted closer to a companion opposite him at the table to explain there was a mistake. *You don't want me, sweetheart. You got the wrong boy.*

But now, watching Oh talk to the EMTs and exhange information with the police who had also arrived on the scene, Jane realized exactly when she knew for a fact that Lou Piccolo was dead. When Jeb switched on the lights, an alarm inside of her did go off. But it was when Jane and Oh walked together through the sliding door that she knew. Their shoulders had touched and they walked side by side, still touching, and Jane knew that she was no longer walking toward Lou Piccolo. She knew, instead, that together, she and Oh were walking toward Lou Piccolo's body.

Now, as always when there is an emergency, excitement was in the air. Neighbors were wandering over, wondering whether to be scared or thrilled, relieved that whatever bad news those flashing lights signaled, it was not happening behind their own gated driveways. Jane was touched to see Tim offer Bobbette his handkerchief and pat her shoulder before coming over to Jane.

"She's afraid someone will say it was her food," said Tim when he arrived at her side. Jane had placed herself away from the fray so she could watch the B Room interact with the curious onlookers as well as with each other.

"I told her it was probably a heart attack. I mean, we all heard Bix go over the list of reasons he was due," said Tim. "Right?" he added, when Jane didn't immediately agree.

"Bix was comprehensive, all right," said Jane. "Nellie has all these refrigerator magnets with the seven signs of stroke, the eight warnings of diabetes, the ten behaviors that signal heart attack, all those cheerful kitchen sayings, and Bix sounded like she had memorized magnet number five when she recited Lou's shortcomings," said Jane.

"So?" asked Tim.

"They weren't true," said Jane. "At least not all of them. What were they? He didn't relax? Didn't relieve stress? He had a place in Ojai where he stayed completely disconnected. He told me he went up there and chilled and hung out in some bookstore. And he worked all the time? If that's the case, he sure was lying to us when he told us about taking the work that the phantom kept sending him. I got the impression he liked being a hack, as he called himself. He wasn't worried about anybody ruining his reputation. And he might have smoked cigars, but I didn't see him take a drink tonight and he turned down cake. Looked fit enough. And he had hobbies. You saw his office. He was a collector. First editions, Depression glass. Paperweights, letter openers.

"I'm not saying that he didn't have a heart attack or a stroke or whatever," she continued. "It just seems odd that Bix was ready to give a whole litany of reasons that this shouldn't be considered a suspicious death. I mean, no one had brought up anything about it being anything but natural."

"She doth protest too much?"

"She doth indeed," said Jane.

Jane watched Skye confer with Bix. It might have seemed suspicious, Skye's frantic whispering, but if it did signal anything criminal, Jane would have to also pay attention to Rick and Greg, who were whispering to each other. Jane looked around for Jeb, who had been reassuring neighbors and playing gracious host to the emergency medical personnel and police. She saw him near the sliding door to the house, now talking on his cell phone. Jane suggested to Tim that he continue comforting Bobbette and see if she knew anything about Lou's health, if he ever requested special food, if he had any medical condition that they all discussed. Since Oh was still busy with the police, Jane thought she might as well see if Jeb had anything to tell her. The B Room gave her canned speeches whenever she tried to learn anything about them and their stalker or prankster or whatever he or she was. Maybe Jeb, with his defenses down, would give her something closer to the truth.

Jeb hung up with whomever he had been speaking when Jane approached. He looked tired, his tanned face sagged despite the fact that he was working his mouth and eyes to erase any anxious lines, any signs of worry. But why erase anything? An acquaintance, if not a close friend, a fellow writer, and adjunct member of his group, had just died sitting next to his pool. Why was Jeb making such an effort to hold in emotion?

Jane considered Oh's method of listening and not beginning a conversation with a question, no matter how badly one might want to hear answers. Now, standing close to Jeb, her face inches from his so she could see his eyes in the less-than-illuminated patio area, she rejected Oh's method and implemented her own. Relentless nagging questioning merged with a disconcertingly clear memory.

"Why did you tell Bix to get me out here on the pretense of doing a movie about me?"

"Chain of events and thoughts," said Jeb. "Not very coherent thoughts, at that. Too confusing to explain."

"I'm smart," said Jane. "Try me."

"I'm the leader of this group, like a father, a . . . guru . . . whatever. And things were getting so complicated. Out of hand. These threats, which I'm sure were because of Lou . . . hell, for a while I thought they might be coming *from* Lou . . . stopped being funny. And I had to act like I had it all under control."

"Why?" asked Jane. "I don't understand this controlled response to everything."

"Janie, I am a huge phony. You of all people should know that. I peaked as an actor in college and I peaked as a writer when I did *Southpaw and Lefty*. You know why? Not because I was the best writer on the show. All of them"—Jeb paused to gesture to the group milling around the yard—"could outwrite me any day. But they all are so damn insecure about it. I could fake it, they couldn't. And I can edit. They might be able to produce the stuff, but I can make it better. So we fell into this routine where I still edited everybody's work, was their private story editor on everything they did, even after *Southpaw and Lefty*."

"How can you live like this, if they all went on to do other shows and you just edit their work?" asked Jane. She had a vague idea of syndication and the idea of being paid for TV shows in reruns, but how much could that be? Jeb seemed to live pretty well for someone just helping out his friends.

"I take a cut for editing scripts. They pay me. And I sell story ideas. It's sort of like I provide a creative space, improve their work, even help them get story ideas and jobs sometimes, then they pay me back."

"It's a pyramid scheme," said Jane.

Jeb laughed. And to Jane, it sounded like the first real laugh she had heard since her arrival in Los Angeles. It wasn't that fake tinkly actress laughter, or that self-deprecating chuckle that everyone had perfected. Jeb sounded truly amused.

"Yeah," he agreed. "I guess it is. But I do provide a service. I love this group of people. And I help make their work better. They think they can't do it without me and I don't disabuse them of the notion."

"So maybe you're more like the Wizard of Oz than the Shaklee vitamin salesman?" Jane asked.

"Maybe," said Jeb. He asked Bobbette, who was heading past them into the house, if she would mind putting on a large pot of coffee and throwing together some food to serve to the neighbors, who seemed to have turned a tragic night into a come-as-you-are block party.

"So, continuing the chain of thought . . . ?" prompted Jane.

"I saw you on TV and thought you might be able to shed some light on what was going on. I didn't think you'd uncover anything sinister, just maybe see who was sending these notes. I figured it was Patrick Dryer who Lou had pissed off, and since Lou was associated with the group . . . I figured you'd find out something that we could use against Patrick and shut him up." Jeb paused. "I also truly thought your story might make a good movie. That story about the farm in Kankakee? It seemed like a great movie idea for one of the women's cable channels, if not for something bigger . . . so, you know . . . two birds with one stone."

Jane finally got hold of her inner Oh and didn't respond. She just waited for Jeb to keep going. Funny how once people got rolling, they were unstoppable.

"And I wanted to see you again. You looked so cute on TV. All confused and talking so fast and getting ahead of yourself, and I just remembered how much fun we had together in college and, you know, we never had closure on anything, I never got a chance to—"

"Hold it. I got closure." Jane took a deep breath. "I came over and Linda Fabien answered the door in a bath towel. That was closure enough for me." So much for Jane Wheel as the strong silent type.

"You thought Linda Fabien and I were . . . Wait a minute. That night you were supposed to be out of town giving your paper. That was you who came to the door all dressed up and Linda answered and you didn't give your name? Yes?"

Jane nodded.

"So . . . you put two and two together and decided I was cheating on you. I hope you're a better detective now than you were then." Jeb laughed. "Linda and I had a botany class together. We had been working in the greenhouse all day long and she drove me home, came in for a beer, called her roommate and found out they didn't have hot water at their apartment, so asked if she could shower."

Jane was glad she could see the ambulance from where she stood. The fact that Lou Piccolo's body was being loaded in plain sight kept her grounded in the present as Jeb spoke. If there hadn't been flashing lights and people milling about talking about cholesterol counts and the importance of cardio workouts, she might have felt herself transported back to college, back to when she was twenty-one years old and the girlfriend of the handsomest man on campus.

"You weren't sleeping with Linda Fabien?" Jane asked, completely puzzled about why this mattered to her now.

Jeb opened his mouth and Jane could tell by the way his left cheek twitched he was about to tell a lie. It was clearly his tell. She only wished she had noticed it earlier in their relationship, twenty-five years earlier, so she could sort fact from fiction. Then, just as suddenly as the tic began, it stopped. Jeb's face relaxed and he looked into Jane's eyes.

"I wasn't," he said. "But," he added after a pause, "I did."

Jane waited.

"After we both had showered, we had another beer. Linda mentioned someone had come to the door, probably selling something, and we hung out, and one thing led to another, and that night . . . you know." Jeb actually looked like he might be blushing, although it was a tough call to make in the night shadows.

Jane felt a weight lift off her shoulders. She had been right and she had been wrong—in all the best ways. Jeb hadn't cheated on her, but he was about to, so she ended things before she was betrayed. Why did something so silly make all the difference in the world? The Jeb Gleason baggage she had carted around . . . the of-course-he's-so-handsome-and-talented-so-why-would-he-want-to-go-out-with-me-anyway bullshit she felt even now on occasion—when she had lost her job, when she had allowed that disastrous kiss with her neighbor Jack Balance, when Nellie questioned her parenting skills, when Charley introduced her to a graduate assistant who was half her age. Jane allowed herself a moment of unconflicted joy, then firmly brought herself back to the present.

"Just like college, Jeb. Nothing really sinister was going on until I showed up. Then Bix gets injured and Patrick Dryer gets murdered. Looks good for you, doesn't it—you get me involved because you're worried about everyone, then when I come and things get lethal, no one is looking your way because you, after all, called in a detective. Never mind that she's an old girlfriend who you probably thought you could make believe whatever you wanted, just an amateur sleuth who you thought seemed cute and scatterbrained on television."

"I figured Patrick Dryer was behind all the notes and the stunts. He was crazy. Jealous and crazy. But I didn't think Lou would kill him," said Jeb.

Jane opened her mouth to argue, but changed her mind. Jeb seemed to still be in truth-telling mode. Did he really believe that Lou Piccolo killed Patrick Dryer? If Patrick was behind everything else, if he was the crazy phantom writer that was tormenting Lou and Bix, and Lou killed him . . . that would end the notes and pranks. What about the mobile? They had found it in Bix's hospital room closet late in the afternoon. Patrick was killed early in the morning. No reason he couldn't have planted it there the night before. Skye was supposed to be keeping an eye on things, but Jane had watched her in action at the hospital. The nurses kept her busy at their station all the time to entertain them, to sign autographs, to regale them with stories of the glory days of *Southpaw and Lefty*. Right after they found the mobile, Jane checked out the sight lines of the room. Patrick Dryer could have popped in the night before and placed the mobile in the closet without being seen while Skye was down the hall. Bix was sound asleep. He was the most likely person to have had those advertising postcards for his new book. And he was a writer . . . he would have known how to make that phony blurb sound like a blurb. He had even cited another novel.

"Are you an Agatha Christie fan, Jeb?"

Jeb gave Jane a blank stare. He shrugged. "What's she been in?" Then he smiled and winked.

So maybe he didn't make the mobile. Jane saw Oh shaking hands with the policeman he had been talking to since his arrival. They exchanged business cards.

"Okay, so why did you steal the mobile?" Jane remembered one of the other reasons Tim didn't trust Jeb. "And the scalpel?"

"I took the mobile because it seemed creepy and scary. I didn't want Bix to see it. I thought it was probably some Patrick trick and if Patrick was dead, Bix didn't need to know about it. She was getting spooked. So was Louise . . . everybody." Jeb rubbed his eyes. "I took the scalpel because Skye said Lou had a gun. I thought he had already killed Patrick and I figured if Lou had snapped, he might come after me. He and I have never liked each other. It seems really stupid, but I saw it in the tray and I took it. Impulse."

"I'm so sorry about your friend, Mr. Gleason," said Oh. He had walked across the lawn, nodding to the neighbors, who smiled at him, assuming he was just another guest at this midnight gathering whom they hadn't yet met.

"I'm sorry you had to get involved in this, Professor," said Jeb. "Poor old Lou."

Jane could see Jeb had slipped back into his L.A. version of hail-fellow-well-met persona.

"You certainly were involved in a long discussion with the police officer who was here," said Jeb.

"We traded some stories," said Oh. "I feel terrible asking a favor now, Mr. Gleason, but I haven't been able to get some of your book titles out of my mind. May I borrow one to take to my wife's uncle's home? I know I won't be able to sleep tonight and I'm afraid the only books they have are silly popular novels. I would much prefer to lose myself in one of your research volumes."

"Anything you want, Professor. Help yourself."

Oh gave just the hint of a bow and walked into the house. Jane continued to be dazzled by how Oh immersed himself in a Japanese persona when he wanted to be trusted as a harmless academic.

The policeman who had been "exchanging stories" with Oh came up and asked Jeb if he could speak with him for a moment and Jane excused herself. When she stepped into the house to look for Oh, she found him apologizing profusely to Bobbette, who looked angry and near tears.

"I didn't mean this as any kind of insult, I beg your pardon." Oh was as close to being unnerved as Jane had ever seen him.

"On a night like this, you would ask such a question? What kind of rude person are you? Who are you? Why are you stealing this book from Mr. Jeb?"

"I assure you I am not stealing—"

"You see how it feels to be accused of something? You understand how rude?"

Bobbette took Tim's handkerchief from her pocket and dabbed at her eyes. She straightened her shoulders and picked up the tray of cookies she had been bringing outside when Oh apparently attacked her with his barrage of rude accusations.

Oh looked a bit ashamed. He shook his head at Jane's smile and shrugged.

"I didn't mean to be rude," he assured Jane.

"Of course not," said Jane.

"I simply asked her when she last dusted the bookshelves," said Oh. "I hadn't thought about it being a reflection on her housekeeping."

Rick poked his head in the door and told Jane and Oh that everybody was getting ready to leave. The ambulance had taken Lou. Bix had called the Piccolo family back in New Jersey and left word with Lou's sister, who would notify the rest of the relatives.

Skye and Louise and Bix were sitting on a chaise by the pool several feet away from where Lou had been sitting. They sat shoulder to shoulder to shoulder, holding each other upright, it appeared to Jane. The evening had certainly taken a turn. Bix, after her speech about Lou's negligence of his health, had been mostly silent. Even while Jane was deep in conversation with Jeb, she had tried to keep an eye on everyone else. Skye and Louise alternately talked and cried. Until Louise and Skye joined her a few minutes ago, Bix sat by herself, with someone coming over to check on her every few minutes. Each time, she would wave whoever it was away. Rick and Greg talked and argued quietly. Jane was certain that she saw Rick refer to his notebook, which meant they were back to working on their script.

Except for a large man in a bathrobe, the neighbors had all left. Jane watched the man padding across the lawn adjoining the pool, saw him wince and draw his foot up in pain. He bent over and picked up something which he turned over in his hand. Jane looked around and noted that no one else was watching, so she approached him before he could locate Jeb and start toward him.

"Can I help? Are you okay?" asked Jane.

"Fine, I'm fine. I stubbed my toe on this. Dog toy or something. I don't know. It was just by the table over there where the man had the heart attack, so maybe I should give it to Jeb. I can't really see it very well. Came out without my glasses, but—"

"I'll give it to Jeb," said Jane. "Are you sure you're okay?"

"Serves me right for coming out barefoot to be a gaper with all the other gapers," he said, yawning.

Jane watched him pick his way through the grass to his house next door.

Tim and Oh were standing at the door to the guesthouse, so Jane went over to join them. Jeb had asked everyone to come back for a late breakfast so they could plan some kind of memorial service for Lou. Jane heard him tell Bix that they'd have to call the lawyer in the morning to figure out the next step for Bix Pix Flix. Skye and Louise told Jeb they'd spend the night with Bix. Rick and Greg walked to the driveway together.

"I never got that nightcap. Did you?" asked Tim, rummaging through the guesthouse kitchen cabinets. He poured vodka for Jane and himself. "Detective? Anything?"

Oh shook his head.

"Hey, what did you do to Bobbette anyway?" asked Tim. "She came up to me and told me you were an awful man and she warned me to stay away from you."

"I removed this book from the bookshelf and noticed something unusual, so I asked her a simple question about which day she dusted the shelves and I fear I was in over my head before I knew what happened to me," said Oh. Jane thought that might be the longest sentence she had ever heard him speak. Bobbette had clearly unnerved him.

"What did you retrieve from the neighbor, Mrs. Wheel?" Oh asked, happy to change the subject.

Jane took the object out of her pocket. Lou Piccolo's leather cigar case.

"I'll give it to Bix tomorrow," said Jane.

"May I?" asked Oh, holding out his hand. He opened the hard leather case, which could hold three cigars. Only one was missing. Oh smelled the two cigars that remained in the case.

"Let's not give this to Ms. Bixby yet. Put it somewhere safe here in the guesthouse, so if someone asks about it, you can say you simply forgot about it."

"Why?" asked Tim. "Exploding cigars? We didn't hear anything."

Oh shook his head. "I have some reading to do tonight. We should discuss this in the morning. Clare's aunt is holding on at the hospital. I spoke with her a few moments ago. I'll come back in the morning, since I have to return the book to Mr. Gleason."

Jane wanted to talk things out, to tell Oh and Tim what Jeb had told her. She realized there was more to discuss with Jeb—they hadn't gotten to Heck. If Jeb was convinced that Patrick had been behind everything, Lou had killed him, then died of a guilt-induced heart attack, where did Heck fit in? Was he just a delusional man who jumped off the roof of his house? Or was Patrick involved in his death, too?

Oh took Jane's hand. It was an unusual gesture. Twice in one night she was aware of physical communication between them—when they had run out together to find Lou Piccolo dead, and now as Oh held her hand and studied her face.

"I am tired, Mrs. Wheel. And at the risk of offending another woman tonight, I believe you are tired as well. Only this morning you were finding Mr. Dryer at the flea market, and now another death. It has been a long day and we both need to go to our beds, rest so we can make sense of it all tomorrow. Good night."

Oh nodded good night to Tim and then he was off toward the driveway. He might be tired, but Jane saw him hold the book as if it were precious cargo. He was anxious to get home to read, to figure out something he probably already knew. Well, Jane was tired—exhausted, in fact. But she, too, had some figuring out to do. She abandoned her vodka and fished out a Coke from the back of the refrigerator. Caffeine and sugar were what she needed right now. She found the bound galley of Dryer's novel, *The D Room*, under the dish towel where she had left it, and kissed Tim on the cheek.

"Going up to read in bed, Timmy boy."

From upstairs, Jane heard him switch off the light. When she heard the door open, she looked out the bedroom window and watched Tim rap softly on the kitchen door of the main house. Bobbette opened it, wiping her hands on a dish towel. With her window open, Jane heard Tim say he couldn't sleep so he had come over to help her with the dishes. Jane laughed out loud. Jeb Gleason could add one more worry to his list. If Tim Lowry did move to L.A., as he was threatening to do, Jeb would be advertising for a new housekeeper. Bobbette would be unpacking Tim's vintage Louis Vuitton trunk within ten minutes of his arrival at his Silver Lake cottage.

16

"Move over, Belinda, I've got something else to read to-night," Jane said, tossing her copy of *Hollywood Diary* on the floor next to her bed. Jane scooted down in the bed, plumped her pillows, and opened *The D Room* by Patrick Dryer. Normally, on a flea-market-murder-detecting day, Jane would have been more than ready for sleep, but tonight she was wide awake. Something about a second death? Alone in her room, slipping into sweats and a T-shirt for sleeping, Jane tried to sort out the events of the day . . . what had happened and what she had heard.

Lou had not struck Jane as a man who could drive to Pasadena from Ojai, stab Patrick Dryer with a letter opener, then coolly spend an hour spinning a mediocre alibi and background story for Jane and Tim in Bix's hospital room. Why was that her first impression? She reminded herself that he was holding a gun on her when they were introduced . . . shakily, yes, but a gun nonetheless. When he and Skye had arrived with Bix earlier that night, Lou was solicitous of Bix, polite with Skye, but slightly removed from everyone else. He avoided Jeb entirely. Jane sensed an agreement to back away from the B Room meetings—whether out of respect for Bix or a general wariness after Patrick's murder.

When Oh, Tim, and Jane had taken their dessert to the guesthouse and Lou had declined to join them in favor of a cigar,

Jane was surprised he had not taken advantage of the opportunity to either explain his surreptitious exit from the hospital or to socialize with them, add his speculations to the discussion of Patrick Dryer's murder. He had become so expansive when they spoke at the hospital, it surprised Jane that he would choose to sit alone after the events of the day. Trying to draw him out, Jane expressed surprise that someone as fit and healthy as he appeared to be was a smoker.

"Only these Padróns," he had said, holding up his leather case. "I don't smoke just any old cigar." Those were the last words anyone heard from Lou Piccolo.

> If I had just killed someone and wanted to make everyone I knew think I hadn't, I wouldn't sit outside of the group twiddling my thumbs and looking worried while they sat and watched a movie or played a game of trash-the-other-writers. No, I'd sit with them and talk about how horrible the murder was and try to flesh out my alibi, convince people to like me best, encourage them to trust me more. But then again, that's me.
>
> I forget. We weren't talking about a literal murder. Not that night. Not yet. The D Room killed people, killed ideas, killed talent, and killed ambition, but for those crimes, none of the members of the group would ever stand before a judge. Unless you believe in heaven and a final judgment, those people will get off scot-free. It's enough to make an atheist like me get religion. Or a gun.

If the narrator in Patrick Dryer's novel was a thinly veiled Patrick Dryer, he sounded like one bitter Betty. Ironic that Dryer the novelist, in the first paragraph of his soon-to-be-published novel, gave a perfectly logical reason to believe that Lou Piccolo was not the one who stabbed Dryer the murder victim. Lou had done just what Dryer said a murderer would not do—remain aloof from those discussing the crime. And in the second paragraph? Dryer's narrator revealed enough bile to make it very likely that if and when the murders began in this Hollywood noir novel, the first-person narrator would be high on the list of suspects. Instead, Patrick Dryer had become the number one victim.

Jane tried to turn off the monkey mind full of questions that ricocheted inside her skull so she could concentrate on Dryer's novel. Why did Lou confess his writing—or lack of writing—secrets to Jane, then slip away like a thief with Bix? Did Louise pour her heart out to Jane about Heck's illness and death because she sincerely needed to talk it out? Or did Jeb give Louise the assignment to deliver to Jane that piece of the puzzle? Why did Bix assess Lou's fitness level so publicly, so immediately, and so incorrectly when they found him dead? And those were just the homegrown starters. Jane knew once the medical examiner filed his report, a whole new set of questions could begin. Detective Oh had also mentioned that both the LAPD and Detective Dooley, whom Jane had met over collectible autograph books and the fresh corpse of Patrick Dryer in Pasadena, would probably want to speak with her again. Jane closed her eyes, took a deep breath, and concentrated on page one. Patrick Dryer was going to have to be one hell of a mystery writer to take her away from the real-life mystery laid out before her.

Not so many blocks away, in a small but well-appointed house in the same Los Feliz area that Jeb Gleason called home, Bruce Oh looked in on his wife asleep in the guest room, retrieved his reading glasses from a worn leather briefcase, and repaired to the den next to his wife's relative's kitchen. He allowed himself a small sigh as he unfolded the reading glasses that Claire had recently purchased for him.

"These are for you," she had said, placing them on top of his morning newspaper. "Wear them."

Claire's efficiency was a trait he had admired from their first meeting fifteen years earlier. She anticipated his needs and those of their household, and she took care of whatever needed to be done. He enjoyed the pleasant hum of the well-oiled machine that was their marriage. When she handed over the eyeglasses, however, the machine paused midwhirr. Oh felt the first glitch, heard the first clanging in the pipes.

If Claire, not a tea drinker herself, somehow knew when to replace the tin of strong black breakfast blend that he preferred, he admired her prescience. That Claire had noted he had begun holding the newspaper farther and farther away from his face and felt she could quickly remedy the situation with a pair of wire-framed spectacles with a 1.25 magnification troubled him. A precise man, it puzzled Oh that he could not point out exactly what bothered him about his wife and her presentation of the eyeglasses. Until tonight, he had settled for the fact that he was a human being, after all, and aging presented a universal human challenge. Most people, if literature and popular culture and the preponderance of ads for anti-aging creams and potions were accurate indications, were uncomfortable, at least at first, with their bodies getting older. Oh, a practitioner of Zen meditation since he was a boy, had been shocked when he realized he might have a visceral response to such a natural process, but he knew that this response would pass and acceptance would come.

But tonight he realized it was not the passing years that he feared or responded to in such an uncharacteristic manner. Oh accepted aging and the weakening of the eye muscles that led to the need for magnification. That was as logical and predictable as the seasons. It was Claire's wordless acceptance of the process that gave him pause. In their fifteen years of marriage, he realized he had never seen her unprepared for what the day would bring. Even when she had been a suspect in the murder of a Chicago antiques dealer, she had combed her hair and applied her lipstick, matched her clothes with precision, and although she had behaved somewhat testily toward Mrs. Wheel at the time, she had essentially remained the soul of composure. Tonight when Mrs. Wheel blushed and became flustered over Lowry's revelation that Jeb Gleason had been her college boyfriend, Oh realized that his wife's gift of the magnifier eyeglasses, although he disliked wearing them, was not in and of itself the problem. With complete clarity, Oh reached the puzzling conclusion that the ever-so-slight discomfort, the smallest pebble in his shoe, was the fact that he had never seen his wife, Claire, blush.

Now that he had solved that puzzle, Oh adjusted the eyeglasses and opened the book he had borrowed from Jeb Gleason's library. It was a large reference book. If anyone had noticed the title, he or she might have found it an odd choice for bedtime reading. Oh was interested in the book for two reasons. First, it was the only book on a rather dusty shelf that had recently been removed. Oh could tell this by the fact that the dust had parted into a trail where the book had been removed, then replaced. Also, the tops of the pages had been relatively clean compared to its neighboring volumes. This book had been opened and closed, scattering the accumulated dust, and there was a makeshift bookmark inserted between pages thirty-six and thirty-seven. Oh decided to begin his reading of *Death in the House: A Book of Common Poisons* where the last reader had left a blank index card as a bookmark, in the middle of chapter five.

> ...this causes vomiting and nausea, headaches, difficulty breathing, stomach pains, and seizures. Each of these symptoms can be traced back to excessive stimulation of cholinergic neurons. With organophosphates, acetylcholine builds up at synapses and ... overstimulates the neurons. Because it is so similar to acetylcholine, and binds to ... receptors, in excess produces the same overstimulation and toxicity.

Bruce Oh nodded. *The more it binds to the receptors, the more is released and . . . yes.* If one had been up at this still-dark morning hour to peer in at Oh, reading this borrowed book in his in-laws' den, nodding and almost smiling, one might think he had found a fascinating novel, an inventive history, an inspiring biography. Or a clue.

Tim Lowry dried the fragile wineglasses that Bobbette hand-washed. She assured him that she needed no help and actually seemed confused that he insisted upon helping her.

"It's a midwestern thing," said Tim. "We insist on making ourselves useful no matter how little use the person we're helping finds us to be."

"Really?" asked Bobbette. "Doesn't that actually make you more trouble than you're worth?"

"Exactly," said Tim. "We ingratiate ourselves with mean-ingless gestures so that we are virtually indispensable for absolutely nothing."

Bobbette laughed and shook her head. She was charmed. Tim was delighted. He was winning.

From the moment he had stepped out of the airport terminal, following the limousine driver Bix had sent for him and Jane, he felt he had reached his place of destiny. He assessed the quality of the luggage of people returning home to L.A.—a full set of vintage Louis Vuitton sat on the curb, something he had been desperately searching for since he had found his orphan piece seven years ago cleaning out the attic of a Kankakee physician, and this set guarded by a limo driver who looked like Brad Pitt—and inhaled the smoggy air of excess. It filled his lungs and filled his heart. This was where he was meant to be.

Hadn't he tried every scheme in the world to make Kanka-kee the hometown USA of his and Jane's childhood? Hadn't he tried to inject small-town charisma into the roots of this once-vibrant industrial town on the river? Yes, by God, he had done his part. To Tim Lowry, making Kankakee whole again had been a mission and he had given it his all. He had served it well, thank you very much, and now it was time off for good behavior. He was a gay man at peace with himself and he deserved to live in a city that appreciated his taste, his wit, and his talents. He had made money at every business he had started—his floral shop that had lifted Kankakee into the land above grocery store bouquets and mum plants, and T & T Sales, his house sale company, which was more of a public service, really, helping people sort through and get rid of their old stuff. Sure, Jane said he went into business in order to worm his way into the old monied houses and basements and attics in town, and yes, maybe it was a plus to have first dibs and all, but he priced goods fairly, he paid well, and if he made a buck or two turning around an early American fruitwood table that had belonged to someone's grandmother and was now being used to hold an old television set on the back porch, well, that was just good business.

It wouldn't be so easy to unearth the treasure in Hollywood. He would have competition. The collectors, the dealers, the stylists, the trendsetters who lived there already would, with their head-start knowledge of locations and custom, race him to the point of sale, display their own considerable charms, and whip out their generous checkbooks. It would be a fight, a struggle. Tim smiled to himself. It would be the challenge he had been missing. Jane, in Chicago, had her foes, her rivals, but Tim had pretty much outplayed most of the buyers and sellers in Kankakee County. He needed new territory to conquer. This train of thought filled him with pleasure and desire—new attics and basements—brightly colored California Pottery vs. the muted Midwestern Roseville. Mid-century modern furniture vs. farmhouse primitive. Yes, he was ready to move on. Westward ho. Wiping the glasses efficiently, he beamed his winning winner's winningest smile on Bobbette, who had her back to him, carrying a tray into the pantry. He would hire her away from Jeb and she would keep his California bungalow clean and neat, help him wash his Bauer plates one at a time, and stack them on open shelves where round-bellied pitchers would line his kitchen.

Tim's reverie was interrupted when Bobbette, standing on top of a small kitchen step stool, made a horrified retching sound and held up two old Waterford tumblers she had fished off the top pantry shelf where she was stashing the extra dessert plates. Tim went over to help her step down from her perch and see what had made his new employee so distraught. He gagged. So maybe she wasn't the perfect housekeeper. She held out to him two glasses, each filled with sticky black-brown goo. Helping her down, he took the glasses from her and set them on the pantry counter. So? She missed a few things. No matter. He knew his way around a broom and a mop. He would still hire her away from Jeb Gleason. For sport. Besides, he loved chocolate cake.

17

The D Room by Patrick Dryer was what some might clas-
sify as a quick read. Lots of dialogue. Sentence fragments. Par
for the course, Jane figured, in a popular mystery with a dash of
Hollywood thrown in for good measure. The book, in Jane's
opinion, was lacking a few important ingredients. First and
foremost, Patrick Dryer had neglected to inject any humor into
his characters or their situation. Didn't he realize that readers
would have a difficult time buying the outlandish murders? The
convoluted story? Jane, back in the day of her advertising career, recalled how her creative group composed a campaign for
a product. Their work was most successful when they accepted
their real task—not explaining their product, not even selling
their product, but instead creating a story about their product.
Jane knew that most young professionals couldn't tell one pre-
mium beer from another, so she and her group gave their beer
a history, a personality, a sense of humor. Jane's direction to her
team? Tell a story that speaks to the intelligence of the con-
sumer, and in the course of spinning the tale, make them smile
in recognition.

Patrick Dryer's rule in writing The D Room? Create—or
report on—a group of narcissistic, unlikable people and pound
away at them. Dryer himself had said in his introductory note
that these were real people. Perhaps that was the problem with
the fiction here. Jane had taken a few writing classes in college

and she remembered a particularly affected young man who had written a story about religious awakening which included eight pages of dialogue between two roommates after a night of smoking marijuana and drinking tequila. When the instructor kindly suggested that the eight pages of dialogue seemed somewhat excessive and didn't always ring true, the writer, filled with passion, hoisted a state-of-the-art circa early seventies tape recorder the size of a small suitcase onto his desk.

"It's all true. I turned this on when we talked because it was getting so intense. You all just don't get it because it's so real," the student said, his finger hovering over the play button, threatening to prove his point to the horror of the other students, who by this time realized they had another hour of class and they might be subjected to a poor-quality tape of the late-night stoned-out philosophy of two twenty-year-olds.

"Just because it's true doesn't make it real," said the teacher. "Fiction has to be more real than life. Whatever happens, whatever anyone says has to be true to the story."

If Patrick Dryer had only taken a class taught by this woman. Or any class, Jane thought, since she figured these were pretty standard rules for writers to live by. Patrick, though, had an ax to grind and grind away he did. Ben, the Bizarro World Jeb Gleason, leader of the group of writers, was described in painful detail, down to the kinglike robes he preferred to lounge in when at home. And Ben's home, down to the last detail in the blue bedroom in the guesthouse, was identical to the one where Jane, from after midnight until now, had done a lot of reading and little sleeping.

Tim's door was still closed when Jane went down to make coffee. She had heard him tiptoe in a few hours after she immersed herself in *The D Room*, but hadn't called out since she knew that any excuse for her to escape from the deadly writing would make it that much harder to finish the book by morning. Jane was sure that somewhere in *The D Room* would be the key to the story playing out before her. She meant to finish it now over coffee and impress Bruce Oh by announcing Patrick Dryer's murderer by lunchtime.

When just enough coffee had dripped through to make a cup, Tim arrived, posing in the doorway of the kitchen. Sleepy, disheveled, but still maddeningly put together, a magazine model in a pair of plaid flannels and a rust-colored waffle-weave shirt, he ignored Jane standing in front of the coffeemaker, a blue Bennington pottery mug in her hand, took a cup from the shelf, and helped himself.

"Coffee?" Jane asked.

"Yeah, got some," he said. "How's the book? Weird to read a story by a dead man?"

Tim's question provided the wake-up jolt that she missed when he stole the first cup of coffee. She had been reading it as if it were the tale *of* a dead man, not written *by* a dead man. A murdered man. Patrick had become so present, whining about his life and hard times, that she had lost all perspective. The fact that she was operating on bits and pieces of stolen sleep might have also contributed to her single-mindedness. Although she was aware while reading the book she might find out who had a reason to kill Patrick Dryer, Jane hadn't been thinking about the fact that Patrick wrote this to destroy others. He didn't know anyone was going to kill him first. *The D Room* was not a diary, it was a novel.

"One that he planned to be alive to promote," Tim reminded her when she told him what she was thinking. "Remember the postcard on the mobile?"

"Remember Bix told us that his first novel had some promise, was critically well received?" Jane asked. "He lost something along the way to this one. This reads like a child tattling on the other kids who won't let him in the game."

Even if Patrick's book didn't tell the exact story, since he may not have anticipated his own early exit from the cast of characters, it seemed to reveal more details about the members of the B Room, which in turn might lead to the real-life murderer of Dryer. And as Jane read further, she began to think that whoever had killed Patrick might also have had a reason to kill another character who, in Patrick's book, was named Sam Sagella. Sam Sagella was Lou Piccolo, down to his curly dark hair and love of Padrón cigars.

Lou Piccolo freely told Jane that he accepted the work of an anonymous writer and was willing to give him credit and money if he would reveal himself. Patrick Dryer, in the novel, made it clear that the character of Sam accepted the work of another under different circumstances.

In *The D Room*, the poor struggling novelist who met Sam Sagella through a distant relative showed him television scripts he had written on speculation, hoping that if it didn't actually get him work, it would at least get him an agent. Sam agreed to read them, make comments and, if he deemed it worthy, show them to his own agent. Sagella, however, stole the work, and after a few minor changes, passed it off as his own. Because Sagella worked with a partner, he involved her—Margaret Luckenby, whom everyone called Lucky—unwittingly at first, in the stolen scripts. Sagella kept promising the writer that he would reveal him as the genius behind the work when the time was right, paying him, fairly handsomely, to keep quiet for the time being. When the ghostwriter found out that Sagella and Lucky were nominated for a major award for a script he had drafted, he became unhinged and began doing away with Sagella's group of writer friends one by one, since they all, knowingly or not, had used his work as their own.

The way things worked in the D Room of the novel was that alpha male Ben convened weekly meetings of a group of writers who had worked together on a phenomenally successful show twenty years earlier. While working on that show, they made a pledge to always support each other professionally. In Hollywood, for them, that meant to keep each other working. Since most television writers reached an age where they were considered no longer valuable, there was a fear among writers, no matter how successful they had been in their early days, that there was a younger, and more affordable, crop of writers pouring into L.A. every day. Writers were always replaceable, and with the current emphasis on reality television, they were now expendable. Ben's group, the D Room, their name born from the same circumstances as the real B Room, included Sam Sagella even though he didn't share their history, because Lucky, in love with him, brought him in.

Although his relationship with Lucky cooled, Sagella made himself invaluable to the D Room because of his endless supply of answers. Treatments, story ideas, scripts—anything anyone needed, Sam could produce. Rewrites, polishes—anything anyone had a problem with, Sam could fix. And the wonder of it all, for Ben and the group, was that Sam wanted nothing more in return than to be included in the D Room meetings. A single share, like everyone else received, of the group money. He claimed he had no ego involved in his work, but he longed for the security and camaraderie that they all enjoyed.

For a time, it was a win-win-win situation. Sam got membership in the group, the group was more prolific and had no fear of writers' blocks or dry wells, and Ben could keep the D Room fund, which he maintained and from which he took a healthy cut as the grand poobah of the literary pyramid scheme, obscenely healthy.

"So they're all in there, right?" asked Tim, pouring Jane a cup of coffee when he topped off his own. Jane, back into the book, smiled and thanked him, forgetting completely that she had made the pot in the first place. "What did he name them?"

"The first person narrator/novelist/genius goes unnamed," said Jane. "So humble of Patrick not to name him Patrick. Would have been so postmodern to actually name the narrator Patrick, but he resists. Resisted. Lou, Bix, and Jeb are the characters Sam, Lucky, and Ben. Louise Dietz is Dolores Kadow, who is actually treated pretty decently. Dolores is a hardworking writer whose biggest flaw seems to be that she trusts what the people around her tell her. She's got that cynical sidekick wit, but at heart she's a good soul who believes in the talent of all her writer friends," said Jane. "Also, Dolores is the only character Patrick bothers to describe at length. He calls her a fashionable dresser with a good eye for vintage jewelry.

"Greg and Rick are Alan and Fred, squabbling partners who really love each other but are blinded by their own workaholism. Even though they begin getting material handed to them, they work just as hard, transcribing dialogue, changing characters' names, and arguing over each point as if they were the original writers."

"Who does he kill? Or how?" asked Tim, rummaging through the freezer. Finding some frozen banana muffins wrapped and marked with a date and Bobbette's name, he held them up like a prize.

"How did it go with Bobbette last night, by the way?" asked Jane. "I heard you go over there and figured you'd have her packing her bags for the move to Kankakee by sunrise."

"One story at a time, sweetie," said Tim, getting busy with unwrapping the muffins and finding a plate for thawing them in the microwave.

"Patrick's persona favors poisons in the novel. He isn't very specific. You know, he has a subplot that he lays in with a trowel. Before he saves the day by feeding material to Sam Sagella, who gives it to the group, one of the writers . . ." Jane leafed back through the pages. "Alan. Is it Alan or Fred who writes some porno films on the side? Kind of a lark for him, but the money comes in handy when they all hit a dry spell. Part of the thing about this that's interesting, even if the writing is a little clumsy, is that they all desperately need to keep up their peak salaries. When they were all hot, they were making a lot of money and bought big houses and fancy cars and lived high. They hired people to work for them, cooks and assistants, and if they can't keep up with their neighbors, it's a fast downhill slide. Patrick maintains that to be successful in Hollywood, you have to look like you've remained successful."

"You think he did?"

"What? Who?" asked Jane.

"You think Greg or Rick wrote porn?" asked Tim, buttering a muffin and handing it to Jane.

"Possibly," said Jane. "It really doesn't go anywhere in the book. I mean, the other members of the D Room act like they don't approve, but they accept the monthly share of the money. He makes the character look like he's going to be his fall guy, you know, pin the murders on him, because of someone he worked with in the X-industry, as Patrick calls it, looking for revenge. So Alan or Fred—accidentally—is supposed to kill—"

"Wait, if—"

"I know, it's confusing, but I skimmed some of that part. I admit I didn't get every thread of the plot. From the story he tells, I'd have to say, right now, that it would be reasonable to believe that Sam killed Patrick. I mean Lou Piccolo killed Patrick," said Jane. "The feud is between the two of them. And if Lou was first stealing stuff, then weaseling stuff out of Patrick, and Patrick threatened to expose him and shut him off, it might have been reason enough to kill him. Since they all go to the flea market every weekend . . ." Jane took a bite of her muffin and sipped her coffee, placing the book down on the table.

"Maybe Patrick went to Pasadena to confront the B Room and tell them what was going on," she continued. "He knew Lou was in Ojai. Remember? We heard him in the outer office looking for Lou when we were there meeting with Bix. So he leaves Bix Pix Flix, plants the little explosive device for Lou to find as a threat. It would scare him, but not kill him. Then he hears that Bix found it and was injured. He goes to the hospital that night to make sure she's all right and plants the mobile in her closet when Skye is out of the room—"

"Patrick planted the mobile?" asked Tim. "Why do you think that?"

"I'm not positive, just thinking out loud. He probably has a stack of those postcards and he could have gotten an old *Southpaw and Lefty* script easily enough through Lou. If he was afraid of getting caught as the one who injured Bix and wanted to frame someone from the B Room, the script pages would hint at that," said Jane.

"Yeah, hint, but the postcard shouts Patrick Dryer," said Tim, putting two more muffins in to thaw.

"That's the thing about reading this book of his. He's an egomaniac. I mean, he can't not stick that postcard on there. He has to let them all know about the book. It's as if he has to sign his work," said Jane.

"Maybe for all the years it went unsigned?" suggested Tim, his head back in the freezer.

"Jeez, they live where oranges grow, for Christ's sake, and all they have here is this?" asked Tim, holding up a frozen can. He found a white ceramic pitcher in the cupboard and reflexively turned it over to look for a mark.

"For all the years it went unsigned," repeated Jane. She looked at the book cover on the advance copy. "Ever hear of Pendant Press?"

"Sounds familiar," said Tim. "Wait a sec." He went over to the table by the stairs and took his BlackBerry out of his briefcase. "I'll Google—"

"Wasn't it the publisher on *Seinfeld*?" asked Jane. "Where Elaine worked? That can't be a real place, can it?"

"Nope," said Tim, "doesn't look like it."

"But Detective Oh got this from a bookstore," said Jane.

"So what?" asked Tim. "Lots of people self-publish. My friend Elliot wrote a book on vintage telephones and self-published. He got it distributed to bookstores and it's sold in antique malls and at shows."

"Try Patrick Dryer," Jane said.

"Hits are about his first book, some reviews, library holdings, it's out of print but available, used, online. Doesn't seem to have a Web page or anything except old mentions of the novel."

Jane got up and stretched. Looking out the window toward the main house, she could see it was another perfect day. The sun was bright, the breeze was warm and dry, the water in the pool blue and pristine. When was she ever going to have an opportunity like this again? The convenience of stepping outside her door and enjoying her private paradise? She turned to look at Tim, pleased to see that he had buttery muffin crumbs on his shirt. Any little thing to break up that GQ image gave her pleasure.

"You look rather cat-full-of-canary," said Tim. "Solve the case?"

Jane shook her head.

"What's next, then?"

"A swim," said Jane, surprising Tim, surprising herself.

* * *

Jane did not particularly love the water, but she found the draw of that pool overwhelming. It was so empty and beautiful and, she had a feeling, chronically unused. It went against her nature, finding something perfectly good and beautiful going to waste. It was not exactly the same as finding a handful of colorful tie-aprons with prints of ducks and geese on them, gingham checks, dancing vegetables, all folded in a drawer at a house sale, clean and forgotten. But it was related. If Jane didn't buy those aprons, they would go unworn. If Jane didn't take a swim, that pool would be wasted for another day. She helped herself to a black tank suit in the pool house, pleased that it fit, even more pleased that there was no full-length mirror. She had not put on a bathing suit in at least three years and she had no desire to do a then-and-now comparison. In fact, if she had thought about this impulse more than a minute, she wouldn't have jumped into the water at all. Jane wasn't a great swimmer, but she could manage a serviceable crawl, and cutting through the water now was the perfect antidote to last night's minimal sleep. She would be invigorated for the whole day if she could resist lying down on a poolside chaise and closing her eyes when she got out.

"You didn't rest for half an hour after eating," said Tim from the doorway of the guesthouse.

Jane waved at him. Spoken like a satellite Nellie, who would surely see the dark side of swimming in a perfect pool on a beautiful sunny day.

Since she wasn't in shape to do more, she decided that ten laps would be more than sufficient to stretch her limbs and clear her head. Something was wrong about Patrick Dryer's book. Not the self-publishing part. That wasn't so surprising. It was the novel itself. There was a hitch in the story. What was it? Jane thought if she moved her body, her brain would follow along and give her the information she knew she had, but could not assemble. On her last lap, she felt better than she had in days. She hadn't realized how good it might feel to actually move. She lifted herself out of the pool and sat on the side where she had thrown an oversized towel. Draping it over her shoulders, she realized she was sitting in front of the table where Lou Piccolo had been sitting last night. She turned and faced the table, clean and empty except for the heavy ashtray, the same one, she supposed, that Lou had been using last night.

Jane tied the towel around her waist and sat down on one of the lounges. She would not close her eyes. She shook out her hair, grateful that Tim had suggested this shaggy style before they arrived in California. How long ago had that been? Her preparation day at the spa? At least a hundred years ago. The amazing thing about being drawn into a mystery was what it did to time and routine. Jane and Tim had only spent a few days in Los Angeles, and she felt as if Evanston and Kankakee were lifetimes away. Looking up at the blue sky, the clouds so perfect that they were surely painted on by the set designer, Jane felt an almost overwhelming sensation. She was being seduced. And it wasn't just any one thing drawing her in. It was just promise, that old shape-shifter, promise. You want to be a movie star, this place can offer you the dream. You want success as a writer? You'll be hammering out a script out by the pool in no time.

Patrick Dryer arrived here, his published novel in hand, and was seduced by the promise. He wrote a script and handed it over to someone he thought he could trust. Then, line by line, his ideas, his writings were drained from him. He was murdered in Pasadena, but his writing was killed much earlier. That book was workmanlike at best. How could he have dazzled Lou with all of the so-called brilliant material used by the B Room?

"What the heck are you doing out there?" yelled Tim. "You're not used to that sun, you'll fry."

"What?" Jane asked, sitting straight up.

"You need sunblock, sweetie. I don't know what's gotten into you. Wearing a bathing suit, swimming, for God's sake. You're from Illinois, have you forgotten? We don't go for dips in other peoples' pools. We don't even—"

"No, what did you say before?"

"I asked what you were doing sitting out here in the sun," said Tim. "What's wrong with you? Sunstroke already?"

"You said what the heck . . ." said Jane.

"Yeah, I meant what the fuck, but I'm trying to clean up my language since you told me that my godfather credentials with Nick would be revoked if I didn't—"

"Everyone is in Patrick's novel. In *The D Room*, he has a character to represent everyone in real life, everyone in the real-life B Room . . ." said Jane.

"Yeah?"

"Heck. Everyone except Heck."

Jane asked Tim to get her another towel. She looked down at her legs and realized Tim was right. What was she thinking? A pale Illinois lass sitting out by a pool? In a bathing suit? For a moment California had her, but there is nothing like the lack of a suntan, that pasty doughy look of one's own skin, to remind you of your roots.

"Henry Rule is not a player in Patrick's book. Why not? He was part of the group when Patrick arrived here. Heck's illness separated him from the group this year, but Patrick's been hanging around out here for at least five years. If the novel is true, they've been bleeding him for at least five years."

"Why do you keep saying that? About the novel being true?" asked Tim, throwing the towel on top of her.

Jane shook her head.

"It's a novel, not a memoir," said Tim. "I mean, he might have based it all on his life out here, but he didn't write a Hollywood memoir or anything. You know, like Belinda St. Germaine. She came out here and got burned by people and wrote *Hollywood Diary*, and even though she probably exaggerates the stuff, she doesn't pass it off as fiction. Maybe Dryer just took the B Room as a subject for fiction, then made stuff up."

"No," said Jane, standing up, wrapping one towel around her waist and draping the other one over her shoulders.

Jane walked into the guesthouse, motioning for Tim to follow. She picked up Patrick's book from where she had left it on the table.

"It's not made up and I can show you why," said Jane. She opened to a page in the middle and began reading.

"Why do you need another rewrite of that script, Sam?" I asked, waving away some of his cigar smoke. It never ceased to amaze me that he insisted on smoking even when I told him it made me sick. One more strike against the bastard.

"The producer's interested, he just wants to see if you've really got the stuff, you know?" Sam gave me an oily smile.

"I've got the stuff," I told him. "I can give you three more drafts of this script if I need to, but I'm beginning to wonder why the producer doesn't want to meet me." I knew then that Sam was using me, but I wanted to see him squirm his way out of it again.

"That sucks," said Tim.

"That isn't even the worst of it," said Jane. "He goes on for pages, having Sam make up phony reasons that Patrick can't be brought to meetings. This is real. It's terrible fiction, but it's real, true-life dialogue. I was thinking, when I started reading this, about a fiction-writing class I took in college. Just because something's copied from life doesn't mean it rings true. It makes for bad fiction." Jane held up the book. "And this, my friend, is bad fiction. And you know what bad fiction is, right?"

Tim shook his head, moving to make more coffee.

"Bad fiction is real life," said Jane.

Jane didn't know whether or not to credit the swimming with clearing her head, but she did now know why the novel was self-published. It was because Patrick couldn't write anymore. The book was poorly written. He had either lost what talent he had or he was simply written out. If Patrick felt that Lou Piccolo and the B Room had drained him of his best work, it was understandable that he would snap. Jane wondered if all the threats and the harassment that Patrick had rained down on the B Room really constituted threats on their lives or if he was referring to his novel. Was he just threatening them because he knew they would recognize themselves in *The D Room?*

For the first time, Jane had some real sense of Patrick's desperation. Not only did he feel he was used and used up by the group, he actually still believed in the power of words. He thought he could hurt them with this. Jane looked at the book and began paging through it again. Where was Heck? Had Patrick left him out because Heck had already punished himself? Maybe he thought the dishonesty, the appropriation of his material pushed Heck over the edge, so Patrick would pardon him from an appearance in his tell-all book.

Jane turned to the chapter that introduced the writer who turned to pornographic films. Last night, Jane had skimmed the sections that dealt with this subplot, since she was only trying to find any facts about the D Room/B Room characters that might point directly to whoever killed Patrick. If it was Lou, and Lou died of a heart attack, the crime was solved and, to some, it would seem that punishment had been swift and clean. Instant karma.

It wasn't a long chapter. The character Ben was hosting a party. Speaking in the very cadence of Jeb Gleason, Jane noted, Ben told a story about a friend of the group, a writer who had fallen on hard times. He had written an X-rated movie under a pen name, turned a quick profit, and had so much fun that he kept at it, found he had a knack for it. He was a prolific writer, but found that the better he was known in the porn circles, the less people wanted to know him in any other circles. Jane had thought last night, even skimming this section, that it was a cut above the rest of the novel. She had also remembered, incorrectly, that the character who wrote the X-rated movie was Alan or Fred. She must have been dozing through it. Now she realized the story of the inadvertent pornographer whom everyone had loved, then shunned, was written with compassion. Maybe, Jane thought, Patrick saw in him a comrade in arms, someone who couldn't get credit for his legitimate work. Now, reading more carefully, Jane noted that the writer/narrator listened to Ben's story with so much attention because he knew who he was talking about. The wayward writer was the narrator's cousin—the relative who had introduced him to Sam Sagella and the rest of the D Room writers. The cousin's name was Hank. How could she have missed that last night?

When a knock at the door roused Jane from her immersion in her second reading of *The D Room*, she looked up, noticed that she had a fresh cup of coffee by her side, but Tim was nowhere in sight. Assuming it was Jeb knocking at the door, feeling refreshed and celebratory since the two thorns in his side, Lou and Patrick, would no longer be around to disturb his own sweet scheme, she sat where she was and reluctantly called out for him to come in. It was, after all, his house.

Detective Oh, holding the giant book that he had borrowed from Jeb last night, nodded a good-morning to Jane.

"Perfect morning for a swim," he said.

Jane opened her mouth, but knew that no words would form. Instead, her skull was filled with the wretched silent screaming of a fortysomething midwestern woman sitting at a kitchen table in a borrowed bathing suit.

"May I boil some water for tea?" asked Oh.

"I dnt . . ." Jane tried to say she didn't know if there was tea, but only garbled sounds escaped.

"I bring my own," Oh said, holding up a tea bag he had taken from his pocket. "I take no chances."

He is pretending not to notice that I can't speak and that I am about to burst into flames, Jane thought. Tim walked in, saw Jane trapped at the table, blushing red from scalp to toes, unable to get up and run because she was sitting at a vintage Formica table on a matching vinyl chair and when she rose, her bare legs would beg to stay where they were planted. Jane would have to peel herself off the chair. It was a scene Jane knew Tim must be finding hilarious, but Jane's discomfort won him over—besides, she knew he'd make her pay later. Tim grabbed a robe out of the downstairs powder room and tossed it to her while he asked Oh how the rest of his night had gone.

"I read some interesting sections in the book I borrowed from Mr. Gleason," said Oh. "Interesting enough to keep me awake most of the night. And you, Mr. Lowry?"

"No reading for me. I washed dishes with Bobbette and we gossiped about the folks in the big house," said Tim.

Jane and Oh both looked at Tim expectantly.

"Nothing interesting," said Tim. "Sorry."

Jane had wrapped herself in the camel cashmere robe that Jeb provided for his houseguests, and found that as soon as she was covered and comfortable, her words and wits returned. She had a fleeting realization that this must be why bathing suit models were alleged to be bimbos, even though they probably had respectable IQs. It was impossible to speak while wearing a bathing suit. Realizing this was probably the only time she was going to feel any camaraderie with a swimsuit model, she allowed the thought to pass into oblivion.

"Patrick Dryer's novel was revealing," said Jane. "Poorly written enough to tell us a great deal."

"Excuse me," said Oh, looking at his watch. "I'm sorry to be rude, but I have to keep track of the time. I am meeting Claire at the hospital at noon."

Jane tried to give her version of what the novel revealed as quickly as possible. She went over the characters and their real-life twins and the scam Sam/Lou had been running.

"I just found the most interesting part that I somehow missed last night. I thought Heck had been left out of the book because I glossed over a chapter about one more writer, a former member of the D Room named Hank. It's got to be Heck," said Jane.

"Does it say anything about him going off the deep end?" asked Tim.

Jane shook her head. "Unless there's another section that I missed, this is it. There's just a story about him writing some racy material for a party, a comedy roast or something, and it was so well received that he started writing X-rated parodies of television shows, actually getting some produced as soft-core porn features. Remember the television show *Thirtysomething*? In the book, Hank writes a feature called *3-D Something* and gets an actress he knows to star in it and it becomes a cult classic."

"I don't know the television show, but I understand the play on words," said Oh. "May I see the cigar case you retrieved from the neighbor last night, Mrs. Wheel?"

"Nope," said Tim, looking up from his BlackBerry. "No *3-D Something* that I can find."

"Fiction, Timmy. Patrick made up the movie name. Look up Henry Rule and see if you come up with anything, although I'm sure he would have done these under another name," said Jane. She wrapped the cashmere around her more tightly, standing to get the cigar case for Oh. The robe felt incredible. She wondered how much Jeb might bill her for the cashmere if she stuck it in her suitcase.

Jane took the case out of the drawer where she had tucked it away last night. It was made of brown leather, fashioned to hold three cigars, the top molded to slide snugly into the bottom. She opened it and inhaled the aroma of tobacco and leather before handing it to Oh.

"You are an aficionada, Mrs. Wheel?" asked Oh, sitting down at the table. He took a pair of thin latex gloves from the pocket of his sport coat and carefully removed the two remaining cigars. He took out a magnifier and began examining one of the cigars. He first held it up to the light, then slowly rotated it in his hand as he carefully looked over the surface. After he was satisfied he had seen the entire outer wrapper, he picked up the second cigar and repeated the process.

"And you are checking for . . . ?" asked Tim, looking up from his BlackBerry.

Jane, too, was fascinated by the precision with which Oh conducted his examination. She looked at the second cigar that he laid down next to the first, compared them as well as she could without touching them, then shook her head.

"I give up, too. What is it?"

"Last night I borrowed a book from Mr. Gleason's library, the only one that had been removed from the shelf recently. It was a book on common poisons. Someone had left a marker on the page where nicotine poisoning was discussed. It occurred to me that Mr. Piccolo might have smoked a cigar that had been laced with an overdose of nicotine, which could have triggered a seizure, an arrhythmia . . ." Oh let his voice trail off as he picked up the first cigar again. "But I don't see any evidence of tampering. I was hoping that there might be a small puncture where a syringe might have been used to inject a concentrated dose."

"Where do you buy an overdose of nicotine?" asked Tim.

"Grocery store, Mr. Lowry. A simple pack of cigarettes would do it, although probably easier with some chewing tobacco. One could soak ten cigarettes, say, in a glass of vodka, and extract enough nicotine to kill someone, particularly someone with any history of heart problems. I spoke to the police this morning and they told me Mr. Piccolo had an episode a few years ago, according to his medical records."

"Cigarettes and vodka as murder weapons?" said Tim. "I like."

"What makes you think that Lou Piccolo was murdered?" asked Jane.

Oh shrugged slightly. "So convenient. His friends accepted him as the murderer of Mr. Dryer, then he dies. Very neat. No one seemed terribly sad last night to learn of his death. Even his partner, Ms. Bixby, who had just been through a shock herself, seemed to take it all in stride. I wondered if, perhaps, a member or members of this B Room group might have scripted Mr. Piccolo's death."

"Would one loaded cigar be enough to kill someone?" asked Jane.

Oh nodded. "But I don't think these two have been doctored. And I don't know how someone could count on the good fortune of having Mr. Piccolo choose the one lethal cigar in his case."

Jane asked to borrow Oh's magnifier and leaned in to look at the cigars herself, careful not to touch them in case they did become evidence.

"I think now is when I'm supposed to say 'aha,' " said Jane, holding up the magnifier.

"You've found an entry point?" asked Oh, surprised.

"I read the labels. These are Macanudos," said Jane. "Lou preferred Padróns. He said Padróns were his favorite. Someone who knew him well enough to have access to his cigars would know which one to inject with the nicotine, which one he'd smoke first. If anyone was suspicious and checked the other cigars in his case, they wouldn't find anything wrong with the Macanudos."

"Excellent, Mrs. Wheel," said Oh. "I'll call the detective I spoke with last night and let him know what to pass along to the medical examiner."

"We still don't know for sure," said Tim. "And if someone did poison Lou, does that mean Lou didn't kill Patrick?"

"It doesn't mean that necessarily, but it always seemed pretty obvious to me that a letter opener was missing from Lou's office, identical to the one found in Patrick Dryer's back," said Jane. "Lou claimed he was a hack writer and Patrick claimed Lou was a thief, but even the world's worst Hollywood writer would create a better scenario than that. In fact, it makes a lot more sense that someone else would take the letter opener from Lou's desk in order to frame him."

"Remember there was a letter opener sold that day at the flea market? The one in Patrick had a tag on it, didn't it?" asked Tim.

Jane reminded Tim how easy it would be to get a tag off any of the things they had purchased and tie it onto Lou's letter opener. The B Room went to the flea markets every weekend. They were all shoppers and collectors.

"Besides," said Jane, "maybe the murder weapon really was the letter opener purchased that day at the market. Maybe Patrick's murder was spontaneous. Someone saw him there, he told them about the book being published, that person had just bought a beautiful silver letter opener, and lo and behold, the perfect opportunity for its use presented itself. Then," Jane continued, "either the murderer or someone who wanted to protect the murderer took the opener from Lou's desk to make it look like it was Piccolo who finally got rid of his ghost and tormentor."

"And the guy who had been doing all the writing for everyone," said Tim. "Pretty screwy to kill the goose who was providing the golden eggs."

Oh carefully replaced the cigars in the case, then peeled off his gloves and tossed them in the trash. Jane shrugged. *Sometimes a cigar is just a cigar.* Jane looked at the kitchen clock. Oh was going to have to leave for the hospital to be on time to meet Claire. Tim had scheduled a cooking lesson with Bobbette. Jane needed to get dressed and wrap this case up. She grinned to herself. She loved thinking in detective-speak.

10

The "leave-behind," the material you leave for the network executive who has listened to your pitch, should be brief. It has to be catchy, memorable, to the point. Brief is the key. They'll be upset if you leave them more than one page to throw away.
—FROM *Hollywood Diary* BY BELINDA ST. GERMAINE

Jeb Gleason had suggested that someone other than himself show Jane and Tim around L.A. He would be tied up all day.

Wren Bixby had suggested another meeting to discuss the possibility of *The Scarecrow Murder*. Even though Jane was there as a detective, her story still had movie possibilities.

Skye suggested a massage. Everyone had been through so much, was so stressed out. She thought Ernie could work Jane into his schedule . . . before or after her own appointment.

Greg and Rick suggested they be left completely alone to finish their current script. Completely alone.

Louise Dietz offered to take Jane shopping.

Jane blew a farewell kiss to Tim, who was wearing an apron identical to Bobbette's and was listening to her lecture on making the perfect croissant. Jane sat outside, watching for Louise to wind her way down the driveway. She thought it would be better if they just took off and Louise didn't get a chance to receive her daily instructions from Jeb. *Not that he wouldn't have already called her and told her where to take me, what to tell me.* Ah well, fair is fair. Jane had given Tim his instructions, too. As soon as Jeb left the house, Tim was to search through every nook and cranny, paying particular attention to the desk drawers in the study to see if he could find an early 1900s arts and crafts silver letter opener. Jane knew that Jeb had been in Lou's office. He had gone in there to make calls when they hurried back from lunch. When Jane returned later to look around, a letter opener was missing from Lou's desk. It was possible that Cynda or whoever had taken it or moved it, but unlikely. The assistants waltzed in and out of the office, waiting for their own careers to begin. They hadn't seemed particularly invested in any dramas that were playing out within Bix Pix Flix.

Jeb had taken the scalpel from the hosptial, he said, because he feared Lou might be coming after him next after Patrick. Highly unlikely that he really believed that, or that he thought he would be effectively arming himself with the tiny blade. *Maybe he just likes shiny sharp objects.*

Louise drove her Prius around the circle drive and stopped it directly in front of Jane. She was wearing well-tailored charcoal gray slacks, a soft cotton, blue button-down shirt, and comfortable low-heeled shoes. Shopping clothes. Her hair was pulled back from her face and she smiled at Jane with the most carefree attitude Jane had seen from any of the B Room since her arrival. Either Louise was the best actress of them all, or she really believed that with Patrick and Lou gone, the trouble was behind them. Despite her cheerful mood and positive attitude, her greeting was serious business.

"Memorial service for Lou is set for Friday," she said, gesturing to the cell phone that lay on the car seat. "I just got a call from his sister. She's the only family member coming for it."

Jane wondered if the medical examiner would be releasing Lou's body by then. No matter, really, if they were just setting up a friends-and-family memorial. On the other hand, Jane found herself struggling not to mention the possibility that

Lou Piccolo had been murdered. Would that affect the eulogy? The eulogizers?

"Was this left up to you to arrange?" asked Jane. "I would have thought Bix—"

"Yeah, Bix is taking care of the details. Place. Food. Format. She just asked if I could make a few calls. Lou's sister said that high cholesterol and high blood pressure run in the Piccolo family, although she didn't know Lou had it. I heard about fifteen minutes of her health history before I got another call that saved me."

Jane would bet the other call was from Jeb. She wasn't ready to trust all of her hunches, but there was something so intimate and immediate in the way Louise looked up at the second-floor window of the house when she was turning the car out of the driveway. As if it were the real ending to a conversation. Jane followed Louise's eyes and saw Jeb, in his royal robe, standing in the window watching them leave. She wondered where he had told Louise to take her.

"How about Long Beach?" asked Louise. "It's a beautiful day for a drive and I know some great little places."

"Actually, I was thinking I'd really like to concentrate on the area around here. You know, since I'm here and toying with showbiz, I'd like to stay close to the heart of the action. I read about some vintage clothing stores, thought we might scout a little jewelry, maybe some Bakelite?" Jane did not want to end up a freeway or so away from Jeb's. If Oh called, if Tim needed her, she wanted . . . what? To come to the rescue?

"Great," said Louise. "I am always up for jewelry."

Jane had seen the look when Louise was on the hunt in Pasadena. Jewelry was definitely one of her passions.

"Maybe we'll do a little trip down Sunset. I'd like to hit Minna's and you'll like Rumor B. Then we'll swing back this way and stop in at Ozzie Dots and Wacko. Those'll give you a taste of what's out here. Anything special you're looking for?" asked Louise.

"Everything," answered Jane. "I just won't know it until I see it."

That was always the truth.

Their first stop was a place on Sunset called The Way We Were. Jane loved everything about the shop, the crowded shelves, the wooden floors that made a creaky old dime-store sound when you walked on them, and the wire bins of billiard balls. What was it about round shapes, spheres, that made Jane go a little weak in the knees? Even as a child, she had loved brightly colored rubber balls—for bouncing, for playing, yes, but more for the way they looked when they were all nested into a box under her bed. Maybe Nellie was right—maybe Jane had been peculiar right from the get-go. The only negative about The Way We Were that Jane discerned was the fact that the title song would now be implanted in her head until an equally tenacious melody reared its catchy refrain.

Jane's tell when she went into shopping/buying/lusting mode was humming. She hummed through flea markets, house sales, not so much in auctions, since the auctioneer provided such an interesting background theme, but certainly she provided her own music in antique stores and malls. Now the searing Streisand "Memories . . ." begged to be released in her own off-key humming. She tried to keep it low.

Jane had worked her way down one aisle of the store, finding several items to touch, but only two to keep. She caressed two sets of paper dolls. June Allyson and Cyd Charisse. They were expensive, but if she could get a discount for buying them both, it would be worth it. Both had been partially cut, but June's folder had three intact sheets. One had dresses and two were accessories—hats, shoes, scarves, handbags—the most difficult to cut out. Jane and Tim, when they were in first grade, had played long hours of paper dolls. Tim had been a master with a scissors even at six years old. Jane knew these sets were less desirable to a collector than they would be if they had been left entirely uncut, but she didn't care about the condition. All she knew was that if she and Tim weren't busy crime-solving tonight, they would be arguing over who got to be June and who got to be Cyd.

Louise hadn't moved from the first jewelry display counter. Jane appreciated her method. Louise was a side-to-side-up-down shopper. She carefully canvassed the cases before calling for help, so she made efficient use of the salesclerk's time while not missing a single item. Jane admired the discipline. Tim called Jane's technique "wild-eyes." Even though she could walk down an aisle from beginning to end, Jane's eyes darted all over the place. She was a reflexive looker—one item led her to another, and only with the greatest effort could she systematically scan a shelf.

Louise found two unsigned costume jewelry pins for a good price. She thought one might be an unsigned Chanel.

"More likely a knockoff, but a good one. See the center? Poured glass. The little stones on the sides are all prong-set. It's nice. Good color." She held it up to the light and turned it slightly. They both watched it cast its rainbow onto the wooden floorboards.

With the exception of Tim, Jane didn't like shopping with other people. Often they wanted to show her everything, hold up each item they saw for her approval. Or worse, they wanted to ask her why she was looking at whatever. *What is it? What would you do with it? Where would you put it? Why do you like it?* It was in the middle of that type of questioning that Jane understood the impulse to murder. She had told Detective Oh that it was probably helpful careerwise that she could put herself in the mind of a killer now and then. He hadn't seemed amused or convinced.

Louise didn't talk or ask questions. She merely smiled at Jane in that dreamy way that said she was happy and she was happy that Jane was happy and wasn't being lost in this stuff so happy? She was tipsy, well on her way to drunk, as was Jane. Stuff was the newest drug, the acceptable drink before five.

Jane might have forgotten all about Patrick Dryer and Lou Piccolo and lost herself in Picker Life 101 for the morning had she not turned a corner and found herself face-to-face with a six-foot-tall, faded, but still colorful wooden cigar-store Indian. His hands were carved so that they could hold a removable tray. On it, the owner of the antiques store had set several other pieces of politically incorrect kitsch. Squaw and Brave salt and pepper shakers, a small ceramic cup with an Indian chief figure attached with the words THE BIG CHIEF'S CIGARS hand-painted on the cup, and several old cigar boxes.

Lou Piccolo could not have sent a more striking reminder. And Jane, watching her drunk-with-love-of-stuff companion pay for her jewelry, figured she should strike while Louise seemed the most vulnerable.

"Let's stash our stuff in the trunk. I want to take you to a great place that has an amazing collection of movie memorabilia and oh wait . . . are you interested in books? First editions? Because I have . . ." Louise began rummaging through her purse looking for a business card with the address of their next stop.

"Lou Piccolo collected first editions, right?" asked Jane.

"Yes. First editions and Depression glass. Vinyl records and, let's see, he liked vintage telephones, too," said Louise. "Lots of other stuff, too. I think maybe the first time I met Lou was at the flea market. Bix brought him to one of our Sundays."

Jane knew that if you can establish the common ground of collecting . . . the thrill of the hunt and all . . . you can get someone to talk and talk. Collectors loved their stuff, but they loved their stories about how they got it even more. And everyone collected the stories.

"Lou was a good shopper. He liked to get under the tables, go through the boxes. I went to a couple of old house sales with him and he could find things squirreled away in cupboards and then make the people holding the sale feel like he had just done them the biggest favor in the world—hauling out the trash for them. Then we'd get to the car and he'd show me an old adding machine, a Victor with Bakelite handle and keys, buried at the bottom of a box of scrap paper and office supplies that the people just missed. He never really lied about what he found and wanted to buy, but he sold the idea of it as something worthless, paid a buck for an alleged box of junk, and walked out shaking his head. Lou was a good actor."

"So Lou was a digger?"

"Exactly. Under the tables, basements, attics, under beds."

"Was he a killer?" asked Jane.

Louise only hesitated for a second. If she was preparing to lie or talk from a B Room script, she, too, was a good actor.

"Maybe he killed Patrick. He had a temper. He and Jeb used to fight like crazy, but that was just jealousy. Territorial pawing of the ground and all that. I mean, Patrick was a pretty slimy guy, and God knows . . . Damn it, I should have turned there. Okay, I'll go around the block." Louise turned down a narrow street. "They used to shoot exteriors for *Southpaw and Lefty* around here. See that alley? That was where Sandy drove, like he was heading home, in the opening credits?"

"Patrick was slimy?" asked Jane.

"Yeah, he was a creep," said Louise, "after what he . . . Hey, there's a parking space."

Jane waited until Louise had parked the car, then put her hand on Louise's arm before she opened the car door.

"It sounds like you knew him pretty well," Jane said.

Louise realized that she had spoken too freely about Dryer. The members of the B Room all claimed to know about Patrick, but denied actually knowing him well. Someone had claimed to have met him on the *S and L* set, but Jane didn't remember

Louise giving up any personal information. Now she straightened her shoulders and turned to face Jane.

"I had an encounter with Patrick once. I didn't like him. He was a user and selfish. He didn't even . . ." Louise stopped. She looked at her cell phone resting in the cup holder. Jane imagined that she longed for it to ring. If only Jeb would call and tell her what she could do to extricate herself from this conversation. Jane knew that both Jeb and Louise had thought shopping would be a safe activity. Jeb might have thought Jane was enough of a detective to calm everyone's nerves about the threats to the B Room when he encouraged Bix to fly her in, but now that he believed the mystery was solved, he figured she was done detecting and her picker instincts would rise to the surface.

"He didn't want to identify the body of his cousin?" asked Jane.

Louise didn't cry. No tears formed. But Jane could tell that it was everything she could do to hold it all back.

"Yes, Patrick was Heck's cousin. He was there that horrible night. Heck had become such a sick man and we couldn't do anything for him. He didn't sleep, he didn't eat. He wrote constantly, that's what he told us. Wouldn't show anybody anything. That creepy Patrick was there, he could have identified the body, but he refused to go in. They made me . . ."

Louise lost the struggle and began to cry.

"Heck probably wasn't the nicest guy in the world, but he was close. I mean, he had his tics, you know? But he'd do anything for his friends. Before he got sick. And Patrick kept trying to weasel his way into Heck's life. It seemed like every time I'd call to check on Heck, Patrick would answer the phone. He was there all the time. Tried to turn Heck against all of us. Thought he'd get Heck's stuff, but he didn't get away with that. Heck left everything to the B Room. He made Jeb and Bix and

Lou the coexecutors of the estate, but Rick and Greg and Skye and me, we're all part of the group that gets everything."

"Did he have a lot of money?" Jane asked.

"That's what's so funny. He didn't have anything, really. Just his house and everything in it. No savings. He spent his money from *Southpaw and Lefty* on his own company. Tried to make movies. No one goes from television to movies easily. Shoot, writers who work on thirty-minute sitcoms can't even move to hour-long shows without jumping through a million hoops. Heck said he was going to do it on his own. He told me he had made a movie. He'd invite us over to see his movie, then he'd say he couldn't find it. Said someone must have stolen his only copy. Talked about it a lot, but it was after he snapped. Jeb said it was just another delusion."

Jane knew that Oh would counsel her to keep listening. He would tell her not to ask a question that offered more information than it sought. But Jane was too excited to listen to her own warnings, even if they came from the smartest voices in her head.

"Is it possible Heck did make a movie, but didn't really want you all to see it?" asked Jane.

"No," said Louise. "Absolutely not. Haven't you spent enough time with us? Every time one of says anything that's remotely amusing, we're repeating it to each other and making sure everyone knows it was our funny line. It's what we do—make stuff up to make each other laugh—or cry, as the case may be. We don't do it for the producers or the actors or the directors. . . ."

"You do it for the viewers?" asked Jane.

"Oh no. Hell no. We do it for each other. If you can make another writer in the room laugh, you've succeeded. All the rest of them who work on the show? The ones who take all the credit when the awards are handed out? They don't know anything. It's the other writers you work for . . . they know when the writing's good," said Louise.

"If that's the case, what if Heck made a movie that he wasn't proud of? That he didn't think you all would like? Would he keep it a secret?"

"What?" said Louise. "What kind of movie would that be?"

Jane hesitated for a moment. If she was wrong about this, it was a lousy thing to say about someone who had jumped to his death. "Maybe it was something off-color or even—"

"Porn?" Louise laughed. "You think Heck got into porno? He couldn't even say—"

"But he wrote those parodies. You told me they were filthy and that he—" Jane's phone rang inside of her bag, and she began digging. Without Nick to change the ring for her, she recognized the no-nonsense bell right away. She had been so busy, so wrapped up in her Hollywood case, she hadn't even missed Nick and Charley, but when the phone rang, she felt their absence like a hard blow to the chest. She had to finish all of this and go back to Illinois so she could miss them properly. They were due home in another week. She'd be there to welcome them. By the time she found the phone and flipped it open, it had stopped ringing, but the message light flashed.

"Interesting bit of information from Bobbette. No letter opener, though. Jeb has got some cool old religious stuff. Fits in with his cult leader image. I'll try Oh. Call when you get the chance. Don't buy any Roseville. The market is flooded with copies."

Louise had dried her eyes with a charming vintage handkerchief, Jane had noted, and seemed hesitant to start the car. She was probably uncertain of whether, after all this serious discussion, they were still shopping. Jane realized that she wasn't ready to end the conversation, not just because she needed information to put this whole puzzle together, but because she liked Louise. Louise had a good eye for stuff and, Jane was beginning to believe, a good heart. On the other hand, Jane wasn't so sure about her judgment when it came to Louise's friends.

"Louise, just hear me out on this. Suppose Heck did make an X-rated movie under a different name. Maybe he liked doing it, but had to keep it a secret because you all wouldn't like it. Jeb told me that you all workshop your writing together and Jeb edits and takes a cut of your money—maybe Jeb wouldn't want to take a cut of that money. Maybe he'd be worried about the B Room reputation. Maybe all that contributed to Heck's breakdown. Maybe he was keeping secrets from you all."

"And that was why he stopped going out and he hid in the house and stopped wanting to see all of us. . . ." said Louise.

"Let's say Patrick, his cousin, came over and gave him some song and dance about blood being thicker than water and Heck confessed what he had done to Patrick. Maybe Cousin Patrick was blackmailing him, and whoever killed Patrick did it to avenge Heck," said Jane, aware of the holes in this, but wanting to see what Louise came up with.

"Lou wouldn't have cared about Heck. I mean, not enough to murder Patrick. Besides, Patrick was pretty scary himself—paranoid and thought everyone was stealing from him. Lou told us that Patrick once accused him of stealing the ideas right out of his head."

"Forget Lou as Patrick's murderer for a minute. Let's just say it could have been someone else. Anyone who was at that flea market, for example . . . Wait a minute," said Jane. "Did Heck and Patrick ever write anything together? Because if they did and someone took it from Heck, thinking he was so crazy he either wouldn't know it was missing or no one would believe him that someone was stealing from him . . ." Jane said, remembering that the manuscript she had seen Rick and Greg working on had *H. Rule* typed across the top.

Jane looked at Louise and saw that she was losing her on this. Jane herself wasn't sure exactly how this would work, but now that she had the idea in her head it wouldn't go away. Fueled by her reading of Patrick's vanity novel, Jane grew more and more certain that Heck and Patrick had come up with some idea, some story that was stolen. And it was probably stolen by someone who didn't know Patrick was involved, someone who felt safe in taking material from Heck. Louise said that Patrick was over at Heck's house all the time. Maybe Heck was churning out material that Patrick helped with, or maybe it was all Heck's and Patrick wanted to take credit himself. Jane looked at Louise, who had her hands on the steering wheel, ready for Jane to tell her where they were going, what they were doing with all of this.

"Louise, will you take me to Lou and Bix's office on the lot?"

"Bix wasn't planning on going in today," said Louise. "She and Jeb were—"

"Doesn't matter," said Jane. "I have a key."

19

The amateur borrows, the professional steals.
—from *Hollywood Diary* by Belinda St. Germaine

Louise remained quiet on the way to Bix's office. Jane had offered up a lot of information, admittedly much of it speculation, but the more Jane thought about Heck and his relationship to Patrick, the more Jane was convinced that something Heck had done, or had been in the process of doing, had set all of this in motion. Patrick discovered that his cousin had a secret and somehow was using it to blackmail someone or some two from the B Room.

As they approached the main entrance to the studio lot, Louise flipped on her turn signal. She was about to drive into the public parking lot across the street that accommodated visitors to the studio when Jane suggested Louise drive past and turn at the next street.

"The private lot," said Louise.

"You're not surprised?" asked Jane.

"I'm guessing that you came this way with Jeb. He said you were with him when he heard about Bix. We're going to have to walk back around, though. I'm not even sure how we'll get in the main gate if Bix's assistant isn't there to okay us. Who do I still know there? I guess I could call Gary in props or somebody on the set of—"

"No need, Louise. I really do have a key," said Jane.

When they got out of the car, Jane looked around and saw no one near any of the cars parked in the annex. She motioned for Louise to follow her and walked to the gate. She unlocked it and gave an open-handed voilà gesture, pointing toward the back door of Bix Pix Flix.

"When we went to the W to pack up your stuff, Jeb told me to keep an eye out for a small old key. He said something about it being an old joke between the two of you in college and he wanted to see if you still had it. Said you'd think it was hysterical if he ended up presenting it to you instead of vice versa."

"Jeb has not lost a step when it comes to improvisation," said Jane. "Truth is I stole it the first day I was here. Jeb must have noticed it missing after I was here with him. I just had a feeling I was going to need it."

"You really are a detective, aren't you?" said Louise. "Or a thief."

Jane knocked on the back door, but there was no answer. It was open, as it had been the last time when she and Tim paid an unannounced visit. The two women stepped in and Jane scanned the hall. She peered into Bix's office. The day, which had begun so brightly, had turned overcast. Bix's office, with the shades partially drawn, was dark and empty. Jane couldn't put her finger on what was different, but she had a feeling someone had been in the place since she had been there. She scanned the shelves and Bix's desk. Some folders that were there before now missing? A coffee cup cleared away? That was it. There had been a pink GlassBake square coffee cup on the desk when Jane and Jeb had rushed over from their lunch after Bix got hurt. Tim had been on the phone and pointed to it when Jane walked in because he knew Jane collected them and was trying to complete a set. An assistant could have cleared it. Lou and Bix could have stopped in on their way back from the hospital.

Lou's office door was closed. Had it been closed when she and Tim had checked it out?

"What are you looking for?" asked Louise.

Jane didn't answer right away. Her first response was the same as it would have been if someone asked her what she was looking for when she went to a flea market. She wouldn't know until she found it. But that wasn't true here. At Bix Pix Flix, Jane did have an idea of what she might find.

"Louise, I swear I just want to keep all of you safe. Can I trust you to keep an eye on the door, warn me if you see anyone coming, while I look for something in Lou's office?"

Louise swallowed hard and nodded.

Jane gave the door a gentle push and stepped in. Her own house had been burglarized once. The garage, where she stored all of her finds to send out to the dealers for whom she picked, had been turned upside down. Boxes were emptied, file drawers where she stored receipts and photos of objects on her search list, every book, pot, plate, vase that she kept in the old bookcases that snaked around the space where a car should be parked had been thrown onto the concrete floor, smashed and shattered. Jane hadn't seen the worst of it—Charley had been there when it happened and managed to clean away most of the heartbreaking mess before she returned from Kankakee.

Jane wondered who would take care of this for Lou.

Every file drawer from the two cabinets behind his desk was emptied onto the floor. His desk drawers were empty, thrown onto the floor, with their contents spread all over the carpet. Cardboard file boxes of manuscripts that he had stored in the closet had been turned over on their sides, pages flung everywhere. The file cabinet nearest to the door, on Jane's immediate left, was ransacked but not totally emptied. Jane had a sense that whoever had done this had begun at that file, hoping to find what he or she was looking for by a methodical sweep of the room. One could read the frustration of the seeker by how much more destructive the search became as it moved around the room. The person who stormed the office wasn't interested in any personal objects belonging to Lou Piccolo. His collections of paperweights, letter openers, and Depression glass remained untouched. Neither, apparently, was anyone interested in Lou's own recent work, since a laptop computer sat on a side table unmolested.

Jane saw no reason to stay and look further, since someone had already done a more than thorough job. The angry mess persuaded her that the search had been unsuccessful. Giving the room one last look, she noticed one thing about which she had been mistaken. She at first thought that Lou's collections had remained untouched. That was incorrect. On his desk, the rows of paperweights remained intact. The row of letter openers, however, had been tampered with since Jane had been there before. The hand-hammered silver letter opener whose outline on the dusty desktop had made its absence obvious was no longer missing. Whoever had taken it, probably in order to frame Lou Piccolo, had decided it was no longer necessary. The letter opener had been returned.

Jane returned to the front of the bungalow, where Louise, true to her word, was looking out the front window. Jane scanned the shelves of first editions in the glass-covered barrister bookcases. Everything she could remember seemed to be there. No obvious gaps in the rows of books. The shelves lined with glass shakers, some with cuttings of ivy and philodendron, remained unscathed. Only Lou's office had been ransacked. And whoever had done it was looking for something that could be filed away, placed in a desk drawer. Scripts? Rewrites? Treatments? Polishes? All of the work Patrick's narrator claimed he gave to Sam Sagella for distribution to the other writers in his novel, the members of the D Room?

Jane had purposely left the gate ajar when she and Louise sneaked onto the lot. If they were caught, she wanted to be able to say they stumbled upon the entrance by accident and wandered in to explore. If there had been anything in Lou's office before, and Jane doubted there was, certainly there was nothing left now. Jane motioned to Louise that it was time to leave. She took the small key out of her pocket and dropped it back where she had found it the day of her meeting with Bix. She wouldn't need it again.

Jane latched the gate and clicked the lock closed. The two women got into the Prius and Louise pulled to the annex parking lot exit and spoke for the first time since they had left Bix Pix Flix.

"Where to?" she asked, awaiting instructions before she turned onto the street.

"Heck's house," said Jane.

Tim was surprised that Jane had not yet returned his call. He had told her it was nothing urgent, but on the other hand, didn't he say he had interesting news? What did a sidekick have to do around here to get some attention?

He and Bobbette had a fine time making the dough for the croissants and while it was resting, Bobbette brought up the subject of the dirty glasses they had found on the top pantry shelf.

"I scolded Mr. Jeb about it today and he acted all Mr. Innocence about it. I will tell you, a man can fool his wife, lie to his lover, and steal from his boss, but he can't fool his housekeeper," said Bobbette.

"What's his secret?" Tim asked, hoping he sounded nonchalant.

"He is smoking cigarettes again. He quit them six months

ago for the fourth time. Every time he gets divorced or something goes bad with his work, he starts smoking, then he has to quit all over again. What is it about men that they are so weak?"

Tim shrugged. "I wouldn't know," he said, smiling at her. "I have no vices."

"Sure, I'll just bet that's true," said Bobbette. "Anyway, I said to him that I had the proof, and he said I must be drinking the cooking wine and I told him that wasn't funny. I would prove it that I could prove it."

Bobbette told Tim that she demanded Jeb follow her to the pantry, where she had left the glasses out in plain sight.

"After you went back to the guesthouse last night, I went to get them to wash. I couldn't figure out what was in them. I smelled them and they were horrible. All tobacco in some drink of gin or vodka. I knew right away what had happened. Mr. Jeb sneaked into the pantry with his drink and smoked, then, when he heard me coming, put out the cigarette in his glass. He knows he can't let me see it, so he sticks it up high in the pantry where he thinks I can't see or reach it. I decided not to wash it. I would show him he can't hide from me. But when we came into the pantry this morning, the glasses were gone. No dirty glasses nowhere," said Bobbette. "Mr. Jeb made the cuckoo crazy sign with his finger to his head and went back to his office to work. I looked all over the kitchen." Bobbette wiped her hands on a dish towel, then folded it by the sink. "Hey, did you come back in and wash them for me?"

"Nope," said Tim. "That's some mystery, huh?" He couldn't wait to tell Jane and Oh that Jeb Gleason had mixed a nicotine cocktail in his pantry.

"Maybe it was those girls. They are always in my kitchen."

"What girls?"

"Those writer women. They always come in and say they want to help. They dry one dish, then wander away when they think of the joke they were trying to write. Ms. Skye is the one who always offers to help first. She tries. She just never learned how to do anything. Ms. Bix and Ms. Louise come in after and help her help me, but then they all get called to help some more in the office meetings. Why do people think that housekeepers want help? Two things we want? To be left alone to do our work and to not be friends with the people who pay us."

Tim nodded. Now that he knew Bobbette didn't want to be friends, he didn't have to finish making the croissants, did he? He needed to talk to Jane and tell Oh that he found the poison and the poisoner. Except that the poison itself was now gone and the poisoner had been tipped off that his poison had been found.

"Bobbette," said Tim, "did you mention that I was with you when you found those glasses?"

"I don't think so," said Bobbette. "I wouldn't want to mention that you were helping. You—you do okay in the kitchen, not like those women. And it was fun with you. But I'm not sure Mr. Jeb would like that I let you work with me. Cooking's another story—everybody wants to cook with me so they can steal my recipes."

Tim and Bobbette stopped talking when they heard the doorbell ring. It was a loud dramatic chord. Since he and Jane arrived yesterday, Tim realized that the house had been full of people who came and went at will. Had he heard a doorbell ring? This was a kind of Hollywood fraternity or sorority house with a bunch of sisters and brothers who all had the key and permanent access.

Bobbette wiped her hands and headed for the door. Tim went into the pantry and took a quick sweep of the cupboards. The housekeeper was right. No dirty glasses. There was a row of Waterford tumblers on the top shelf. Tim counted twelve. The two that had been used to dissolve the cigarettes or chewing tobacco or whatever had been used had been emptied, washed, and put away. As Tim called Jane and left a message on her voice mail about what he'd discovered, he absentmindedly pulled open the drawers. Maybe there was something else—a tin of chewing tobacco or some pretentious French cigarettes that belonged to Gleason or something he could offer Jane and Oh in order to tie the creepy old boyfriend to Lou Piccolo's death.

"Hello?" Tim said in his best James Bond–speak. The drawer he had opened had random bar accessories and kitchen utensils. Two tarnished sterling silver individual lemon squeezers which he would love to pocket to add to his collection of beautifully rendered, yet truly gratuitous dining objects, but he resisted temptation. The object he instead lifted out of the drawer, using a linen towel to pluck it from among the other items, was a four- or five-inch plunger and tube device, almost an inch in diameter. If one were prone to doctor's office nightmares, this would be the instrument with which the evil nurse would approach to give you a flu shot. It was a syringe-type infuser, fitted with a sharp point, originally intended to infuse meats and poultry with a marinade. Now it was half filled with a viscous brownish goo, dried onto the sides of the tube.

"Looks like Jeb Gleason has found a use for all those cigarettes he gave up," said Tim out loud, "or he's been mainlining cocoa."

When he heard Bobbette's voice, and footsteps in the kitchen, Tim dropped the syringe into his jacket pocket. Finding this little object of evil was going to be good for a promotion. What came after sidekick? Costar? God, Tim Lowry loved Hollywood. When he turned to go back into the kitchen and saw the gun pointed at him, he sighed. *Sidekick* to *costar* to *special appearance* and *in memory of*—all in one episode.

Detective Oh had performed the role of dutiful husband on the trip to California. His wife, Claire, had an affection for this elderly aunt and felt obligated to be with the odd remnants of family who had collected together out here for the vigil at her bedside. Oh had agreed to accompany Claire when she asked, since they so rarely traveled together. Oh did not like to leave his home and his work and Claire preferred, on her antique-buying trips, to work alone. This time, however, as she was making her reservations, she announced that the airfares were excellent and she would appreciate his support. Always a gentleman as well as a husband, Oh had agreed to the trip.

He left Mrs. Wheel and Tim Lowry at Jeb Gleason's house in plenty of time to arrive at the hospital at the promised hour. A few minutes before noon, he walked into the family lounge on his wife's aunt's floor and found his wife having a disagreement with a cousin over some family heirlooms.

"Bruce, please give us your thoughts," said Claire, standing, using her full six feet to impress her opinion, and, she hoped, her husband's, on her second cousin. "Is it morally right to keep museum-quality porcelains hidden away in private homes or should they be made available to the public for viewing and study? How do you feel about this?"

Bruce Oh studied his wife's face and took a deep breath. "If you are referring to your great-aunt's collection, I believe, at the appropriate time, you should talk to her eldest son, your cousin, and see if she made her wishes known. If not, then the vases should be appraised as part of her estate, distributed as her will instructs, and the fortunate person who takes possession will be left with that difficult decision."

The cousin gave just enough of a satisfied smile to signal to Oh that his wife would no longer be soliciting his opinion. Oh excused himself to take a solitary walk around the hospital. It had become a daily ritual, while visiting Claire's aunt, to wander though the corridors. Oh found each waiting room, with its domestic scenes, mysterious tears, odd pairings, compelling. It was addictive, this daily drama that unfolded before him.

There were recurring players, the nurses and assistants at their stations, who had become familiar, nodding to him, smiling as he passed—and the changing cast, the new weeping sons and daughters, shocked parents, patient spouses.

Oh was thinking about the people who worked here, their complete immersion in an important and precise world each day, wondering if everything outside of the hospital became so much less important to them, when he found himself standing in front of a nurses' station where a friendly argument was going on.

"Celie, played by Skye Miller, was still a regular character when the show went off the air, she just wasn't in it all the time. She was supposed to be away at college or something. But she was in the credits, she was still a star," said a nurse standing with her back to Oh, who became very interested in a wall chart next to the station that enumerated a hospital patient's rights.

"I heard she was Sandy Pritikin's mistress by the end of the run. She broke up his marriage," said a man with a plastic carryall filled with labeled vials of blood.

"Bullshit," said the standing nurse. "She was as sweet and innocent as—"

"As an actress who hasn't had a role since her hit show went down the tubes," said another woman, who was seated at the desk in front of a stack of charts.

"She's a writer now," said the nurse who was Skye's champion. "She was here taking care of her friend, who is a writer, too. They worked on *Southpaw and Lefty* together. Those rumors about Sandy Pritikin, I remember them. When Skye was here, I asked her about him, what kind of guy he was. And she said she shouldn't speak ill of the dead, wouldn't gossip. Remember, he had that heart attack two years ago? But she did say that the rumors about her weren't true. She was real upfront about it. Said that the publicists were always trying to put something out there about her and people on the show, but it was because they wanted them in the news, didn't care what kind of news it was."

A nurse who was working at a computer at a counter behind the front desk had her back to the group. She turned around and Oh glimpsed her face. So tired and drawn.

"I am finally out of here," she said, standing. "I've worked enough doubles to last me a lifetime. And, my little Hollywood reporters, I was on duty the night the famous Skye Miller stayed with her friend and she might be all smiles and generous with the autographs, but she's tough as nails, too. Some guy got in, after hours, to see her friend, Bixby, and when she came back up to the room with food and found him, she flipped. She tossed his ass out. Threatened to call security and have him arrested. Gave all of us a piece of her mind after he left."

The tired nurse waved good-bye, picked up what looked like a heavy purse, and walked toward the elevator. Oh followed and got into the car with her.

"I am so sorry to admit this, but I was caught by the conversation back there," said Oh. What would Mrs. Wheel do in this situation?

"I am such a fan of the TV show I heard you talking about. Was the man who came here an actor from the show, too?" Oh did his best to look like a real television fan. For reasons he couldn't explain, he slumped his shoulders and nodded his head as he talked. He felt like a bobble-headed doll, but it made him feel more like the television watcher he was pretending to be.

The nurse shook her head. "He was a writer, I think. Said everyone was going to be a lot nicer to him when his book came out."

"Wow," said Oh, possibly for the first time in his life. It just seemed like the correct word for the circumstances.

"Yeah." The nurse yawned. "I don't really watch television, but I read a lot. I paid attention when he mentioned a book.

Skye just laughed at him and said it must be great. She heard he had a heck of a publisher."

"A heck of a publisher?" Oh asked.

"Something like that. I just remember the phrase because I noticed she wasn't swearing. Heck of a world when you actually take notice of the words that aren't swear words, huh?"

"Yes," said Oh, "heck of a world." He held the door open for her as they exited the hospital together. For good measure, he added, "Wow."

20

Save everyone's business card. It comes in handy to know where people used to work.

—FROM *Hollywood Diary* BY BELINDA ST. GERMAINE

"Heck lived in Los Feliz, too? In Jeb's neighborhood?" asked Jane as Louise headed her Prius back the way they had come from Jeb Gleason's that morning.

"Who doesn't?" asked Louise. "I have a place there, too. Bix, Skye . . . we all live within a mile of each other. Greg and Rick live in Echo Park."

"How about Lou?" asked Jane. "Was he part of the neighborhood?"

"No, but not so far away. I think his house is in Silver Lake. Never been there. He never invited anybody. Not to his place in Ojai, either. Except Bix, of course."

Jane listened for the third time to Tim's answering tape, but didn't leave a message. Where was he? Probably house-hunting with Bobbette. Why wasn't he picking up, though?

"Why 'of course'?" asked Jane.

"They were an item. As were Bix and Jeb," said Louise.

Jane figured since Louise had faced a bit of breaking and entering with her and hadn't seemed all that protective of her friend Bix's office, perhaps her friend Bix wasn't that much of a friend. Maybe it was time to break down the script and figure out who was really who in this cast assembled by mentor-turned-Svengali Jeb Gleason.

"I know that Jeb got me out here under false pretenses," said Jane. "My story had no real movie potential, but since I was an old friend and a PI, he thought I might be able to figure out what was going on without making any waves. But two people are dead. Three if you count Heck as part of all this." Jane paused, hoping this was having the right effect. "So, before we go into Heck's . . . anything you want to tell me about your B Room meetings?"

"Jeb works magic. He pulls stories and pilots out of the air," said Louise. "I am not kidding about this. He has kept us all working, all successful, because he has never run dry. He is a genius."

Jane knew this wasn't true. It wasn't true in college and it wasn't true now. The statement told her nothing about Jeb, but everything about Louise. She was in love with Jeb. And if one loved someone, it was easy to lay the mantle of genius on his shoulders. Jeb was glib and handsome. His style exerted a powerful influence over his fellow writers from his early days as a writer on *Southpaw and Lefty*, but Jane knew that did not make him a genius. If Patrick and/or Lou had been providing Jeb with the source for his genius—and they were both gone—Louise was going to know the truth about Jeb soon enough, so it wasn't up to Jane to blurt anything out. Jeb had a bank from where he drew his genius material and Jane had a feeling, as they pulled into the drive of a small stucco home with an arched roof over its porch, she was about to discover it. There was a low second story and a squared tower on top of that with a platform all around it. Two orange trees dominated the small front yard. Grass had gone to weeds. A homeless person was a sad sight, but, Jane thought, an abandoned home gave off its own sense of loss.

Louise shifted the car into park, but made no move to shut off the engine. Her hands remained on the steering wheel.

"Right back there, around the corner of the house, is a brick patio. I know the second story doesn't look very high. Heck went out the window of his little observatory. He must have been pacing on the platform, then slipped under the railing to get onto the roof. The police said he must have really thrown himself off . . . with an effort, they said. He landed facedown, broken neck. Dead. The funny thing is, the house isn't so tall, is it? If he had landed on the grass, he might not even have broken a finger."

"Did the police investigate this as a suspicious death?" asked Jane.

Louise shrugged. "They were inside the house. I think they made up their minds."

"What do you really think?" asked Jane.

"I'm not going in," Louise finally said.

"Is there an alarm system?" Jane asked, opening the car door.

Louise shook her head. "I told Heck he should get one, since he always thought people were after him. He said an alarm system was the first step to letting them control you. He was paranoid and mentally ill. He never even locked his doors."

"You're the owners now, right? Do you?"

"Side door is always open. I'm not sure about the front. We don't come here," she said. "We haven't touched it."

Jane got out of the car and walked to the front door. The doorknob turned easily enough, but the door itself was difficult to push open. Once Jane was inside, she saw newspapers stacked to the side that she had caused to slide over and scatter by opening the door. So far, Louise had set her straight. Heck's friends used the side entrance.

The living room was crowded but manageable. There was no single object in the room. Everything was in multiples. On the coffee table were six identical hobnail glass ashtrays. Three baskets all filled with pencils were under the table. The pencils were all sharpened to a fine point although most of them were tiny stubs, no bigger than two inches. Rugs lay on top of other rugs. Jane noted that some of them were quite valuable; two beautiful old Persians caught her eye. She was embarrassed to notice them, but it was the same as what happened at any estate sale. She entered the house with respect for the person who had lived his life within, she felt sorrow for his loss, and then she began eyeing his property. She wasn't proud of this behavior, but she had come to accept it in herself. She was drawn to the stuff of peoples' lives and even after the person departed, the stuff remained.

The living room had four large wooden desks. On each were stacks of scripts. There were a few title pages, shows Jane had never heard of. Heck had spent the last ten years writing every day for shows that played in his head. He must have ended up with enough new programming material to run three networks out of his living room. Jane picked up a few pages. The script pages were in no particular order. Or at least the order was not decipherable to Jane. Each page was coded and numbered in the right-hand corner. Jane took a breath and looked around the first floor. She needed to see the big picture, find the key to all of this.

The kitchen was small and every bit of limited counter space was filled with stacks of food. Cans of pickled beets were stacked ten high. There were three towers of chicken gumbo soup. Jane opened a cupboard to see if Heck had filled it with similar foodstuffs and found mixed nuts. At least a hundred pounds of mixed nuts. The containers were large gift tins and Jane picked one up. It wasn't heavy enough to hold five pounds of nuts, but it did feel like it was full of something. Jane pried open the lid.

The first tin held pieces of card stock, hand-cut to the size of business cards. On each card was written a title. The titles sounded like television show titles, but Jane didn't recognize any of them. Jane tried to imagine Heck sitting in this house, cutting up pieces of cardboard on which to write the hundreds of titles that floated into his mind. Jane wondered how it worked for him. Did he draw out a card and did the idea for the show come to him as a whole piece?

Jane opened another tin and in it were the same types of cards, this time all light blue, with character names and brief descriptions printed on them. *Sue Rennicker, unmarried attorney who gives up work to raise daughter. 10 years old, disappears. Sue's back to work to forget. Hard, haunted.* There were hundreds of cards in the tin and at least twenty tins in the cabinet.

Jane looked at the tins she had just opened. The title cards were in a container marked "unsalted." The characters and descriptions were in the "salted nut" tins.

It was like an elaborate parlor game. Draw a card here, pick a card there. Put together a show by a kind of lottery system. No wonder Heck never left the house. He must have been busy every minute of the day.

Jane heard a noise above her head at the same time she heard a car. Had Louise driven off? Jane looked out the window and saw the Prius. Louise wasn't in the car. Maybe she was out looking through things in the garage. Jane noticed that the side door was open.

Patrick Dryer had either figured out Heck's code or persuaded his cousin to explain it to him before he took his fall off the roof. Jane didn't think Dryer killed Heck. What was it Tim had said? You don't kill the goose who can lay the golden eggs. Of course, Dryer could be guilty through sheer neglect. He knew Heck had lost touch with reality, but his derangement was so damn profitable to everyone else. He was crazy, but he was a character and plot machine. If Dryer's novel, *The D Room*, was any indication of what was left of his talent, Patrick Dryer himself was finished as a writer. With Cousin Heck's material, though, he could be Hollywood's newest writing sensation. If only he hadn't tied himself to Lou Piccolo and made himself into the fount of wisdom for the B Room.

So Patrick Dryer was a user, a thief, and a bad writer. Those added up to make him a creep. People disliked him, for sure, but was being unlikable enough to drive someone to murder him? The work he stole from this house and passed off as his own was really written by Heck, but Heck couldn't be the murderer—he had been dead for months. Lou and Patrick were fighting, but Lou needed Patrick's access to the material and figuring out how the pages worked—for Lou's own career and for what he could now supply to the B Room. Lou, if he had the key to everything in this house, could be the new Jeb.

Jane dialed Tim again and this time she left a message. "I'm standing in the middle of a giant file drawer of television writing. We have one crazy genius, one greedy dried-up cousin who didn't inherit the family fortune or talent, apparently, one Machiavellian who wants to take over the kingdom—and they're all dead. Who profits? Timmy, where are you? Get over to Heck's— the house is three blocks from Jeb's."

Jane opened a kitchen drawer. Inside was a wooden flatware divider, but instead of knives and forks and spoons, Heck had used it to store pens. Black pens, blue pens, and red pens filled the compartments. Hundreds of pens. Jane noticed he separated the plastic ballpoints with advertising on them from the simple Bics. There was a highly evolved sense of organization to his madness. Jane found herself admiring the efficiency with which he channeled his manic energy. If only it had given him satisfaction.

Jane heard the faint chiming of a cell phone. It was the sound signaling a message had been left. Could Heck still have a working cell phone somewhere in the house? A battery would have expired, so the phone must be plugged into a charger. Jane would check upstairs. Might be interesting to see who was a good enough friend to have his cell number, but not close enough to know he was dead.

Okay, Jane thought, *let's just say Lou figured out that he could access the writing Heck left behind and didn't need Patrick, who had become a pain in the ass, was suing him and trying to publicly humiliate him. Plus get his money. Why wouldn't Lou kill him?*

Jane had to admit that he might. It was the method used to kill Patrick Dryer that Jane questioned. Lou might call himself a hack writer, but he was savvy enough about story and structure to know better than to choose a murder weapon that was one of his favorite collectibles. Also, he loved his letter openers. No collector would use a Kalo silver arts and crafts letter opener to kill someone—not if it meant leaving it with the body anyway.

Each room downstairs—living room, dining room, and den—was similar. Multiples of objects filled every surface. Jane noticed in the den that six towers were built floor-to-ceiling with See's candy boxes. Jane went over and carefully extracted one of the boxes from the middle. It was light, no candy. Jane was relieved somehow that Heck had eaten the chocolates. It made her think Heck had at least experienced some sensual pleasures. She shook the box and heard the swish of paper. He must have left the wrappers. Jane lifted the lid.

Jane needn't have worried about Heck enjoying sensual pleasures. The ten photographs in the box were of a naked woman. Although the woman, more a girl, really, had a game smile, she seemed sad and uncomfortable. The pictures were taken in Heck's living room. The same coffee table was in front of the couch. For some inane reason, Jane noticed that there were only two ashtrays when the photo was taken. Jane thought perhaps she would be able to put the boxes of photos—she was sure now that's what all of these boxes held—in some type of chronological order by the number of objects visible in the pictures. Jane opened a few other boxes and found the same types of photos, all with different women. The oldest couldn't have been more than twenty-one.

There were no names written on the photos, although written in marker on the inside lids of the candy boxes was the word *audition* with a letter and number code next to it.

Jane wondered if there were any Hollywood actresses who had gone on to stardom who had fallen for Heck's "auditions" and come into this living room, scared and embarrassed. Were they desperate? Did he offer them money? Jane looked at the towers of boxes. There must be two hundred of them. She felt sick and at the same time, relieved that Louise hadn't come in with her. Louise would know about this soon enough, they all would have to know, but Jane hoped Louise wouldn't have to see it for herself.

There was that chime again. Still holding one of the candy boxes, Jane headed for the stairs. In the upstairs hall, she searched for a light switch. When she flicked it on, she saw that although the downstairs held evidence of a manic, frenzied writer, it was upstairs where Heck truly became the mayor of crazy town.

Every inch of wall space in the hall was filled with notes pasted on the walls. Some of them looked like actual notes on scripts. Jane noted some *Southpaw and Lefty* scripts that were marked with red pen, then the notes were answered again in black pen. Heck had given notes on his own notes?

There were three small bedrooms that radiated from the center hall, all filled with paper. Stacks and stacks and boxes upon boxes. If the place burned down, it would be a forest fire, thought Jane. In the middle room, Heck had gotten crafty. *Southpaw and Lefty* scripts, many still bound in folders, were stacked along the window wall. The ones that had been un-bound had loose pages that were scattered around a small table and chair in the middle of the room. Most of the loose pages had been recycled, however, shaped and folded into swans . . . hundreds and hundreds of origami swans. Jeez, Patrick not only couldn't do his own writing, he didn't even do his own folding. Jane pictured Heck downstairs at one of his desks, writing, writing, flinging the pages into a pile, then coming up here to unwind by transforming all the old writing into something else entirely. This man must have been unable to ever still his hands. His mind and his body had to be in constant motion.

Jane's phone rang and she got it out of her pocket and flipped it open before the second ring. A record. "Tim?"

"He's with you, hon. We're on our way."

"Jeb?" Jane said into the already dead phone.

Jane had seen enough scary movies to know that the hero—that was her—should not be in a house alone when the possible villain/murderer—that was Jeb—was on his way. Jane looked out the window and saw Louise's car but still no Louise. She said she lived only a few blocks away—she probably went home and called Jeb herself. Jane dialed Oh's number, but the phone was off. Of course, he was at the hospital, and phones needed to be turned off. She left the message for him to come to the house and decided she'd better get outside herself. Not only did she know enough not to get caught inside, she knew that it would really be stupid to get caught upstairs with no escape.

That damn cell phone chime. Where was it coming from? Jane moved into the next, much smaller bedroom. This one, no surprise, was filled with more paper. At first, in the dimly lit, dusty room, Jane thought it might be stacks of newspapers lining the walls underneath the windows, climbing straight up toward the ceiling in places, but when she went closer to inspect them, she saw they were more typewritten pages. Stacks and stacks of manuscript pages. This house was both a writer's dream and a writer's nightmare. *H. Rule* was typed in the corner of each sheet Jane picked up, with a number and letter code following the name. She tried to read two consecutive pages from a stack to see if she could understand what she was reading, but the two sheets were not from the same manuscript. The corner codes were different.

The chime again. From behind some messy stacks in the opposite corner. Jane walked over, carefully stepping around the paper that had drifted from the piles against the walls.

Jane expected to find, what else, more pages behind pages. She did not expect to find Tim Lowry, unconscious, fully dressed, yet scantily covered in random pages of sitcom dialogue. His cell phone chimed. He had a message.

"Tim, wake up, we've got to get out of here," said Jane. Her friend was breathing, and to Jane's untrained ear, it seemed normal and regular. She started to take his pulse, then realized she wasn't wearing a watch and for some reason nurses always looked at their watches when they laid their fingers on your wrist, and even if Jane could feel anything, she had no idea what she was supposed to count, for how long, or what the final number would mean.

"Damn it, Tim, just wake up."

She heard a car in the driveway. Three blocks away and the damn B Room drives over. Well, California, what would you expect? Jane had been there, what? Three days now? Long enough to stereotype and generalize and denigrate. "Timmy," said Jane, unbuttoning his collar. She rushed into the bathroom, where there were no towels, and took off the linen shirt she had worn over her tank top. "You will buy me a new shirt, Lowry," she said out loud, soaking the sleeves in cold water. She ran back and placed the wet cloth on Tim's neck and face. "Wake up!"

Jane tried to dial 911 on her cell phone while she was patting Tim down. If he ever did wake up, she knew he was going to kill her for the water marks on his silk shirt.

"Tim!"

"Phone down, Jane," said Jeb, who had climbed the stairs silently. Either that or her own heart had been making enough noise to drown out his footsteps. "You don't understand what's going on. This is just a meeting."

"No," said Jane. "I won't."

"He's okay, he's just drugged, and I am not giving you an option," said Jeb, grabbing her wrist and squeezing until she dropped the phone. It slid under a manuscript cover sheet. *Plan B: When Life Happens, a one-hour comedy drama.*

"Have you stolen that one already and pitched it, Jeb?" Jane asked.

"Not one of Henry's best, but it has a great female character. Spunky, determined two-time loser who rises from the ashes to become a success in her second career," said Jeb.

"Drivel," said Jane.

"Yeah, who cares?" said Jeb.

Bix and Skye walked in, shaking their heads at all the pages everywhere. Bix knelt down next to Tim and held a vial up to his nose, which roused him and made him sneeze.

"This is frightening, Jeb. Like being inside Heck's brain," said Bix. "Let's go back to your house."

"You've been here before," said Jeb, pulling Jane up, kicking her cell phone across the room, and still holding on to her wrist.

Bix shook her head. "Never came in. I used to bring food and movies over once in a while, but Heck always met me at the door. Said he was in the middle of something."

"And he was," said Jeb. "Let's go downstairs. We can clear some chairs in the living room and have our meeting. Rick and Greg are on their way. Louise's car is here, but I haven't talked to her. Did she drop you off, Jane, then walk to her house?"

Jane watched Tim blink and try to place where he was.

"Why's my shirt wet?" asked Tim.

"I was saving your life," said Jane.

"Do you have any idea what this cost? It's custom."

Since Tim seemed to be recovering, Jane turned her attention to the threesome in front of her. Bix and Jeb were calm, talking to each other about various projects. Skye had opened a closet and was looking through the stacks and boxes crammed into the tiny space. Jeb let go of Jane and helped Tim to his feet. Jeb patted Tim's shoulder and apologized.

"You're going to have more of a headache than you started with," said Jeb to Tim, who looked totally perplexed. "Now, we just can't have you both talking about all of this for the next few days. After that, none of it will matter," said Jeb. He sounded upbeat.

When Tim stood up, he immediately put his hand in his pockets and reeled. He leaned against the door to steady himself.

"Pretty dizzy," he said.

"It will fade," said Skye. "You'll actually feel pretty refreshed. It's a deep-sleep drug—don't know its name, but when I had that awful insomnia in '96—remember, Bix?—I went to a herbalist who said if you could deeply rest your body, I mean put it out, the actual time mattered less than the quality if—"

"Please," said Jeb, looking at Bix. "Make her stop."

"Okay, hotshot, I'll stop, but after the meeting today, I think you'll be happy to be allowed to listen. The tables are going to turn, my friend—" Skye stopped when Bix put her hand on her arm.

"Honey, save it for the meeting, okay?"

Skye nodded, smiling.

The group made their way downstairs and Jeb began shoving pages off chairs.

"Are we prisoners here?" asked Jane. "Can I just walk out that door?"

"No and no," said Jeb.

He finished setting up the room and smiled at the sound of another car in the driveway. "You want to know what this is all about and I want to tell you. After our deal goes through tomorrow, none of this will matter. It might not even matter now, but I want all the paperwork finished before we say good-bye," said Jeb.

"You're as crazy as Heck," said Jane. "Do you think you can get away with murder?"

Jeb laughed and greeted Rick and Greg, who arrived together. Jeb asked Bix to call Louise again.

"We're going to start. I talked to Louise this morning and filled her in, so she's up to date anyway." Jeb took a deep breath and stood tall. "As of tomorrow, when the final papers are signed, I will be the new president and CEO of Bix Flix, which has signed a gigantic deal with a major studio. We will also be going public, which is why all of this has to stay hush-hush for the next few days. We are all set, my friends. Job security, complete creative control, and corner offices. Whatever your hearts desire. I promised you ten years ago if we stuck together, we'd own this town. And, of course, I was wrong, but we own our corner of it now."

"How can you possibly get Pix out of Bix Flix this fast?" said Jane. "You haven't even had Lou Piccolo's memorial service yet."

"Lou signed off on this months ago. He wanted out for the past two years. Just recently he told me he had finally cracked the code on what he wanted out of life," said Bix. "I figured he was moving permanently to Ojai."

"Did he actually say 'crack the code'?" asked Jane.

Bix nodded.

"Don't you see? He learned how to put all this stuff together," said Jane. "He cracked Heck's code. Or rather, Patrick Dryer did and Lou somehow got the information out of him. Lou planned to become the new you, didn't he, Jeb?"

Jeb smiled so cordially that Jane thought he must have lost his mind. She looked around and finally locked eyes with Tim. Here they were, in the crazy house of a crazy man with a bunch of crazy people, and they were having a pleasant little meeting with the crazy town citizens.

"Jane, I didn't care what Lou had or hadn't discovered. I knew Lou was getting this stuff from Dryer and Dryer squeezed the crazy-ass filing system out of Heck before he died. I wanted you to come out here because I thought you might find something on Dryer so that we could get an order of protection or something. These pranks were driving us nuts. And in the case of Bix's arm, they were getting scary. Doesn't matter anymore. The B Room has developed enough projects to keep us all busy for the rest of our lives. We're done with Heck's work. Time to let that poor man rest."

Skye snorted.

"So why'd you have to kill Patrick if you were done with all of this?"

The B Room turned as one and looked at Jane.

"Man, you are good," said Rick. "You solve the Black Dahlia yet?"

Jeb looked horrified. If he was acting, this was a much better performance than she had ever seen him or any of this group give.

"You think I killed Dryer?" asked Jeb. "Haven't you been paying attention? Lou Piccolo killed Patrick. He didn't want to share all this, so once he got Patrick to give him Heck's system, he got rid of him."

"With a Kalo letter opener?"

"I admit that was strange, but Lou probably just bought that one at the market, then saw Dryer, who, incidentally, had been following him all over town, making scenes," said Jeb.

"You remember the yelling at the office during our first meeting?" asked Bix. "That was Patrick."

"Yes, I know. I also know that someone took the Kalo letter opener from the collection off Lou's desk."

Jeb and Bix looked at each other. Tim shook his head at Jane. She could tell that he was worried she was talking too much. He might be right. She wasn't sure she knew anybody in any cavalry that would be riding in to save them. She hadn't been able to reach Oh, she hadn't called the police.

"I did do that," said Jeb. "When we ran back to the office after the explosion, which was clearly a Patrick trick, I saw those openers and noticed the Kalo. After I saw Dryer at the flea market, stabbed with what looked like Lou's opener, I went to the office to see if his was still there. When I saw it still in place, I took it. I figured he did it with one he bought there, but just in case the police couldn't prove it, I'd help by making his own disappear."

"So why did you put it back?" asked Jane.

Jeb looked blank.

"I put it back," said Bix. "I saw it on your desk last night, Jeb. I took it and put it back in Lou's office this morning. The poor man's dead. No reason to point the police in his direction any more than they will be anyway. It's over. I didn't want you involved in it, Jeb," Bix said.

Jane realized that they were telling the truth as they saw it. They believed that Lou killed Patrick and that he then died of a heart attack by the pool. They had all been television writers so long that they accepted this without question. Three acts and a conclusion. Time for a twist.

"So Lou killed Patrick?" Jane asked.

Bix and Jeb nodded. Greg and Rick shrugged. They were bored and clearly wanted to be doing their own work or, judging from their leafing through the pages on the floor by their chairs, diving into their own decoding of some of Heck's work.

"Who cares? He was a prick and he's gone," said Rick, patting his pocket, looking for a cigarette. "Damn it. Didn't Heck used to smoke?" Rick began opening desk drawers. "Jesus, there are pages of dialogue all over the damn house. Poor bastard. How many voices in his head did he have to listen to all day?"

"Yeah, poor Heck," said Skye. "Let's all feel sorry for the bastard."

Bix walked over to Skye and tried to put her arm around her, but Skye shook her off.

Rick was going through a built-in corner cupboard in the adjoining dining room, muttering to himself, when Jeb got a call from Louise. "Yeah, we're right here in the house. Why? Bring it in. Yeah, they're all in here. Okay, in a minute."

Jeb told Greg to go help Louise out in the garage. "She's got something out there and it's too heavy for her to bring into the house. Can you see what's up?"

"Eureka," said Rick, bringing out a cigar box.

"Don't open it," said Jane.

"Why? You think Patrick rigged them all up to explode?" said Rick.

"In a way," she said. Without thinking, Jane had carried the See's candy box upstairs, put it down when she found Tim, but picked it up and brought it downstairs with her. She still had it tucked under her arm. The last thing that box contained was cigars. It, too, was probably full of the sickening "audition" photos.

"Boom," said Rick, flipping open the lid. "Wow. These are great. Here's a note—*Heck, I know you used to like a good cigar. These are from my private stash. Enjoy. Lou.* The note is dated . . . hey, when did Heck jump?"

Jeb took the note and read it. "It's dated the day Heck killed himself."

Skye began to make noise. Jane thought she was crying until she looked over at her. She definitely wasn't crying—whatever she was doing was closer to nervous giggling.

"Can I ask a question before this goes any further?" asked Tim.

He was sitting next to Jane, rubbing his temples, the fog beginning to clear.

"If everything is all worked out and we're just here for your little love-fest meeting, how come I had a gun held on me and was made to drink that shit? How did I even get here?"

"He must be hallucinating," said Jeb.

"No," said Skye. "I caught him snooping around in the pantry and I thought he was stealing stuff. I wanted us to have the meeting here, remember, so we could see Heck's stuff before the house got sold? Worked out great, too," Skye said. She looked at Tim. "You were loopy after you drank my special potion, but I got you over here, you were walking. You just don't remember."

"You have a gun?" said Jeb. "You told me he was looking for something for a headache and took the wrong thing by accident out of your purse."

Skye reached into her knitting bag. "Sure, I got Lou's gun. He had it at the hospital and I took it. I have wanted one for protection for ages. A girl can't be too careful these days."

"Anybody got a match?" asked Rick. "You want one, Jeb? They're Padróns."

"No," said Jane and Tim at the same time.

"Sure," said Skye, taking out a lighter.

Jane grabbed the cigar from Rick. "If these are Lou Piccolo's, you don't want to smoke them."

Skye raised the gun she had taken from her bag, pointing it at Jane, but taking a step back so she could cover the whole room.

"Yes, they do, Jane Wheel. All the boys want to smoke a cigar. They want to celebrate the big new change in the company, right? You anti-smoking people are ridiculous."

"Oh, Skye," said Bix, putting her hand to her mouth. "Heck liked to smoke cigars."

Jane looked around the room, something about the smoking . . . right. The ashtrays. There were six of them lined up on the desk, but they were all clean. The house hadn't been cleaned, there were dishes in the sink, but there were no ashes in the ashtray, the house didn't smell of tobacco. But Heck was a smoker. He liked cigars. And in order to butter him up, Lou sent him cigars from his private stash.

"How often did Heck smoke? One a day?" asked Jane.

Bix was crying. Jeb looked at her, puzzled, but didn't say anything.

"Every night, after dinner," answered Bix.

Skye ignored Bix's tears and, with a big smile, gave Jeb and Rick each a cigar. She nodded and pointed her gun at Rick. "You first, sweetie, let's have a light."

"It's going to explode, isn't it?" asked Rick, looking at Skye. "You're trying to kill me, kill us." He began backing out of the room.

"No, it's not going to explode, silly," Skye said. "We're all right here, too." She flicked her vintage Zippo and Rick reflexively began puffing on the cigar. He nodded to Jeb and gave him a thumbs-up.

"Now you, Jeb," said Skye.

Jeb shook his head.

"It's over, sweetie," said Bix. "Give me the gun."

Jane saw the cavalry arrive. Oh had pulled up in his rental car and was heading for the house.

"Heck smoked outside, didn't he? Up on the platform of his observatory?" said Jane. "Lou gave him some of his cigars from the stash you had already doctored, and he took one up on the roof. Heck had a seizure up there, didn't he? That's why he went off the roof so oddly, he was rigid and seizing when he went over the side. . . . For God's sake, Rick, put that out."

Rick was holding his stomach and was beginning to look dazed. Bix grabbed the cigar out of his mouth and pushed him into a chair.

"You can smoke or I can shoot you," said Skye. "Your choice how you die. Bix and I are taking over everything and we're burning down this house. This filthy house. You boys are going to get sloppy and drop your cigars and this place is going to go up in smoke so fast. Everybody felt so sorry for that poor Heck? He was crazy, all right. And he worked hard, all right. He also had a business on the side . . . and when I was fourteen years old . . . Uncle Heck told me he could get me in a movie. . . ."

"You don't have to talk about it, honey," said Bix, "it's over."

"It's over when I say it's over, Bix. I am finally in charge. This says so," she said, waving the gun. "And I'm stronger than you losers, so don't get any ideas. I've been working out since I was a teenager to keep the weight off, to stay strong, to be ready for when the next Celie role came along. None did, though, did it? You know what good old Uncle Heck told me?"

Jane knew that Oh could see in the window. The door was open; their voices, Jane hoped, were carrying. They were framed there, acting out their roles, and Oh stood watching the scene unfold. He was nodding his head and Jane could see him raise his phone. Yes, an ambulance would be coming in time for Rick and a police car for Skye. Jane saw Louise come out of the garage, helped by Greg. Now Jane was the watcher and the window her frame. Jane could tell by looking at Louise that she had found an even bigger stash of Uncle Heck's other business. By the look on Louise's face, the total collapse of her features and form, Jane could tell she had been wrong about one conclusion she had reached earlier. Louise wasn't in love with Jeb. Louise had been in love with Heck.

It was as if Jane and Oh were watching an episode of some bizarre chapter of the B Room, or maybe it was Patrick's version, *The D Room*, from two sides of the screen. Jane's version was the story of the brokenhearted Louise finding out the truth about the man she loved, whose death she would now experience all over again. Oh, from his vantage point, was viewing the Skye Miller story, the child actress who was used up by everyone before she was old enough to catch on.

"Uncle Heck was such a sweetie, wasn't he?" said Skye. "He told me my big chance was to make a grown-up movie. That's what he called it. Sandy Pritikin drove me over here, told me it would be great for my career. Told me Heck knew what he was doing. Sandy smoked those cheap cigars, he reeked of them, he . . ." Skye stopped. Her words were bitter and angry, but tears streamed. "I let Sandy, what was it Heck told me to say . . . be my costar . . . yeah . . . and I let Heck film the whole thing. I was fourteen years old. And the next year, when I put on weight, who was the prick who tried to get me fired? Sandy Pritikin. I told him I'd tell what he did, what he did to me, and he just laughed. He said no one would believe it and Heck filmed it so his face was never in it, no one could prove it was him, but everyone would see what a little slut—"

Bix put an arm around Skye, but she wouldn't or couldn't stop talking.

"Sandy was smoking one of those crappy cigars when he called me that. I made sure that the box I sent him two years ago were good ones, such good cigars that he wouldn't be able to resist lighting up, even though he'd had the bypass, even though he wasn't supposed to smoke. I wish I could have been there when that hammy bastard lit up. I pray every night," said Skye, looking around at all of them, "that it was slow and excruciating."

"Skye, let's get rid of it," said Jane.

Skye stopped talking and looked at Jane.

"Photos, films. There were other girls, too. It's in these candy boxes." Jane held out the one she had been clutching. "There's a brick barbeque out in the backyard. Let's burn it all, okay?"

Skye nodded and when Jane reached for the gun, she allowed Jane to take it. Jane handed Skye off to Bix, who emptied out a box of papers and started putting the candy boxes into the larger container. Together they carried it out the back door.

Jeb was completely dazed.

The police and ambulance arrived quietly. Oh must have given them the word. Jane handed over the cigar box to the police. Tim stood up behind her and reached into his pocket and handed the syringe over.

"I can't believe she drugged me and held a gun on me and she didn't even search me to see if I'd found anything incriminating."

"It wasn't going to matter," said Jane. "I think in her script we were all going to die anyway."

"Who killed Patrick?" said Jeb. "Lou, right?"

"Skye did it all, Jeb. You treated her like an annoying little girl, but she was all grown up enough to plan a lot of murders. You were definitely going down."

Jeb looked skeptical. The EMTs wheeled Rick past them through the front door.

"The nicotine she was using to doctor the cigars was in your pantry, probably from your own cigarettes. Bobbette said Skye was in the kitchen all the time, loved to help cook and get recipes," said Tim.

"And she had read one of the best books on poisons I have ever seen," said Oh, "right in your own library."

"Skye stabbed Patrick Dryer? She wasn't at the flea market. She was at the hospital with Bix."

"She wasn't at the flea market with you and the B Room, Jeb, but she was there. Remember how proud she was of having her license? Didn't need anyone to drive her around anymore? Bix was in surgery and it was easy to get to Pasadena and back. I'm not sure why she picked that day, since it was a little more complicated than shooting up a cigar, but—"

"I can help here, Mrs. Wheel," said Oh. "Mr. Dryer had come to the hospital the night before, probably to hang that dreadful little mobile to scare you all, one of his pranks, and he had an argument with Ms. Miller. The nurses heard some of it and he mentioned that he had a book coming out and that his cousin Heck had helped him publish it. I suspect she feared that the book detailed her appearance in some of Mr. Rule's films."

"One. She only did one," said Bix, who had come in to pick up her purse. "I'll be going down to the police station."

Jeb went over and embraced Bix. "I'll go with you. We'll get her a lawyer and—"

Bix shook her head. "I'm not going just for moral support, Jeb. I knew about the cigars. I figured it out and I didn't stop her. It's why . . ." Bix looked over at Jane.

Jane smiled slightly. "It's why you didn't mind that I was here. You didn't think I was a very good detective. You saw me babble away on television when Jeb brought you the tape and so when this went down, you thought I'd be perfect to help skew all the facts here. You realized that the explosion was meant for Lou. Even though you got hurt, you still thought Patrick was harmless. But Skye didn't know that. And Patrick threatened Skye. He knew about Heck's other life. So did Lou. She killed Patrick because you were the only person she trusted and he hurt you and she thought he was going to hurt her. Then Lou showed up at the hospital with a gun and the script wrote itself. She could get rid of Lou and let the murder be pinned on him. Especially if Bix helped."

"I didn't want to do it at first, but Lou was so cruel about all this. He threatened our deal—the Bix Flix deal. He wanted more money to keep quiet about Heck. Heck was already dead, I didn't want . . . I didn't tell you about it, Jeb. He would have blackmailed Skye. She asked me to put the cigars in his case for her. I didn't ask her, but I knew she must have laced them with something."

"Did you know what kind of cigars Lou smoked?" asked Jane.

"No," said Bix. "I never paid any attention."

"That's why there was only one Padrón in the case. You were letting fate decide which one he smoked."

Bix shook her head. "It doesn't matter."

"It might, Ms. Bixby, when you speak with your lawyer," said Oh.

"And you couldn't possibly have known about Heck and the cigars," said Jane.

"No. Or Sandy," said Bix. "I had no idea about Sandy. Or Heck. Oh God, what will I say to Louise?" asked Bix. She touched Jane's arm and walked out the front door, where another police car had arrived.

Jeb followed Bix outside. He looked back at Jane, wanting very much to say something, but Jane could tell that he had no idea what it would be. Unfortunately, no one had written or decoded this script for him.

Jane, Tim, and Oh looked at each other and gazed around the room at the stacks of pages, the overflowing desk drawers, the candy boxes that remained behind. Oh's cell phone rang and he studied the number. He nodded and answered,

"Yes. Yes. I am, too. I'm on my way."

Jane and Tim looked at him. Who was left that hadn't been accounted for?

"My wife's aunt," said Oh. "She's passed."

Jane and Tim gave their condolences and the three of them walked out of Heck's house together. So many stories buried in those rooms, feverishly written by Heck, then hidden away until someone could figure out how to tell them. Yet they were all really the same, weren't they? Life, love, betrayal. Greed, loss, and death.

Jane put her hand through Tim's arm and, in a bold move, did the same with Oh, who walked on her other side. Was it something related to the closure, the resolution of this drama? A wave of good humor came over her despite the weight of the last several minutes. It struck her that the three of them were a strange variation of one of her old favorite television shows. *The Mod Squad*, where every promotional trailer focused on the three twentysomethings who went undercover as high school students—Linc, Pete, and Julie—walking down the street while the announcer intoned, "One black, one white, one blond." This version, more of an odd squad, Oh, Tim, and Jane now walked the same Hollywood streets, sort of. One Asian, one gay, one—what was she today? Jane Wheel, girl detective? Wife, mother, friend, picker? All of the above?

Time to go home.

Music.

Credits.

Fade to black.